Missing Barbados

Willem Pain

D1517022

.

Smashwords Edition
Copyright 2013 William Kuypers

License Notes: This ebook is licensed for your personal enjoyment only. This ebook may not be re-sold or given away to other people. If you would like to share this ebook with another person, please purchase an additional copy for each person you share it with. If you're reading this book and did not purchase it, or it was not purchased for your use only, then you should return to Smashwords.com and purchase your own copy. Thank you for respecting the hard work of this author.

Table of Contents

Dedicated to Hendricus and Mia Kuypers, two shining lights in the darkest hours of life, and to my editor, the lovely Lisa Nicholson.

Merry
Christmas '19
Dorothea!

Love
Lea

PROLOGUE

"What you are is what you have been. What you'll be is what you do now." - Buddha

Actual Bridgetown, Barbados Historical Record

Written October 25th, 1757
Barbados House of Assembly - Legal Document
"On the motion of Francis Bell Esqr. It was ordered that the Clerk prepare an address to his Excellency in Council for an order on the Treasurer for payment of One hundred Pistoles to Charles Hollingsworth Esqr. Commander of his Majesty's Brigantine called the Speaker for taking French Privateer infesting the Coast of the island, and for other good services done on his Cruises, which are duly regarded by the Publick: And that a Copy of this minute be delivered to Mr. Hollingsworth by the Clerk.

November 22nd, 1757
Letter from Charles Hollingsworth Esqr to the Assembly
It is with the greatest satisfaction and acknowledgement, that I have received from Mr. Duke, Secretary to your Assembly, their Minute of the 25th of October, so much in my favour, and I beg leave to take this opportunity of expressing the just sense I have of the kindness; to which I can take no other merit than a good inclination, to do justice to the commission

The present you intend me, is of that nature which leaves me not at liberty to accept it, and I hope from the goodness you have already favoured me with, that my excusing myself from such an acceptance may be received with a favourable construction, and not lessen the esteem, the publick have already honoured me with.

I am, Gentlemen, your most obliged and most obedient humble servant,

CHAS. HOLLINGSWORTH.

November 25th, 1757

Barbados House of Assembly

"So laudable a spirit as Captain Hollingsworth has discovered on this occasion must not be passed by either unnoticed, or unhonoured in this Assembly, I therefore move that it is the opinion of this house that Captain Hollingsworth has shewn no other than a noble Principle of Conduct by his refusal to accept the sum of money offered him in acknowledgement of his services, - I further move that, in lieu of the 100 Pistoles which we had voted him before, we should now send to England for a gold-hilted Sword of that value to be presented to Captain Hollingsworth, a thing more worthy his acceptance and which we shall desire may be worn by him as the Instrument of his own Glory, and our publick gratitude."

CHAPTER 1

Susan Berg passed by the ninth floor like bird poop falling out of the crystal blue Miami sky. At 32 feet per second, most would think that the building would be moving by very quickly. Funny how the mind works in an unusual circumstance like this, she thought. It all actually slows down, almost to a snail's crawl, perhaps because your body and mind have entered some sort of shock.

Robert Merchant looked the same way as he seemed to float on a downward descent next to Susan, his eyes as big as saucers, his mouth agape like a dry-bed guppy gasping for air. How was she to know he wasn't Luther Stein, the weasel bastard whom she was sure had broken into her eleventh floor condo to steal the evidence she had on him? They were both roughly the same height, and in the dim light of the South Beach moonlight, one could argue that they looked a lot alike as well. Yes, she could perhaps be accused of using a bit too much force when she tackled him in a dead end sprint, throwing them both through her plate glass window and over her balcony. She would have never imagined it was her boyfriend, there to surprise her on her birthday after returning from a law conference in Minneapolis. For God's sake, a text message would have helped. Forgive a girl for trying, for crying out loud.

She was sure that they were not only going to die, but that this relationship was over as well. Throwing your boyfriend off a building is probably a bigger relationship killer than passing gas during oral sex. Of course it really won't matter much when they reach the bottom floor, Susan thought just as she noticed the shimmer of aqua blue coming up from below. Of course, the frickin pool, she realized. In her haste to fall to earth, she had forgotten about the oversized swimming pool that covered the length of her building's courtyard. The thought of a perfect

Olympic ten when she hit the pool flashed through her mind, quickly discarded in favor of an unflattering but far less deadly feet first entry. Susan pointed down toward the pool as her now ex-boyfriend looked at her with a "Why me?" expression of horror mixed with hate. Robert looked down and attempted a smile of relief. The jack-o-lantern quality of his grin actually caused Susan to laugh, a reaction resulting in an obscene gesture from her accidental prey. Susan braced herself, smoothing down her new Vera Wang dress that she had put on for her birthday dinner with her girlfriends. She pointed her toes straight down as she tried to remember if it was the shallow or deep end of the pool that abutted the building. For the life of her, or the lack thereof, she could not remember. Funny how the craziest thoughts go through one's mind as an unexpected death approaches. Susan actually wished she had balled Robert Merchant before accidently throwing them to their deaths.

And then it was there. The hard splash of water greeted them both, Susan entering like a supple yet strong feather, her body going in at the slightest of angles. She immediately arched her back, having spent too many of her school years on the Pine Crest Dive Team. The momentum carried her toward the bottom of the pool, her good form causing her to curve away at the latest moment. Susan glided like a bullet across the pool bottom until coming to a subtle rest at the shallow end of the pool. She lay at the bottom of the pool for a moment, her mind and senses working overtime to synch. Susan then sprang up from the water, her lungs finally registering that they were out of air. She gasped for air, trying to order her thoughts regarding what had just occurred. It was then that she thought about Robert, for unlike her he had not spent any time on a dive team, in school or otherwise. Robert Merchant had landed at a bad angle, his feet neither pointing down nor held tightly together. The force of hitting the water at that speed effectively gave Robert the all time greatest wedgee, his body crashing into the unforgiving concrete of the pool bottom while his attention was diverted to his pounded gonads. Both of Robert's legs broke on impact, his femur on the left and his ankle on the right. Robert lay on the bottom of the pool, physically and mentally paralyzed. Susan swam to him as fast as she could, diving down and with all her might lifting him by his shoulders to the surface. As many drowning victims do, Robert thrashed and grabbed at her, doing anything to stay afloat. And as any well trained lifeguard knows, the best tactic in this situation is to subdue your subject, which Susan promptly did with a stiff forearm to Robert's jaw knocking him unconscious. Yes, Susan thought as she floated Robert to the steps of the pool, if the eleven story fall did not end their relationship, her right cross surely did.

"Now is the time for me to take her." Reginald Carrington checked his watch by the light of the half moon, the only sound being that of the gently rolling waves on the sandy shore. The night air had a chill-to-the bone effect on him despite the thick soup of warm humidity that clung in the air. The once familiar beach now seemed ominous in the darkness as he crept along the side wall of the Wellington Bay Club Resort on the West side of Barbados. Thoughts of his plan passed through his mind as he steadied himself against the coquina wall. He downed the twenty ounce soda and tossed the plastic bottle into the weeds. Reg, as everyone called him on this remote rock of English heritage, hoisted his lanky six foot three frame into the arms of an old banyan tree. He surveyed the Wellington Bay Club Resort as the sound of something creaking, mixed with the rhythmic chirps of crickets, floated through the air. Reg looked down for the source of the sound just as the branch cracked in half, sending him head first over the wall and onto the grounds of the resort. With a mouth full of grass, Reg looked up toward the guard gates at the front entrance, the guard casting shadows of movement as he casually read the Barbados Advocate newspaper. Reg spit the grass plug out, his sweaty face dripping with the rich dirt he helped put down during his summers working at the resort for a landscape company. Reg pulled himself up to a crouched position, looking like a garish stick figure come to life. He pushed his blonde bangs out of his eyes as if that would allow him to see the details of his plan more clearly. Reg knew full well that the guards at the Wellington Bay Club meant business. Their Ruger P series pistols were carried for more than just display. He learned that not less than two years ago when he and two of his friends on the basketball team stole a bottle of Mount Gay Rum from their coach's locker at school. It was their freshman year, and feeling like the most wanted of criminals, they took to Reg's seventeen foot Prindle catamaran. Although Reggie knew the Barbadian waters like a fish, having sailed for years, a half bottle of rum can addle the best of sailors, to say nothing of a first time drunk. The boys caught an unfortunate onshore wind and found themselves aground at midnight, smack dab in the middle of the club's beach. Before they could right themselves, much less the boat, two security guards had all three in the sights of their revolvers. Not appreciating the seriousness of their situation much less the guards' intentions, Reg attempted to disembark at which point both guards discharged a round squarely at his feet. Reggie, as startled as he was drunk, immediately pissed himself much to the delight of his two drunken friends.

For most kids like Reggie, life in tranquil Barbados as the son of an expatriate barrister was nothing if not perfect. Until now. Until he had laid eyes on her. It was more than lust to Reggie, more than love; it was rapture, a total surrender of his soul. He had to know her, to be with her. In that moment he knew as sure as there was a God above that he would be with her. That was certain, if nothing else. He was convinced that their destiny was to be together, regardless of how it came to be or what he had to do to ensure it. All of his proper upbringing, the private schools, the private karate and sailing lessons, his stately father, it all became moot. Now, none of that mattered anymore. The only thing of importance to him was Lady Melody. Even now, her eternal scent overpowered that of the tall grass and ocean breeze.

Reg felt for the comfort of the broken off broom handle in his rear pocket, the clear choice of any serious criminal. He tried hard to control the racing of his heart, breathing hard. He moved between the buildings with zero stealth, stumbling and tripping like a drunk on holiday. Reg softly cursed himself, always ending with a reaffirmation that he could pull this off. The chill in the air that he had earlier felt was now a clammy sweat, like a sticky glue to his skin. Reg vigorously rubbed his open palms across his face and then his shirt tail to wipe it away.

His summers of working at the resort had given Reg an excellent knowledge of the buildings, his destination etched in his mind. Those carefree days seemed like a lifetime ago, mowing the grounds and pulling weeds, taking causal dips in the ocean between trimming the plants. He arrived at building number three and checked his watch. Only ten minutes until one. His breath kept pace with his racing pulse, a nervous need to pee pushing on his bladder. Reg cursed the large sized soda he had drank. He did his best to quietly relieve himself on the condo wall, feeling as awkward as he felt scared. The sudden flash of light illuminated him, Reg unable to stop in mid relief.

"You there, stop what you're doing!" the guard ordered. Reg's mind raced to keep up with his pounding heart. He quickly zipped up his pants, his foreskin getting caught in the process. Reg bit his lip as tears of pain welled in his eyes. On pure instinct, he began to run, moving serpentine through the grounds, the overweight guard struggling to stay in hot pursuit through the moist earth. Running full speed through the lush grounds, Reg lost track of where he was until he collided face first with the chain link fence that encircled the beach. The impact bounced him like a rubber ball, landing him on his back with a thud. Reg forced himself up as the beam from the guard's flashlight approached from a distance. Reg frantically looked about, cornered on the beach. He grabbed a coconut off the ground and with all his might hurled it at the approaching guard, the projectile lodging itself in the low lying fronds of a palm tree. As Reg looked up at his misfortune, the guard's light discovered his face.

"What the hell?" the guard laughed out loud at Reg's face criss-crossed in red checker board from his collision with the fence. "Okay kid, don't you make another move."

Reg slumped down in defeat as the guard approached, dreams of his one true love fading away with every step the guard took toward him.

"When are you kids going to learn? You can't sneak in here and use the pool at night," the guard said just as a rustling of the palm fronds above his head was heard. The guard and Reg both looked up as the coconut rolled from its position and came straight down, smacking the guard squarely in the face. The guard emitted a momentary expletive and then dropped to the ground with a thud. Reg looked about with disbelief and then cautiously approached the sprawled out guard. He checked the man's pulse. Convinced that he was only unconscious, Reg ran back toward the building of his destination. He arrived just in time to hear the front door of the top unit open.

Reg pulled out his sturdy stick, the time for indecision now gone forever.

"And to all of you, Ladies, Gentlemen, Haves and Have Nots, I salute you! Not for what you have done, but for what you have not done. Not one drink you have offered, and not one drink I have drank! Not rum, not whiskey, not beer!" Richard "Dutch" Holland guzzled the remainder of his boilermaker and slammed the glass down on the bar.

Crane Luk, a toothpick of an Asian man, sat on a nearby bar stool, his dark brown eyes showing concern as he measured Dutch Holland. "I will buy the next drink," he softly said to Dutch.

Dutch pointed an accusatory finger at Crane. "You, my dear sir, are a gentleman and a scholar. Unlike the other swill that populate this unseemly place of ill repute!" Two young sailors in their twenties from the dry goods cargo ship, Lorelei, cast baneful stares in Dutch Holland's direction. Their gaze did not go unnoticed by Mr. Crane Luk, the Vietnamese shifting uncomfortably on his bar stool next to Dutch Holland.

"Hey old man! Old man, why don't you just shut up and let us drink in silence?" one of the sailors said.

Dutch stopped midway in downing his eighth or ninth Boilermaker, everyone including the bartender having lost count.

"And what _old_ man would you be talking to, dipshit?" Dutch's gaze settling in on the two young sailors.

Crane stood up and gently took Dutch by the arm. "Dutch, it's getting late. We've really got to get going, to meet you know who."

"No, no, that's okay. You know who can wait until who knows when." Dutch's gaze returned to the two sailors.

"You better listen to your yellow friend there old man," the other young sailor advised with a snicker.

"And what old man would you be talking to a-hole?" Dutch replied, his voice as wavering as his stare was steady.

The two young sailors rose from their seats and crossed the bar toward Dutch. "We're talking to you, _old_ man," the first one said.

Harris Beerli, the bartender and owner of the Bridge Bar and Grill, as short as he was stocky, set down his tray of empty beer bottles and moved in between Dutch and the two men. "All right boys, this does not need to go any further. He's just drunk, that's all," Beerli said, pointing to Dutch. "Really, it's not worth it, believe me. Been there, done that, know what I mean?"

The sailors stopped their advance and considered the bartender's words. Crane Luk backed away from the bar.

"This is not good," Crane said to no one in particular, "No, this is bad. Not good."

Dutch smiled as he approached the pair, waving the bartender to the side. "I'm really glad that you boys have reconsidered," Dutch said, "because I would hate to kick the living life out of both of you."

The two men laughed with bravado. "And just how would you do that, old man?" the first sailor asked. Dutch stood motionless, his eyes closed, no one certain if he was savoring the moment, considering his options, or falling asleep. Dutch finally smiled, like the Cheshire Cat from Alice in Wonderland.

"You know, you boys are right. I'm just drunk, that's all. I apologize, really. What was I thinking, an old man like me?"

The two men puffed out their chests, victorious smiles and nods to all in the bar as Dutch moved in close.

"This is really, really bad," both Crane Luk and Harris Beerli muttered as they stepped even farther away.

"Hey, no hard feelings," Dutch continued. "Let me buy ya'll a beer." Dutch reached behind the bar and pulled out two Coronas. "You like Coronas, boys?"

The two smiled and nodded.

"So do I. Know why?" The two sailors shook their heads. "Because they're light beers, which makes them easier for an old man to swing!" Dutch swung the beers forward like a windmill, each squarely landing on the sailors' heads, the beers exploding in a hail of glass and spent suds.

The first sailor stood stunned, but the second instinctively threw a punch, his fist landing a glancing blow to Dutch's forehead. Dutch picked up a stool and crashed it against the man's side sending him flying across the floor. A blow from the other sailor struck Dutch squarely on the jaw, Dutch staggering against the bar. Dutch picked up several of the empty beer bottles on the tray and began hurling them at the pair, hitting everyone other than his intended targets.

The shrill sound of a police whistle signaled their arrival, bartender Beerli's night stick on Dutch Holland's head signaling Dutch's departure.

Susan Berg strode down the hall of 610 Brickell Avenue and pushed through the front door of her office, feeling happy to be alive. Besides that, she was sure of only one thing. That her relationship with district attorney Robert Merchant was over. And she suspected, being a member of the Florida Bar herself, that at a minimum every DA and judge in Dade County would know what she did to him, if not every attorney from Miami to Tallahassee. "Frick," she muttered to herself, the shine of being alive already starting to wear off.

"Nine sharp," Patrick announced, as always. He stood and handed her a tall half-caff caramel latte, light soy, one sugar, cinnamon sprinkles. As always. "And I picked up your Vera Wang dress from the cleaners. It's in your office."

Patrick followed Susan into her ninth floor office, its wall of windows offering a panoramic view of the inter-coastal waterway, Miami's South Beach, and the ocean beyond.

"Patrick, what have I told you about coming into my office when I'm not here?" Susan said.

"I'm sorry Ms. Berg, I must have had an aneurism, blinded by that dress. It's so beautiful!"

"It is beautiful," Susan said as they admired the dress. "Were they able to save it?"

"Yes, although Mr. Enrique wanted to charge you double. But when I explained what happened, he was all forgiveness."

Susan looked about her desk as she sat down, a nagging sense that something was amiss. Although she was the last of a breed, coming from a long line of morning newspaper readers, she would always go through the paper looking for leads on possible clients as she sipped her morning latte. "Patrick, the morning newspaper. Where is it?"

"Oh that? Well they ran out of news so they decided not to print a paper today." Realizing his reply might land flat, Patrick bit his lip as Susan considered his failed attempt at comedy. She gestured with her hand for the newspaper to come forth, Patrick begrudgingly taking it out of the nearby trash can.

"What, did they report that Armani stopped carrying chartreuse shirts for men?"

Patrick frowned as he held the newspaper in his trembling hands.

"Come on, gimme," Susan said as if coaxing a bone from a dog. Patrick regretfully complied, handing her the paper and then stepping several feet back. He chewed his thumbnail as Susan opened the newspaper and began reading the front page. Susan stopped and stared, as if she had been hit between the eyes with a stun gun. There on the front page, featured item, was a large photo of her and Robert Merchant falling through the air, her condo building as the backdrop. As the effect of gravity tends to do when mixed with falling, Susan's Vera Wang dress was up around her ears, followed by her underwear and long legs spread wide apart. "What the frick!" Susan shouted as she read the headline out loud, "PI falls for DA." Susan held the paper out for Patrick to see. "It's not enough that I throw my boyfriend out the window, there's got to be a god damn shutterbug hanging around as well. What's the chance of that?"

"Damn camera phones," Patrick surmised.

"Look at me! With my dress over my head, my legs spread apart!" Patrick leaned in to study the photo closer.

"At least you're wearing underwear this time. And look, it's your pretty ones!" Susan gave Patrick a dead pan look which substituted for yanking his tongue out.

"I've got to get out of here," Susan said as she aimlessly searched the drawers of her desk. "I've got to get out of town!"

"What are you looking for?"

"An escape door for Christ's sake!" Susan shouted back. "My passport. I need my passport! Where is it?"

Patrick hurried over to his desk and opened a drawer. He took out a passport and a letter-sized mailer, both of which he held up for Susan to view. "Now Susan, I can give you this passport. And yes, you can scurry out of here."

"Yes, gimme," Susan said as she gestured.

"Or, together we can try to find this girl." Patrick held out the full color flyer, on it a large photo of Susan seated at her large mahogany desk. She was framed by the view of South Beach through the picture windows behind her. In one hand she held a Mount Blanc pen and in the other a .38 pistol. With her cold blue eyes offset by her princess nose, smooth brown skin and a thick mane of hair, she looked more like a super model than a top detective. The bold title read "Caribbean Detective Corporation" followed by the line "Twenty Years of Professional Discretion". Susan studied the flyer for a moment, her eyes going back and forth between it and the passport.

"You are a star Susan. A survivor, and a top detective," Patrick encouraged.

"You know, you're right," Susan finally said. "I'm not going to let a little story in the morning paper chase me away." Patrick smiled in relief. "Besides, who reads the newspaper nowadays?"

"No one," Patrick replied.

"Ok then, what's on the agenda today?"

Patrick opened his appointment book, thumbing through the pages. "You have a meeting at ten with Mrs. Harris."

"Let me guess. She wants another update on her husband?"

"Yes. I'm starting to think she's starting to get off on the photos you took of her husband with that cross dresser."

"Maybe she's looking for fashion tips. What can I say?"

"Oh, and you got a call from, of all things, the British High Commission in Bridgetown."

"Barbados?"

"Yes. A Mr. Engleton. He said it was a very discreet matter. That he could only discuss it with you. Very mysterious. I told him you would call him back, first thing. Seemed very British, tally ho and all that."

"I just knew that flyer would pay off! All right then, let's get Mr. Engleton on the line. Pronto!"

"Right away." Patrick scurried off and within minutes he rang through Mr. Engleton.

"Mr. Engleton, how can CDC be of service?" Susan asked in her most professional demeanor.

"Ms. Berg, so glad for your prompt call back. It seems that we have a very delicate issue here. Very confidential, to say the least."

"Mr. Engleton, please tell me what you can."

"It's one of our most prominent families, Ms. Berg. Royalty, to be exact. It seems one of their children has gone missing."

"Missing?"

"Missing, abducted, run free, we are not sure yet. The authorities here are, well, not the most capable, or trustworthy. We can't have this kind of thing leak out to the press."

"Yes, I understand. How can we help, sir?"

"I have been asked, rather the High Commission has been asked, to arrange to investigate. Discreetly investigate, you understand. No such nonsense as in the Dutch islands. The British interests on the island would not stand for it. Tabloid sensationalism would not due at all."

"Of course not. I can assure you, CDC prides itself on being discreet," Susan replied.

"Yes, that is why I contacted you, Ms. Berg. The family had seen your flyer. We would like to discuss you taking the case. At the very earliest. I must stress that this cannot become a public matter."

"What about Scotland Yard or MI5? Have you contacted them?"

"No, the family, rather the father, has requested that they not be brought in."

"Can you give me the details?"

"I would rather discuss it in person, for the sake of confidentiality. Can you arrange to be here today?"

"Today?"

"Tonight then. I'm having a reception, and the father of the missing person will be available then."

"Well I'm not sure. I will have to arrange a flight, reschedule some things." Susan's mind raced through her schedule as well as what kind of fee she could charge.

"I have already secured a flight for you out of Miami. It departs in two hours. I can assure you, with this family confidentiality is tantamount, and cost is not an issue. When it comes to the royal family, we must resolve this issue quickly."

"Okay Mr. Engleton. I will be there. I will see you at the reception tonight."

"About eight, formal attire. It's at the Grand Hilton Hotel. I'll make sure you're on the guest list."

"Formal attire, of course Mr. Engleton."

Susan hung up the phone and reviewed the conversation in her mind. Rarely, if ever, would she take a case with such little information, but like an itch between her shoulder blades, this trip would scratch what was currently irritating her. Besides, she couldn't pass up an engagement with the British High Commission. Opportunities like this did not come up every day. The referrals alone could be worth the effort.

Susan Berg's father, Ben Berg, started the Caribbean Detective Corporation, or CDC as those with a habit for acronyms called it. He started CDC with the money he had "collected" by divulging names of the major cocaine dealers and their lawyers to the DEA while working as a Miami detective in the eighties.

Through Susan's skill, connections and perseverance, CDC had become one of the top detective and security companies in

Miami and the Caribbean. Susan had created a network of the highest skilled detectives throughout the Caribbean, as well as discreet muscle when needed. Most of their cases were running down errant husbands or swindlers. These types always had a habit of running off to the islands to disappear with their lovers, other people's money, or both. But this sounded like a real case for a change, an opportunity for her to do some real detective work.

On most of Susan's jobs, her company was able to get their retainer fees up front. But unfortunately, she often had a hard time collecting the rest of the fee when the job was done. Government jobs for royalty were different. Sure money in the bank, and right now that was the perfect place for that money to be as far as Susan Berg and her company were concerned.

Watching the bottom line made a tough job tougher. And Susan Berg was tough. All business, all the time. It earned her the name of "Ice Berg," spoken behind her back by competitors, employees and most of the men who had dated her. She was certain Robert Merchant would now join those ranks. However, there was only one person brazen enough, or crazy enough, to call her that to her face. A person she often despised more than anything.

"Patrick, who do we have available for Barbados?" Susan yelled out as she impatiently drummed her fingers on the desk. "Patrick!"

"I've got it," Patrick hollered as he hurried into her office, rifling through a stack of files. "It seems that all of our usual assets are committed on other islands."

"Well, who is close? Who can be there by tonight?" Patrick held out a fax, the paper shaking in his trembling hand. "What is it, Patrick?"

"It's a fax. It just came in. From Barbados."

"Well, read it to me!"

Patrick put on his pair of expensive pink reading glasses and read in a quivering voice. "Ice Berg. You still owe me money. Send bail. In jail. Dutch Holland. Bridgetown, Barbados."

CHAPTER 2

Susan stewed about her last minute trip as she suffered through three hours on a cramped flight to Barbados. It was just like the British to book her a coach seat, the cheap bastards. Money was no object my ass! She would get them back twice when she charged them. That is, if she took the case.

What had Mr. Engleton meant by royalty? She knew that royalty to the British could mean anything from the queen mum herself to a stable boy of some distant earl of nowhere. And why so uncertain regarding who and what had happened? Could the authorities really be so out of it that they had no idea?

Susan reviewed all that she had read on the plane from the travel book her secretary, Patrick, bought for her. Of all the islands in the Caribbean, Barbados was one of the oldest and most well ordered. Dating back to the 1600's, Barbados had been a bastion of British rule in the Caribbean. And since America was a British colony at that time, the ties between Barbados and Colonial America had also been strong. Bridgetown was the only city outside of America where George Washington had ever visited, staying there for several months while his older brother recovered from tuberculosis.

To this day, Barbados remains a refined and well-run island. Dressing for dinner, tea time, low crime and very stable. A stalwart of British civilization and a favorite vacation destination for many Brits on holiday.

Nothing so far made sense, but these cases rarely did until Susan got her hands dirty. Susan winced as the thought of Richard "Dutch" Holland crept back into her mind. Like a bad penny, he always found his way back into the pockets of her mind, and her bank account. Of course she still owed Dutch money from his last job. But she felt totally justified in not paying him after he completely screwed it up. It was a simple job, even for him.

All he had to do was pick up some land deeds from a lawyer in Costa Rica for a home in the Guanacaste region that a client of hers was building. The last she heard, Dutch had been run out of the country and the papers had somehow disappeared. That had been three weeks ago and Susan had not heard a word from "Dutch the Drunk" until receiving the fax. It was as if the Devil and Dutch conspired to make her life a living hell. Susan ordered a double scotch from the flight attendant, her nervous system prickling over the thought of Dutch Holland.

"So, you going to Barbados on vacation?" asked the middle aged businessman with the bad comb over sitting next to her.

Susan studied him like a lion considering her next meal. "Why do you ask?"

"No particular reason. Just making conversation." Susan stared at him, steely eyed. The man uncomfortably shifted about in his seat. "It's just, well, I'm single, and I see that you're single," the man said, pointing to her ringless hand. "And I was thinking, perhaps we could see some of the island together?" Susan ran her eyes up and down the man, as if shredding his skin, along with any sense of dignity he might have had.

"Not if you were the last man, on the last planet, in the last universe," she said in a decisive monotone. "You understand me?" The man nodded as he swallowed hard. He stood up on quivering legs, and headed toward the back of the plane, Susan fully expecting he would jump.

It was after three by the time the flight to Barbados landed and she bullied her way through customs. She had no idea of how or where to reach Dutch Holland or his better half, Crane Luk.

She decided to take a cab straight to the Bridgetown Police Station on Coleridge Street. Susan expected the worst, having to see Dutch Holland again, but hoped for the best; maybe he would be stone cold on a slab. As her cab driver maneuvered down the narrow winding streets from the airport toward Bridgetown some thirty minutes away, Susan sat back and let the breeze calm her racing thoughts. The distinctive scent of musky vegetation and burning firewood filled her senses as it mixed with the sea air, its smell always present on the islands. One of the best features of Barbados was its location. As the farthest eastern lying island in the Caribbean, it was not only the first port of landing for the sailing ships of old, but it also enjoyed a constant on-shore breeze.

"You going to the jail to meet your man?" the stubble faced cab driver asked as he wrestled with the steering wheel.

"Shut up and drive," Susan said with a smile. The middle aged cabbie squinted at the road ahead, visibly on the verge of tears.

The dense fields of sugar cane slowly gave way to the rows of packed houses and shops on both sides of the H1 Highway, crowded in like pups at their mother's teats. The cab recklessly bounced through the pot holes, nearly colliding with pedestrians and vehicles as they sped through the town of Hastings. The intermittent views of the ocean finally gave way to Carlisle Bay, easily the longest stretch of sugar white sands forming a perfect crescent to the clear azure of the peaceful ocean.

Susan slumped into her seat as she struggled with the urge to jump out of the cab and dive headfirst into the irresistible blue. Thoughts of her murdered father arose. She imagined how he would have enjoyed being on the islands and sharing another case with her. Instead she was left with Dutch. She felt sure that her father would have approved of her giving up the chance to again be the public defender so she could carry on in his place. Memories of that night pricked her conscious, when some cowardly coke dealer shot him in the back. "Son of a bitch," Susan muttered to herself, causing the cabbie to drive even faster. Her fingers curled into fists as the thought of discovering who had shot her father and emptying the clip from her Glock into his head overcame her.

The sound of snarled traffic jolted Susan out of her thoughts as the cab entered the congested streets of Bridgetown. Tourists from the cruise ships' clogged the streets and bridges, the cruise ship's upper decks visible over the crowded roof tops from the port at the edge of town. Bridgetown was a tourist's delight with a quaint mix of stucco buildings piled next to each other. Many of the streets included narrow bridges over canals which were fed by the ocean. Except for the cars, one could imagine being back in the 1800's when tall ships ruled the oceans and men of courage ruled the day. Whether by accident or the result of the British pension for tradition, Bridgetown had remained much as it was and always had been. The narrow streets, crowded in by the buildings, which randomly housed anything from the exquisite to the mundane, provided a homey feel even for first-time visitors. The lack of American tourists added to the special feel, as the streets were primarily filled with Europeans and South Americans.

The cab took a sharp turn and after a half mile abruptly stopped at the police station on Montefiore Fountain Square next to the public library and synagogue. Susan recalled reading in her tour book that many of Barbados' first settlers in 1625 were Jewish, their influence steadily growing until the devastating hurricane of 1831 when most of them left for Philadelphia. She wondered how strange this island must have seemed to them upon arriving from the capitals of Europe. It's hard to believe during that time, the Protestant religion strictly forbade making a profit on the loaning of money to others. The Jewish religion, never feeling so inclined, was always there to serve that need, charging a reasonable amount of interest for their money lending services. And with Barbados as the primary port of trade for the British Empire at the time, it is no wonder that the Jewish population thrived in Barbados.

The cab driver wrestled Susan's bag out of the trunk. He nodded toward the police station. "You buying or selling?" he asked with a smile, hoping his attempt at conversation would result in a tip.

"I guess I'm buying," Susan replied, handing the driver the exact amount of the fare. Susan wrestled her bag up the steps into the small lobby of the police station as the cabbie peeled away, leaving obscenities in his wake. She was greeted by the sole desk sergeant who dolefully stamped paperwork behind a counter. Crane Luk was primly seated on a wooden bench on the other side. "Crane?"

Crane immediately came to attention, taking Susan's hand in a polite gesture as he always did. "Thank you so much for coming. When your secretary called, I couldn't believe it. It's so kind of you, really. But you could have just wired the funds."

Susan moved in close to Crane, her five foot ten inch frame towering over the diminutive Vietnamese. "Right," Susan smirked. "Crane, how long have we known each other?"

"Oh, I don't know Ms. Susan. Let me think, going on five, no, six years. Right after your father, God bless him, passed away."

"And after all that time you still think that I would just wire money to that half-wit Dutch Holland?" Susan's mood lightened. "If it wasn't for his past with my father, I wouldn't even be here, much less work with that idiot."

"Well, I don't know. It's just that, well, Dutch said you owed him some money."

"And he owes me some land deeds. I've been taking nothing but crap over those missing papers."

"Not to worry, Ms. Susan. I have them, for sure."

"You have them with you, right here, right now?"

Crane whistled through his teeth, a sure sign that the answer was not nearly as easy as the question. "You see Ms. Susan, that is where it becomes somewhat, well, difficult."

"Difficult? How difficult can it be? Either you have the deeds or you don't! And if you don't, then Dutch Holland can just rot here for all I care."

Crane gestured in his gentle way for Susan to sit next to him on the bench, leaning toward her in confidence like a priest counseling a new bride. "You see, I have been given instructions to guard those papers, and when payment is received, to give them. They have been through quite a journey, a very harrowing journey, just to get here. That much is true."

Susan bore her steely blue gaze into Crane's timid eyes. "I want those papers Crane."

"So many lives have been saved by those documents. That I can tell you. I am sure when you know it all, you will be as proud of those papers as anyone could ever be."

"Crane, has the sun fried your brain? What the hell are you talking about?"

"It all started with the lawyer in Costa Rica."

"Mr. Mercado?"

"Yes, he invited us to lunch, and not one to be rude, Dutch accepted. Of course, he invited me along, because you know how much I enjoy lunch."

Susan rolled her eyes. "Not that Dutch has ever missed a free meal in his life as well," Susan said as she waved Crane onward toward his point.

"Over lunch he explained that the love of his life, a Ms. Heidi Costanza, was being held captive, and since Dutch was a detective, he asked if we could free her."

"Captive? Free her? Free her from what? From who?"

Crane crouched in close to Susan. "That is the difficult part. It seems that the lawyer, well, let's just say that he met her at her place of business. A terrible place, where men go to be with women."

Susan shut her eyes, her head back, as she took in Crane's delicate recounting. "Okay, so this attorney, Mr. Mercado, wants you and Dutch to rescue this prostitute, Ms. Costanza, from a cathouse. Is that what you're saying?" Susan worked hard to suppress her desire to squeeze Crane's neck until his head popped off.

"Yes," Crane replied in an embarrassed hush. "So Dutch makes a few visits to the house."

"A few visits? I can just imagine. He probably slept with every girl there."

"No Ms. Susan, Dutch called it reconnaissance."

"Reconnaissance my ass," Susan spat back.

"You know Dutch only has love for Ms. Vicky. She is his true and only."

"You mean one and only. And besides, have you ever met this Ms. Vicky? I haven't. I think she's some figment of his pickled imagination."

"No, I assure you, Ms. Vicky is neither a fruit or a spice," Crane said.

"Fruit? Spice? What? Oh, I get it, fig...ment. Very funny Crane."

Crane looked at Susan like a dog hearing a strange noise. "You see, Dutch had a plan. One night we went to the house. He instructed me to plant some explosives that he made from fertilizer under the porch. To be a diversion, so that he could then sneak out Ms. Costanza."

"So what happened? No, don't tell me. Somehow you blew up the deeds instead."

"No, we blew up the house."

"The cathouse? You blew up the whole house?"

"It seems that Dutch had somewhat changed his plan. While I was working on the porch, he put the remaining explosives on the back wall and right after I blew up the porch, well actually most of the front wall of the wooden house, he blew out most of the back wall."

"Why? Why the hell would that moron do that?"

"It's his soft heart. Always getting him into trouble."

"No, you fool. I mean, why the hell did he blow up both walls of the house? What was he thinking?"

"Well, after all his visits he had gotten to know all the girls so to speak. So he decided to rescue all of the girls, not just Ms. Costanza. The only problem was that the night we rescued the girls, half of the judges from San Jose just happened to be there. Must have been a legal conference or something. And of course, when both walls blew down, well, you can imagine. With just two walls, the whole thing started coming down, board by board so to speak."

Susan buried her face in her hands. "What a fool," she muttered.

"Oh, there's more. As the judges, many naked, came running out of the front door, Dutch was leading a line of girls out the back, all dressed in frilly things and such. And black smoke everywhere."

"How many were there?" Susan couldn't help but ask.

"I counted at least six judges, all fat and charred, you know, all black from the soot."

"No, I mean girls! How many were there?"

"There were five. Let's see, there was Ms. Costanza, and Ms. Mary. She didn't have a last name for some reason, just Ms. Mary. And then there was Ms. Martinez, she was from Venezuela."

"I don't need to know their frickin names Crane. For God's sake. Jesus!" Susan shouted, her eyebrows raised like the golden arches.

Crane leaned back from Susan's volume. "You would have liked Ms. Mary."

Susan shut her eyes and then squinted hard, trying to compose herself. "Okay Crane, just tell me. What does this have to do with the deeds?"

"Oh that. Well, we got the girls to the boat, but what we didn't know was that the Madame of the house recognized Dutch, because of his previous visits."

"You think?" Susan sarcastically spat, her glare almost blinding Crane.

"We also didn't know that the owner of the house was the local police chief. You see, prostitution is legal in Costa Rica."

"Frickin A! Was there anything that you <u>did</u> know?"

"Yes, Dutch knew someone might come after the girls. So he tied some anchor chain to one of the pylons under the dock. Sure enough, just as we were pulling away, the police chief with his men show up on the dock. They began shooting and everything was crazy, the girls screaming and all. What we didn't know was that the whole dock would come down. I guess the other pylons were rotted, with the police chief and all going into the water. I think the police chief drowned, but I'm not sure."

Susan took a deep breath. She measured her words using her hands as the meter.

"Crane, how about you get to the part about the deeds? The deeds, okay?"

"Yes, well that is one final thing we didn't know. Or at least count on. You see the lawyer, Mr. Mercado, was to meet us in Aruba. There he would pay Dutch his fee and take Ms. Costanza."

"And ..."

"Well, during our passage through the Panama Canal, well, you know how Dutch is when it comes to women."

"Like a rattlesnake."

"So, the girls were all partying with Dutch, you know, celebrating. Dancing, drinking, flashing other boats, that sort of thing."

"I can only imagine."

"When we get to Aruba, Ms. Costanza says she is not in love with Mr. Mercado. That she is now in love with Dutch. Bad, very bad."

Susan raised her hand for Crane to stop. "Let me guess. The lawyer doesn't pay you the money and you're stuck with five girls."

"Well, you are right about the lawyer, but again, Dutch and his soft heart. He pays to fly all the girls back to their home countries. And that is why we are broke and need you to pay us."

"What an idiot," Susan muttered.

"Would you like to know how we got the papers back?"

Susan again halted Crane with an open palm. "Here, here's the money. Just get him. Don't say another word." Susan stuffed a wad of bills into Crane's hand, closing his fingers over them. "Not another word."

"Thank you, Ms. Susan," Crane said as he stood up. Susan motioned him away as she buried her head in her hands.

CHAPTER 3

Reg held on tight to Melody's hand as he led her through the dense underbrush that clung to the rocky ground. It was clear to see that Barbados was created from a volcano by the nature of the high ground on the North end of the island. On this windward side of the island, the sharp lava rocks towered straight up from the rough ocean, the waters below known to be teaming with sharks. Waves constantly slapped at the stone face, water spraying up through the holes in the rocks, etched over time by the ocean tides. Reg and Lady Melody constantly looked about their surroundings, each for their own reasons. Their clothes were sweat soaked, Reggie pulling her along, a firm grip on her wrist. Lady Melody stumbled on the rocky path that led to what seemed to be the edge of a cliff.

"We're not going down there, are we?" Lady Melody asked in the softest English accent, her voice trembling, as they reached the edge of the cliff. They both peered over the edge at the one-way path etched into the face of the cliff that led down to a small floating dock. At the end of the dock lay an older boat, a 32 foot Hatteras Sport Fisherman. "I can't possibly walk down that. It's way too narrow."

"Yes, we have to," Reg replied. He pulled the broom handle from his back pocket, as if to finalize any further discussion. Lady Melody let out a baleful sigh, her head down. She had always been one of the most athletic girls in her class, the prestigious Perse School for Girls. But ever since that fateful night when Reggie showed his face, she had not had one bit of rest. Her nerves were shot, and all she wanted now was a hot bath and a warm comfortable bed. From her point of view, neither seemed very likely.

Reg had made plans with the captain of the small fishing boat "Kazar" to rendezvous on this side of the island because of its sparse population and isolation. He only hoped that his deposit with a promise of more to come would guarantee that the Captain kept his promise. Having spent his entire life on a small island like Barbados was like growing up in a small town. Reggie had always been his mother's favorite. He was no more than a happy freckle faced ten year old when his mother was diagnosed. It took a year and seven months for the uterine cancer to consume the rest of her. All the while Reggie never sure of what was happening or why. The hole her death left in Reggie's young heart was more than anyone should bear at that age. And one that no one could fill. Nor did they try. His lawyer father, struck down by her loss like a pedestrian in a hit and run, never was one for sharing feelings. The loss of the only love in his life made a bad personality trait even worse. So Reggie was left to bear his grief alone, with no one to understand much less care. Most of the kids he had grown up with were British expats like his family, or wealthy island locals. They all attended St. Michael School located on Martindales Road in the parish of St. Michael. With 800 students, and a penchant for a lot of homework, there wasn't much time for girls. Unusually tall for his age, his time playing on the school's basketball team further curtailed his chances with girls. The school principal's belief in using the strap as a form of corporal punishment sealed the deal. Just the hint of impropriety between the sexes at school would insure the strap for the boy and a stern admonishment for the girl, as well as dire warnings of teen pregnancy to the parents all around. So without a female figure in the home and insurmountable barriers at school, Reggie had entered his eighteenth year of life without any opportunities at lust or love. With Lady Melody it was both.

With a population of around 300,000 it wasn't unusual to end up knowing something about someone from every walk of life, including the seedier side. The Captain, as everyone called him, was one of those. Everyone just referred to him as "the Captain" and Reg had never really wanted to know more. As it is with boys in high school, especially rich boys, drugs are just a part of the curriculum. The Captain was one of the major suppliers of pot which was grown as the number one export on the neighboring islands of St. Lucia and St. Vincent. So Reggie knew of him just like many of the other proper English boys who had the money for a pound or two of pot. And since the Captain regularly padded his income by smuggling in whatever else would bring a price, he wasn't above smuggling a person off of the island as well. A small time dealer who also worked as a doorman at the Club Xtreme nightclub had introduced Reg to the Captain upon Reggie's repeated requests. The Club Xtreme was one of the few nightclubs on the island and was the party destination for many of the young and famous who visited Barbados. It was the same club where Reggie first laid eyes on Lady Melody. She was in Barbados on holiday with a group of girls from school, their chaperone more interested in the handsome waiters behind the bar than her charges.

It was as if a curtain had parted for Reg, with only Melody standing on center stage. From the moment he saw her, with her long blonde hair, crystal blue eyes, and a smile that could warm a heart of ice, he was possessed. She was rhythmically swaying back and forth to the music when he spied her that fateful night, his feeling for her emerging like a cobra coming out of its basket.

Melody was the most beautiful woman he had ever seen, or that he had ever dreamed of. Not even in his post pubescent dreams had he imagined that such a beautiful and perfect woman could exist. He had never known such soul searing desire. Too insecure to ever approach a pretty girl, he had confined his emerging sexual urges to the occasional ladies lingerie catalogue. When he first saw Lady Melody in the club, chatting with her friends, smiles all around, his heart actually stopped beating. He had to force himself to breath, to believe that such a person could actually exist. It took him three more visits to the Club Xtreme before he was able to sum up his courage and manage a casual discussion with her. And even then he could barely take his eyes off the floor, as if he had some type of shoe fetish. He could still imagine her by his side, her hair as fresh as lavender, her skin baby soft. Nothing could come close to her and now he had no greater goal than to do just that.

Fortune finally shined on him by positioning her next to him at the bar that night. "Hi, I'm uh, well, I've seen you here a few times, you know," was his first auspicious sentence that he muttered to Lady Melody, half scared to death. Lady Melody simply flipped the hair out of her face and smiled, so coyly that Reggie turned red with embarrassment, sure he had climaxed right then and there. After an interminable silence, Reggie held out his hand, "I'm Reggie. And you?" he asked, already kicking himself in the head for saying something so lame.

"Melody," she said, taking his hand. The soft wonderful feeling of her dainty, perfect hand against his skin, rough worn from doing landscape work, caused his heart to melt. He held it as an ogre would a baby bird, carefully, looking down at her hand as if it were a rare work of art. Reggie looked up at Melody, his expression one of sincere truth.

"You are so beautiful," he said, not sure of where it came from, but feeling resolved just the same. Lady Melody smiled, this time shyly, as if she were hearing those words for the first time. She blushed.

"Thank you," she managed, her voice breaking.

Now things had changed. And the game was a totally different one. A game that neither could afford to lose. "There's no turning back for me now. It's either down the path or over the cliff into the sea," Reggie said, his expression fixed with determination. Lady Melody began to softly cry as Reggie pulled her along by her wrist.

The two clung to the rocky face as they slowly made their way down the winding trail that was nothing more than a two foot wide ledge chiseled out by some island inhabitant long ago. Reg let out an audible sigh of relief when they finally reached the floating dock, the small fishing boat casually bobbing about in the surf at the end of the dock. He hurried Melody down the dock and into the boat, constantly scanning the surroundings for any sign of the Captain, or anyone else. Reg ducked momentarily into the small cabin and then pointed for Melody to sit on a small pile of fishing nets.

Melody, her face full of fear and regret, sat down on the nets, her arms hugging her knees to her chest. "Why are we taking this boat? It doesn't seem very seaworthy," she said.

"It could be worse," he abruptly stated. Melody slightly shivered as she gazed about. An errant wave slapped the starboard sending salt spray over both of them. "When the Captain shows up, don't say a word, you understand?" Melody glumly shook her head and then curled herself into a tighter ball. All she could hope for at this point was that Reggie may have some faint idea regarding what he was doing, and how to do it.

"Don't say a word about what?" The gruff voice from behind Reg startled him, Reg almost tipping over as he spun around to face the Captain who stood on the dock behind him. The Captain cracked a grin, the state of his yellow decaying teeth matching the rest of his appearance. "I saw you two skulk in here. I was taking a piss on the rocks."

Reg nervously smiled as he felt for the comfort of his broom stick, still snug in his back pocket. "It's getting late. We need to leave now before the seas get much larger," Reg stated, the confidence in his voice cracking.

"You got the rest of the money, son?" Reg nodded, patting the front pocket of his jeans. "Good, because I'd hate to have to throw you and your cute little package overboard." the Captain said gesturing toward Lady Melody, causing her to shiver at his sight. The Captain withdrew a pint of the local Mount Gay Rum from his coat pocket and took a swig. He stepped onto the boat, his eyes taking a walk all over Melody. "So, she worth a lot of money I'd guess, a pretty young thing like that?"

Reg looked over at Melody who now shrank back into the fishing nets. "It's nothing to talk about. Let's get going."

"You young kids, always in a hurry. Hurry here, hurry there." The Captain rubbed the stubble on his scarred chin. He took another swig from his pint of rum and leered at Melody. "I bet you've never even taken the time to taste that there flower, have you son?"

"How about you cut the talk short? We really need to get going, now," Reg demanded, his eyes darting from the Captain to Melody and then back again. His heart began to race as he struggled to keep an expressionless composure.

"Well, I'm just thinking, how would it be if I take over this little game you've got going? The way I see it, I can have her and her daddy's money to boot."

Reg withdrew the broom stick and pointed the sharp end at the Captain. "I don't think so, old man. If you want your money, you'll do what I say." The Captain looked bemused for a moment, and then quickly pulled a tucked Smith & Wesson .45 pistol from behind his back. He pointed it squarely at Reg, its gun barrel almost touching Reg's left temple.

"A gun beats a broom stick every time, son. You rich kids, you don't know shit, do ya?"

Reg's face flushed red with adrenalin and fear, Melody's eyes wide with fright as the Captain chuckled.

"I do know some things," Reg softly said as he summoned all of his courage, the thought of death being more acceptable than losing possession of Melody. Hoping that his years of karate lessons would pay off, Reg swung the open palm of his right hand with all his might as the Captain leered at Lady Melody, his hand firmly slapping the Captain's head right where Reg had been trained, on the left ear. The speed and strength of the slap immediately burst the Captain's eardrum, the concussion emitting a jar to the Captain's brain which stunned and confused. With his other hand, Reg deftly grabbed the Captain's gun and wrenched it away, remembering to simultaneously step back to avoid any blows of retaliation. Instead, there was silence as the Captain momentarily stood stunned, his eyes wide with painful surprise as a trickle of blood dribbled from his ear. Like a building demolished by dynamite, the Captain crumpled to the deck, his eyes rolling into the back of his head. Reg, flooded with adrenalin, pointed the gun at the Captain and then at Melody as he shifted about from one leg to the other. Melody drew back in shock, Reg lowering the gun. He bent over and studied the unconscious Captain.

"You should give this up," Melody softly spoke. "None of this is working out for you, Reggie. You're just going to get caught. There's just nowhere to run. Nowhere for you to hide."

Reg paced about the boat, raking his fingers through his hair as he wildly waved the gun about. "Don't tell me what to do. I have a plan, you hear me! A plan, damn it. Here's what we're going to do. I'm going to drive the boat. Get up," he ordered.

Melody rose, backing as far away from Reg as she could. Reg pointed the gun at the Captain, shaking it as if it were an extension of his index finger. "Come over here and help me."

"Help you with what?"

"We're gonna roll him off the boat."

"Off the boat? You mean into the water?"

"Yeah, that's exactly what I mean." Reg kicked the legs of the Captain as one would a downed animal to make sure it would not strike back. He patted down the Captain, taking the keys from his coat pocket. "You get his legs."

"No, I won't do it. He'll drown. That's just the same as if we shot him. That would be murder. I can't do that. I won't do that!"

"What are you talking about? You heard him, didn't you? He was going to shoot me, and do worse to you. He's a pig!" Reg looked into Melody's eyes which were wide, not with fear, but with compassion. He wasn't sure if it was for him, the Captain, or both.

A nervous laugh escaped his lips, Melody's sympathetic smile slowly calming his anger and anxiety.

"Okay, then we roll him onto the dock. Okay?"

"Okay. I'll do that." Melody walked over and grabbed the Captain's legs, gathering them up in her arms like a bunch of errant flowers. "Thank you Reg."

"I'm going to regret this," Reg said as he grabbed the Captain under his arms. "He deserves the sea."

CHAPTER 4

Susan waited in the police station lobby for over an hour, her impatience growing by the minute. The sound of Dutch Holland's voice cut through her like a razor blade on paper. Susan stood as the desk sergeant appeared followed by Crane Luk and Dutch Holland. Dutch, at six foot two, always seemed to look taller and larger to Susan than his build belied. He was sporting a two-day stubble and faint streaks of blood on his tee shirt. As always, he wore a pair of Reyn Spooner shorts, khaki, along with a well worn pair of Sperry Top-Sider boat shoes. His locks of sandy grey hair always seemed to spill over his face, like an aging Medusa. As he got closer, Susan could almost count the number of battle scars on his face, his nose a history of poorly set breaks.

"Okay, you guys take it easy," Dutch hollered back to the other prisoners down the hall in the holding cells. Susan approached the sergeant, her eyes glaring at Dutch as he approached. Her anger flared like a volcano at the thought of having to pay to spring Dutch while he conducted court in the jail cell like some celebrity.

"Shoot him. Just take your gun and shoot him," she whispered to the sergeant. The sergeant gave Susan a quizzical look and then shook Dutch's hand.

"It's a pleasure to meet another Vietnam vet. You take care Dutch," he said, fondly patting Dutch on the back.

"Just get me out of here," Susan demanded, Crane leading the group out of the station to an awaiting cab.

No one said a word as the cab maneuvered down the narrow streets that wound their way through Bridgetown toward the marina boat docks. Street vendors dressed in colorful prints hawked their wares in front of the white-washed concrete buildings, tourists and locals clogging the streets and sidewalks.

Dutch and Crane in the back, Susan in the front. Susan never cooled off quickly, and this was no exception.

"That sergeant was one nice dude, don't you think?" Dutch finally spoke, a thinly veiled effort to break the ice. Susan turned around in the front seat, her face screwed up in rage as she pointed a shaking finger at Dutch.

"Don't you say a thing! Not one thing. Crane told me what happened in Costa Rica. Oh yeah, he told me all right. Are you totally insane? Don't answer that. Of course you are. If I didn't need you for a case, I would have let you rot in that jail. Rot! You understand me?"

"Come on Ice, it wasn't that bad. Besides, how lucky can you get? You need a great detective, and what do you know, here I am. It's almost like ESP."

"ESP. Yeah, Extra Shitty Person! That's what you are Dutch. And I expect you to be on your best behavior when we meet our client tonight! So help me, if you screw this up, I'll personally see to it that you're hand delivered back to Costa Rica. I mean it."

"Jeez Ice, and here I used one of my two phone calls to get you a reservation at my buddy's hotel. I'm kind of hurt."

"Well, the one good thing is at least you had a chance to sober up in jail. You are sober aren't you, relatively speaking?"

"Like a church mouse. Hey, I tell you what. I'll give you the deeds the minute we reach the boat. How's that? You can catch a cab to my buddy's hotel, and I'll pick you up around seven, just in time to make this meeting tonight."

The cab pulled up to the marina entrance, stopping at the guard gate just long enough for the guard to recognize Dutch and wave him through.

"How is it everyone always knows you?" Susan asked, a note of annoyance in her voice.

"You've got to make friends Ice. It's all about who you know and who you blow. Right Crane?" Crane dutifully nodded without saying a word, his stoic posture unchanged since entering the cab.

"Like the two men in the bar?" Susan quipped.

"Those two had it coming Ice. They called me old, and Crane yellow."

"You are old, Dutch, and Crane, no offense Crane, is yellow."

"I'm just saying," Dutch replied as he stepped out of the cab and headed toward his boat without waiting. Susan and Crane jumped out of the cab, Susan instructing the cabbie to wait before chasing after Dutch.

Dutch's sailboat was a 44 foot Leopard catamaran. Built in '98, he spent more loving care on it than on all the women in his life combined. The catamaran was an owner's version, with one large owner's stateroom including a head running the full length of the starboard pontoon hull. In the other pontoon were two staterooms including a head for each. With a huge enclosed deck area that included the galley, dining area and comfortable living room with a big screen TV, it was as roomy and comfortable as an apartment. And unlike single hull sailboats, the Leopard catamaran was as fast as it was stable. That made it a great long distance cruiser as well as a party boat, the latter feature never lost on Dutch. Dutch patted his boat, "Sailher," as he jumped aboard. "Good to be back on you girl," he announced as he pulled off his tee shirt soiled with blood. Dutch had put every cent working as an "independent ops" agent into the boat. Fresh out of Vietnam, Dutch wasn't sure of much, except that he was working as a hired gun for an international private security company. And just like Nam, it left some deep scars, because killing is killing, whether for God, country or money. So the minute he had begged, borrowed or stolen enough money to get Crane Luk out of Vietnam, and to pay cash for the only lasting love in his life, his boat the "Sailher," Dutch left it all behind. Of course, the outstanding warrant the grand jury stuck him with for the suspected murder of some scum bag cocaine cowboy a few years back also kept him sailing onward. It's hard to serve papers on someone who doesn't have an address.

Crane and Susan boarded the boat, Crane taking a bottled water from the deck cooler. He handed it to Susan.

"Here Ms. Susan. It's important to stay hydrated in Barbados. It's very humid." Susan took the water and sipped it, leaning against the wheelhouse.

"Yeah, good move Crane. He's right Ice, before you know it you could faint from dehydration. Barbados is as close to the equator as you can get. Crane, get me a beer will you?" Crane dug into the cooler and handed Dutch a bottled water, Dutch frowning.

Susan's gaze fixed on Dutch. She noticed how lean Dutch was, like an alley cat, his muscular torso marked with too many scars from so many battles. She studied the bullet scar on his right shoulder, like a twisting whirl, knotted and tough.

"Is that the bullet scar from the drug dealer who murdered Dad?" she asked.

Dutch glanced at his shoulder and nodded as he traced his finger over its rough contour. "Yeah, that's where that little punk shot me. Son of a bitch," Dutch casually replied. "I still wish I would have shot him a few more times."

"I think four was enough," Susan said.

"Yeah, you're probably right," Dutch agreed as Susan and Dutch's eyes met. Susan immediately looked away as her face blushed with embarrassment.

"I've got to go," Susan stated, quickly jumping off the boat and onto the dock. "Don't be late!" Susan called out as she hurried toward the waiting cab. This wasn't the first time Susan felt what to her was inappropriate feelings for Dutch. "For God's sake, he could be your father!" Susan told herself. She would always write it off as a deep defect in her character, some kind of sick "daddy issue," even though her relationship had been good with her father. She would end up with butterflies in the pit of her stomach when those feelings arose. And she always reacted the same way, by running away as fast as she could. "Frickin gross," she said under her breath. Susan climbed into the back of the cab. It was then that

Susan realized she had not gotten the name of the hotel Dutch had arranged for her.

As she began to open the car door, Dutch appeared at the window, his bare stomach, wet with sweat, almost in her face. He ducked slightly down, Susan unable to divert her eyes from his chiseled abs.

"You didn't get the name of the hotel," Dutch smiled. "It's the Caribbean Court. Just past Bridgetown, on the H1 Highway. "Right on the ocean, in Hastings." Dutch rapped the hood of the cab and it sped away.

Susan sat motionless in the cab, flushed by a multitude of feelings that seeing Dutch had arisen in her. And again, the inevitable stomach butterflies. Although she had only seen Dutch occasionally growing up in Miami, her father would always announce Dutch's arrival with the kind of pomp and circumstance that most would reserve for rock stars or royalty. He seemed to be a mysterious, almost mythical figure to her. Never had Dutch ever stayed around longer than the blink of an eye. Since her mother had died during her birth, every time Dutch showed up at their door in Miami it was her aunt who would babysit her when her father and Dutch would take off. She never knew what they did or where they went, but her father would always return with a renewed sense of purpose about his life. As a girl, Susan would often dream about the adventures she imagined they had. That all ended the day her father was murdered, and Dutch showed up to "make things right" as he would say. Dutch represented to her a reckless but heroic figure whose appearance always created opposing feelings of dread and admiration.

Ten minutes later Susan reentered the present. "Crap, I forgot the deeds!"

CHAPTER 5

By the time Susan reached the Caribbean Court Hotel in Hastings, it was one hour until sunset. The advantage, if not monotony, of being on an island near the equator was that the sunrise and sunset, just like the weather, was the same all year long. In Barbados, sunset was almost at seven, with sunrise around six.

The Caribbean Court Hotel sat on one of the nicest stretches of white sand beach in Barbados. With a swim area encircled by coral rocks, swaying palm trees for shade and modest but clean rooms, it was a bargain. All of the rooms sat on top of a rock hillside, with cascading stairs leading down to the pool, the restaurant and tiki bar, and then the beautiful beach. It was a recurring destination for many middle class tourists from England, and especially for Dutch due to its tiki bar which served a really good and cheap rum punch.

As the cab pulled into the parking lot, Susan recalled the story her father had recounted to her several years ago. It seems that Dutch had helped the brothers, Keith and Ted. They had inherited the hotel from their parents who died in a tragic car accident. An aging organized crime lord from Peckham, a tough section of London, had vacationed at their hotel with his twenty-year old bride. He liked the island so much that he sent a few toughs there with designs on making some of the local businesses pay them protection, particularly from those who provided vacation services to the middle class English clientele. The hoods figured that since they put the bite on the middle class in England, they should also do the same where the poor souls vacationed with whatever money they had left. Dutch made short work of the extortion problem, as well as the lives of all those involved in the trouble making. It was rumored that the only evildoer to survive was the twenty-year old bride, with whom he had a yearlong affair. "With Dutch, a favor done deserved ten in return," Susan thought as she surveyed the modest hotel on her way to check in. She wondered who owned the large brightly painted tour bus promptly displayed in the front parking lot as she entered the hotel office.

"So, you're the latest refugee?" the pretty young blonde behind the check-in desk announced in a decidedly British accent.

"Refugee?" Susan replied.

"From the Dutch circus. I could tell he was calling from either a jail or a bar on account of all the men shouting in the background. Wasn't the first time, you know?"

"God, don't tell me. You too?"

"Me three. That's how many times that prat has stood me up! If you see him, you tell him Vicky would like a word with him."

"I'll do better than that, I'll bring him to you. But only if you promise to slap the crap out of him."

Vicky broadly smiled as she handed Susan the key. "Your first drink's on me. Just let Winston at the bar know I said so."

By the time Susan unpacked, showered and squeezed herself into her evening gown, it was almost eight. Although she had packed faster than a bum getting a free ride, she still managed to include her favorite Versace evening gown. With a neckline that plunged lower than the stock market on black Friday, the backless dress made her look like a sparkling jewel. She kept her ears pricked for Dutch's knock on her door, to no avail. As she finished her make-up, the phone rang.

"I'm down at the bar with my old buds Keith and Ted," Dutch announced. "You're late."

Dutch hung up just as Susan was about to unleash a plethora of cuss words his way. As she stormed down the steps to the outdoor bar on the level below, Susan imagined Dutch sitting there in jeans and a dirty tee shirt, rum drooling down his chin. She also imagined exactly what she would say and where she would punch him. Susan slipped on the third step from the bottom and rolled with the grace of a week-long drunk to the bottom of the steps.

Dutch Holland turned around in his seat at the bar, impeccably dressed in a white shirted tuxedo. "Perfect landing Ice," Dutch shouted out as Susan lay splayed out on the landing at the entrance to the bar.

Susan pulled herself up as well as her Versace dress which was fortunately unharmed. She waved off the offers for help from the men all around. "What the hell," she said, her intentions strangled by Dutch's immaculate appearance as well as her red-faced embarrassment.

"Vicky just rang down. I took the liberty of having Winston here serve me your free drink. Hope you don't mind."

"Good to see you haven't changed much, Dutch," Keith added. With an average build and height, and a smile as breezy as the beachfront bar, Keith was always smiling. He stood and extended a handshake to Susan as she wobbled in. "I assume you're one of Dutch's unfortunate friends as well?"

"Unfortunate yes. Friends no."

"Ouch," Keith smirked. "Dutch and I used to pal around in the old days, right Dutch? Before my parents gave me this place and I got married, just to be clear."

"Keith and his brother, Ted here, are just giving me a hard time," Dutch said. "Ted runs that big tour bus you couldn't miss parked out front. Great tour for sure." Dutch wrapped his burly arm around Ted, giving him a bear sized hug.

"How would you know, Dutch? You've never bothered to take the tour, much less get on the bus," Ted replied as he struggled out of Dutch's grasp. Ted, younger than Keith with a lanky build and cool blue yes, had a gentle touch about him.

"Word gets around, Ted," Dutch assured, slapping Ted on the back.

Ted moved to Susan. He kissed the back of Susan's hand, a wink in his eye.

"Speaking of words getting around, the police are still bugging me about the last time you were here. Remember the last time

Dutch? When you burned the tiki hut down," Keith chimed in, always one to poke the bear.

"Come on Keith, I only burned it a little," Dutch said.

"A little? You call the whole roof a little?"

"I know I'll regret this Keith, but what happened?" Susan couldn't help but ask.

"Well, our Mr. Holland decides that he'll tape the conversation of some thugs who are trying to shake us down right here in the tiki bar. All's going well until Dutch, somewhat inebriated, trips over the power cord. Down comes the whole recorder and mic, right out of the palm frond ceiling, smack dab onto the middle of the floor. One of the thugs pulls a gun, and Dutch grabs the tiki torch and sizzles the poor bloke. Next thing you know, the whole roof is on fire. And the goon is running for the ocean like a flaming cocktail!"

"Come on guys, it wasn't that bad," Dutch objected. "It was just the roof. And don't forget, I got rid of those jerks."

"Not that bad? What about Birdie?" Ted added.

"Birdie?" Susan asked.

"Birdie was our pet parrot," Ted sadly said, pointing to a vacant bird cage hanging from the ceiling. "She went right up, like a roman candle. Squawking, burning. Burning, squawking. It was awful, just awful."

"Boy, are we late," Dutch announced, wanting to skip Ted's soliloquy regarding the fate of the late Birdie. Dutch took Susan by the arm to lead her out.

"Do you know how long it takes to get rid of the smell of roasted parrot? Do you Dutch?" Ted shouted after them as Dutch quickly dragged Susan out. "Well I do Dutch. It takes four months. Do you hear me? Four months!"

By the time Susan stopped laughing at Dutch, their taxi had arrived at the Grand Hilton ballroom. A short five minute ride situated between Hastings and Bridgetown, the Hilton was as stateside as you could get. With its modern design and a nice stretch of beach, it held the point between Carlisle Bay and the rest of the island. A primary destination for honeymooners and well-healed Americans, the large ballroom on the bottom floor was often used for large events due to its capacity and close proximity to Bridgetown. Dutch headed straight for the ballroom on the bottom floor, Susan following from behind. Susan caught him just as they arrived at the front door, her hand strangling Dutch from behind by his collar.

"Not so fast Dutch. There are a few things we've got to get straight."

"Whatever you say. You're the boss."

"That's right. I am the boss. So you let me do all the talking. Right?"

Dutch dolefully nodded. "Got it."

"And no drinking," she said, shaking her finger in his face. "No getting drunk, or saying the first thing that comes into your mind."

"You got it."

"In fact, don't say anything. Just let me do all the talking. In fact, don't even think. Just look and listen, like at a railroad crossing. Look and listen, all right?"

Susan pushed past Dutch and entered the ballroom wearing a smile of satisfaction for having set Dutch straight. A reception line of several British officials stood in line and greeted the attendees as they filed into the ballroom.

"Which one's Engleton?" Dutch asked as he grabbed a drink from a passing waiter's tray.

"I don't know. I only spoke to him over the phone. Listen for a British accent," Susan suggested as they made their way down the line.

"Really? They all have British accents." A short man with a slight paunch and regrettable comb over approached Susan from the rear of the greeting line.

"Miss Berg?" the man asked.

"Yes. Are you Mr. Engleton?"

"Yes, please, let's move from the line," he said. Mr. Engleton of the British High Commission took Susan by the hand and led her to the side, Dutch following behind.

"Ms. Berg, I am so pleased to have you here." Engleton hesitated as he looked Dutch over.

"It's okay. This is Dutch Holland. He's one of my investigators." Dutch shoved out his hand, shaking Engleton's without hesitation.

"Looking forward to working with you. Can you give us an overview?" Dutch asked.

"Yes, of course," Engleton replied in hushed confidence, leaning in for effect. It seems the daughter of one of our most prominent royal families has disappeared while on holiday with her school group. We believe she may have been kidnapped."

"Kidnapped?" Susan repeated.

"Yes, that's what it now looks like, based on what we know from her chaperone and some of her classmates."

"What makes you say that?" Dutch asked.

"There was a local boy who had been showing an unusual amount of interest in her. Everyone we spoke to said that the girl had been seen with him several times at a local nightclub."

"How old is the girl?" Dutch asked, Susan giving Dutch a look that demanded his silence.

"Lady Melody was ... is, seventeen years old. Poor thing. My thought is that this boy was infatuated with her. Or something worse."

"Do you have a photo of the girl?" Susan quickly replied, cutting Dutch off.

"No, but her father does. I hope you understand that her father, Lord Hainesborough, will have to approve any additional information you are given. His family has a royal heritage that goes back to the 1600's. So you see, this is a very delicate situation. Anything that would be of any consequence to their family name would be very distressing."

"But he does want her back?" Dutch wondered out loud.

"Of course he does. He's worried sick. It's just that neither his family, nor any of the royal family, needs to have this get out. The last thing we need is a publicity circus. It wouldn't be good for Lord Hainesborough or for getting his daughter, Lady Melody, back. I'm sure you understand how confidential this investigation must be." Mr. Engleton scanned the greeting line. "There is Lord Hainesborough now," he announced, motioning toward the line. "When you speak to him, please address him as Lord Hainesborough the first time. He will then let you know how to refer to him."

Susan and Dutch turned to observe an impeccably dressed man moving through the line of nondescript officials, his tall, lean stature enhanced by a perfect head of hair with the ideal touch of gray.

"That's what a Lord looks like, huh?" Dutch said with a sneer.

"Looks pretty good to me," Susan said as if thinking out loud.

Mr. Engleton discreetly motioned to Lord Hainesborough who acknowledged him with a tip of his head. Hainesborough completed his introductions at the reception line and then casually sauntered through the crowd, glad handing the party goers as he approached Engleton. He greeted Engleton with a proper handshake.

"Mr. Engleton, always a pleasure."

"Lord Hainesborough, I would like to introduce you to Ms. Susan Berg, and her employee, Mr. Holland." Hainesborough took Susan's extended hand, his eyes locking with hers.

"It's a sincere pleasure Ms. Berg. I understand you took extraordinary measures to meet with me, and I thank you."

"It was my pleasure," Susan cooed, Dutch intentionally clearing his throat.

"Does everyone use your whole title or do they just call you Lord for short?" Dutch asked with a grin.

"You can use my first name, Miles," Hainesborough replied without missing a beat.

"Miles, would you mind discussing this over dinner? I'm so hungry, my stomach's gonna climb out of my throat and bitch slap my face." Susan grimaced at the comment, Dutch avoiding her attempt to step on his foot.

"Very well," Hainesborough agreed, leading the group to a nearby table. Susan pushed past Dutch making sure to take the seat next to Lord Hainesborough.

"Miles, I know that this must be very difficult for you," Susan said taking his hand in hers. "However, the sooner we can begin the investigation, the better our chances of success."

"Yes, I understand Ms. Berg." Hainesborough closed his eyes as if summoning some inner strength. "My daughter, Lady Melody, is a wonderful girl. So beautiful and full of life."

"Of course," Susan agreed. "But is there any information you could tell us about her? Anything that would help us find her?"

"I don't really know," Hainesborough replied, as if surprised by the question. "She's a bright girl, and very kind. Is that what you mean?"

"She means, does she like to fool around?" Dutch interjected. "You know, chase boys, do drugs, kiss girls?" Susan scowled as the blood drained from both Hainesborough's and Mr. Engleton's faces.

"Of course not," Hainesborough said with a tone of annoyance. "Lady Melody is a proper English girl, I'll tell you. No such thing here! Where you need to start is with that boy, that island boy who was stalking her, for God's sake."

Susan gave Miles' hand a comforting squeeze. "My apologies Miles, Dutch didn't mean to insinuate anything. We are all sure that Lady Melody is a good and proper English girl."

"I really can't tell you much about what happened here. I was on the mainland and was scheduled to arrive this week for the showing of our family's antiquities. That is why I allowed Lady Melody to come on this forsaken trip with her school. Lady Melody and I planned to meet up for a family holiday afterward."

"I once knew a stripper named Melody," Dutch added, followed by a woman's shrill shriek of delight heard from across the room. Everyone turned to behold the statuesque blonde from the hotel desk headed straight for their table, her shapely figure squeezed into a low cut sparkling formal. And legs taller and more shapely than a champion race horse, but faster.

"Dutch!" the woman called out as she approached their table, all eyes on her.

"Baby!" Dutch shouted, his arms open to accept her bustfull hug, locks of blonde hair flowing everywhere. "Everyone, this is Vicky, Vicky Godown," Dutch announced to the table, everyone's mouth agape. No one moved, as if turned to stone, until Lord Hainesborough stood up, extending a formal hand in welcome.

"Nice to make your acquaintance, Ms. Godown," Hainesborough primly said. Vicky smiled broadly, her teeth brighter than the midday sun. She bear-hugged Hainesborough, an appalled Engleton clutching Susan's arm.

"I hope you don't mind Miles, but I invited Vicky. She just loves these sorts of things. Dancing fool, right Vicky?" Dutch said. Susan tried to reply, her words chocking on Vicky's breasts that seemed to fill the room as well as every man's eyes.

"Oh, I just love to dance. And you Miles?" Vicky traced her finger down Lord Hainesborough's chest. "I just bet a handsome man like you is quite the dancer!"

"Yes. I was known as quite a quick step at boarding school," Hainesborough sheepishly said.

"Well what are we waiting for! Dutch, you don't mind if I show these gentlemen a good time do you?"

"Oh no Vicky, if they don't mind. Gentlemen?" Dutch offered. Both men looked as if they had just been nominated as the target for the firing squad. "Vicky, they're all yours. You can find me in the buffet line."

Vicky grabbed the arms of Hainesborough and Engleton, dragging them toward the dance floor as Dutch quickly disappeared into the crowd. Susan looked about the empty table, completely bewildered.

"What the hell just happened?" she said to herself.

Dutch knew all to well what had happened, as the devil is in the details.

CHAPTER 6

Reg looked about the open waters of the Caribbean, a sinking feeling in the pit of his stomach. He was sure that he had the correct heading when they left Barbados in the Captain's boat. The boat had no GPS or Loran for guidance, as the Captain had smuggled in these waters all his life, and the positioning equipment would allow the authorities to track him. With the high duties Barbados imposed on just about anything, the Captain would have smuggled in cars if he could have gotten them on the boat. The door to the cabin opened enough for Lady Melody to look out.

"You sure you got a course?" she asked in the most helpful English tone.

Reg confidently nodded. "You don't have to worry about that. No sir, my dad and I have done this run thousands of times."

"Thousands?"

"Well, more like hundreds."

"Hundreds? Really?"

"Well, a couple of times, that's for sure. We just head southwest and there it'll be, St. Vincents. You ever been there?"

"No. I've never really been anywhere. This is the first time I've ever left England." Lady Melody said as Reg continued to scan the horizon. "You sure we're not lost?" Her voice squeaked as a feeling of despair hit the pit of her stomach.

"I'm sure."

"It's just that I'd hate to die at sea. Did you ever see that movie about those poor people lost at sea? What was it again? Oh, I remember, "Life Raft," or something like that. Their tongues got all swollen, and their skin baked. It was awful!"

Reg stuck his tongue out and looked down at it. "Their tongues?"

"They got that way because they ran out of water. Everyone got so thirsty that they started drinking salt water. It drives you crazy you know? Drinking salt water. You go raving mad."

"You go mad?"

"Yes, you see your kidneys have to get rid of any excess salt in your body through your urine. But because salt water has more salt in it than fresh water, your body ends up not having enough water to get rid of all the extra salt. So you end up dying of dehydration. Your brain swells up from not enough water. Total dehydration. So you go mad."

"How do you know all that?"

"High school biology."

"I played on the basketball team," Reg said, not one to be outdone.

"And I'm sure you did very well." Melody was always one to believe that you could compliment your way out of any sticky situation, and this was as sticky as gum.

Reg offered an uneasy smile. "There's no need to worry, were not going to die of thirst. We should be coming up on St. Vincent any second now."

"And if we don't?"

Reg scratched his head as he stared out into the horizon. "Are there supplies down in the cabin?"

Lady Melody shook her head in the negative. "All I found was a bunch of wrapped up packages. They all have this weird design on them. Like an Asian symbol or something. Not sure what they are, but I'm pretty sure they're not food." Lady Melody looked about as if she feared being overheard. "I think they're drugs," she whispered.

"What kind of drugs?"

"I really don't know. I didn't even bother to open any of the packages. I've never done any drugs. In fact, I've never done much of anything. Until this."

"Hand me a few of those will you?" Reggie directed. "I've got an idea." Melody disappeared into the cabin as Reg scanned the horizon. She reappeared and handed several of the solidly wrapped packages to Reggie. "We should be there any time now," Reggie assured.

"You know, it's not too late to turn around. No one has to know anything. I'll just go back. I can say I just stayed out partying. That way there won't be any trouble for you. It will be like this never even happened."

Reg pursed his lips, the lack of landfall causing him to consider her pointed suggestion. "And you wouldn't say a thing about me? You wouldn't even mention my name?"

"No, no I wouldn't," Melody said. Reg eased off on the throttle, the boat dropping down into the water.

"You know, I just want to tell you. I mean, I never wanted you to get hurt. Not ever. You've got to know that."

"Yes. I do believe you." Reg began to turn the boat around just as the outlines of the St. Vincent's four thousand foot La Soufriere volcano came into view. Reg pushed the throttle down and the boat lurched out of the water, Lady Melody spilling back into the cabin with a shrill scream. She stayed put in the cabin, preferring its cramped confines to the vast uncertainty that awaited her on deck.

In twenty minutes Reg had the boat running along the northeastern shore of St. Vincent. He brought the boat within one hundred yards of shore and then cut the engine. Reg opened the cabin door and leaned in. "Melody, it's time. We're here. We've got to go."

Melody opened the door of the cabin like a turtle peeking out of its shell. She looked toward the shore, then at Reg, and then back at the shore again.

"Do you have a really long gang plank?" she asked.

"It's the boat. You see, we're going to have to sink it."

"Sink it? Are you crazy?"

"Otherwise, they'll know where to find us. The Captain is sure to find it. It'll lead them right to us. Not to mention the police. No, I've got to sink it."

"And how do we get from here to there?" Melody asked, pointing to the shore.

"We swim," Reg said with a confident smile. Reg went to the back of the boat and took out the transom drainage plugs. Melody watched with dismay as the ocean began to flood into the boat.

"Do you even know if I can swim?" Melody finally asked.

"Well, can you?"

"No, no I can't," Melody said. Reg looked at Melody and then ran to the back of the boat. He struggled to put back in the drainage plugs, slipping in the slosh of water. Melody laughed under her breath, at that moment Reg realizing her ruse.

"Can't swim huh? Funny. Very funny." Reg picked Melody up and unceremoniously threw her into the water.

CHAPTER 7

It was a short cab ride from the Hilton to the British High Commission. Dutch mentally reviewed the layout he observed when he stopped by earlier on his way to Susan's hotel. He had walked into the lobby of the British Consulate dressed in a loud Hawaiian shirt, a cheap camera swinging from his neck. He bolted straight up the stairs snapping pictures as he went, until the guards caught up with him and summarily walked him out, Dutch profusely apologizing for mistaking it to be the museum of erotic art. No passive infrared or ultrasound motion detectors, known as space protection in security terms, were mounted on the stairway leading to the top floor of offices. He decided that a small window on the stairway's mid-floor landing would be his point of entry, just large enough for his body type. Dutch was certain that with everyone from the consulate at the Hilton, his worst-case scenario would be an aging guard, if that.

Dutch had the cabbie drop him a few blocks away and continued through the alley until he reached his destination. He tugged at the drainpipe that ran up the wall and then pulled himself up, shimmying up until he reached the window. A long penknife was all he needed in order to push the old window lock open. Dutch gingerly pulled himself through the window, and dropped silently onto the stairs' landing. "So far, so good," he thought.

He waited for any sounds, the rattling of keys or the beeping of an alarm, before slowly moving up the stairs to the hallway above. The place was so quiet that the lack of sound pounded in his ears. Dutch counted three doors down until he came to the office of Mr. Engleton, a bit of information he had gotten by making a phone call to the front desk earlier in the day. He had discovered long ago that a kind voice and a plea for help to those at the bottom of the office pecking order could do wonders when seeking information. So when he called saying that he was with the Bridgetown Fire Department and that he was updating the building's sprinkler coverage maps, the lady at the front desk was kind enough to answer all of his questions.

Dutch withdrew his tension wrench and inserted it into the bottom of the door lock, gently pushing right and then left, where he felt no resistance. No matter how many locks Dutch picked, his heart always raced as he worked the tumbles. The specter of being caught along with those feelings of fear and excitement always seemed to make life's seconds seem so much more real. Magnified. Dutch pushed the slender lock pick into the top of the opening, pushing upward against each pin he encountered, until the final pin receded, his tension wrench moving fully to the left, unlocking the door.

Dutch poked his head into the office, first examining the doorframe for any magnetic security alarm contacts as well as the blinking of any space protection devices. Dutch noticed the cooling breeze that drifted through the open window from the ocean beyond. Satisfied that all was clear, he quickly entered the office, gently closing the door behind him.

He twisted on his penlight and went straight to Engleton's desk. Dutch had discovered during his many unauthorized entries that most people were just too lazy to neatly put away files that they were currently working on, and Engleton was no exception. Rather than worrying about what was in Lord Hainesborough's file, which he found in a pile of folders, Dutch took out his digital camera and began taking photos of each page in the file. He listened for any unusual noises from outside the office as he completed photographing each page.

Leaving the office as he found it, Dutch quickly headed back down the hall. The glint from a passing doorknob caught his eye, the sight of a padlocked door always proving irresistible to him.

Dutch looked about like a beady weasel, and then set to work, first pushing his tension wrench into the bottom of the padlock's keyhole. He then inserted the lock pick into the top of the lock and jiggled it as he pushed down on the wrench. The sound of a click shortly followed, Dutch pulling down on the padlock and removing it from the door.

He entered the storage room and panned his penlight to look about. The room was loaded with large, wooden storage crates. A creature of habit when it came to sticky fingers, Dutch pulled a shipping document from one of the crates and stuffed it in his pocket. He then noticed a single carton that stood out, about four feet long and rectangular, perched on its own pedestal. Dutch moved around it and saw something that made his heart almost stop, the blinking of the space protection on the wall.

He left the storage room as quickly as he could. The moment he entered the hallway, the beam of a flashlight crossed the hallway from the top of the stairs, followed by the sound of a security guard's footsteps.

Dutch quickly ducked back into Engleton's office and franticly scanned the area for a way out. His only option was the window. Dutch pulled himself through the open window and carefully stepped out onto the narrow ledge, his hands gripping the top of the windowsill two stories above the street. The guard's flashlight shone into the office, its beam panning about and then settling on his crotch, squarely framed in the middle of the window.

"Come on out of there. I've got a gun," the guard shouted in a trembling voice.

Dutch waited as the guard approached the window, his breath racing faster than his pounding heart. With nowhere to go but straight down, Dutch had only one alternative. Just as the guard was upon him, he swung himself into the office through the open window, landing full force onto the rotund belly of the overweight security guard. He pulled the guard's cap over the man's flustered face and then rolled him over. Dutch bolted out of the room and down the stairs; literally flying out of the landing window he had come in. He scampered down the drainpipe and hit the ground running, a bullet from the guard's gun splattering the brick wall just inches from his ear. Dutch didn't stop running until he reached the safety of his catamaran in the harbor.

After about twenty minutes of frenetic dancing, Lord Hainesborough stumbled back to Susan's table, his face flush as his handkerchief worked overtime to dot the sweat from his face. "I've just got to have a break. That young woman is about to kill me."

"I know the feeling," Susan replied, offering Hainesborough a chair. "My apologies about all of this. I had no idea Dutch had invited that woman."

"No need to apologize. She's just full of youth, and with it a zest for life." The Lord's obvious admiration for the trampy blonde bombshell was like pouring gasoline on Susan's blazing temper. She bit her lip.

"She's full of something," Susan agreed.

"She so reminds me of my daughter," Hainesborough said, the smile running from his face. "So beautiful, so young." Tears began to well in Hainesborough's eyes, touching Susan's heart.

"Lord Hainesborough, I know this must be hard on you, but we really need to talk about Lady Melody."

Hainesborough glumly lowered his head, almost speaking into his cumber bun. "I guess it's easier to pretend it hasn't happened. Just like when her mother died. I have to not think about it. Otherwise it's all too much. I'm sure you must know what I mean?" Hainesborough's grief connected with Susan, dredging up her feelings over the loss of her father.

"Of course, I know this is tough on you. How about you just tell me what you know?"

"Well, that proves to be somewhat embarrassing. You see, Lady Melody is a fairly free spirit. She pretty much has free reign, as most kids do nowadays. After her mother's passing, I must admit that I threw myself into the parliament, running the estate, that sort of thing. I can't help but feel responsible for this in some way. After all, it was my decision to let her come to this forsaken island."

Susan took Hainesborough by the hand and cast a look of reassurance. "We'll find her. Don't worry. How about her chaperone, or the other girls that were with her? Do you have their contact information?" Hainesborough wiped the first tears from his eyes with a napkin from the table.

"Yes, of course. That would be the best place to start. I spoke over the phone to the chaperone, Ms. Harris, when this terrible thing took place. That's when I heard about this man, this boy, whom they suspect. Other than that, there's not much to tell. I ask you Ms. Berg, please find her. Please find her and bring her straight back to me. Will you do that for me?" Susan felt the pain that showed in his face. She couldn't image how powerless this very powerful man must feel, perhaps for the first time in his life.

"Yes, I will do that. I promise. I will bring her straight back to you."

"Miles, are you hiding from me?" Vicky Godown's shrill voice echoed in Susan's ears like the shrill bells of hell.

"Oh no Ms. Godown. Just taking a break."

Vicky draped herself over Lord Hainesborough from behind, Susan giving her a look that would drop a charging water buffalo. "I'm afraid Mr. Engleton has had enough," Vicky said. Everyone at the table looked over toward the dance floor, Engleton collapsed in a chair, furiously fanning his beet red face. His strands of combed over hair stood askew in every direction, his shirt blotted with sweat.

"Shall we, Ms. Godown?" Hainesborough politely offered, extending her a gracious hand as he rose from his chair.

"Absolutely," Vicky replied in delight as she led him toward the dance floor, Susan's nerves as strained as a cheater's marriage.

After another two hours of enduring the lord of the dance, Susan skulked back to her hotel. She had given up any hope of

Dutch showing again, not sure where he had gone, but certain that it would be good for no one. As her cab pulled up to the front of the Caribbean Court Hotel, Ted was exiting his tour bus parked in the front parking lot.

"Where's your old ball and chain?" he asked as Susan approached him.

Susan managed a tired smile as she held down her gown against the stiff breeze coming off of the ocean. "You mean odd ball and chain don't you?"

"Come on, you look like you could use a drink. It's on me." Ted threw a friendly arm around Susan's shoulder and escorted her down the steps to the tiki bar. They both stopped short at the sight of Dutch at the bar.

"What took you so long?" Dutch shouted. "I've been drinking for the last hour waiting for you Ice."

Susan's anger shot through her body, charbroiling her soul. "You shit head! I can't believe it! You leave me with that blonde bimbo, Ms. Godown, just to come here and drink?"

"Now be careful what you say about Vicky Godown. She's very sensitive you know," Dutch countered.

"Give me a break. Can you believe that?" Susan asked turning to Ted. "Ms. Godown, really?"

"Actually, that is her real name. I'm guilty of introducing her to Dutch. She was one the guides on my tour bus. Quite a good girl, really. Now she helps manage the hotel. She's just young, full of life."

"Yeah, I've seen her full life." Susan sat down on a bar stool and sighed in resignation. "I need a drink." She took a long sip from a rum punch, her eyes never leaving the arrogant grin covering Dutch's face. "Okay, I'll bite. What is it?"

"What's what?" Dutch said with the innocent tone of an executioner.

"That shit eating grin of yours. I know that grin. You've been up to no good, haven't you?" Susan asked as she took another sip of her drink, her mind working overtime on the answer. She pointed to the manila folder on the bar in front of Dutch. "It's the folder, isn't it?"

Dutch smiled back, the proverbial canary in his cat's mouth.

"Don't tell me. Let me think for a moment." Susan furrowed her brows in thought. "Right, first your bimbo shows up unannounced and distracts us all while you disappear."

"He likes to break into places, you know," Ted added, soliciting a smirk from Dutch.

"No, you did not? You did, didn't you!" Susan grabbed the folder on the bar and scanned its contents. "Crap, you did. You broke into the frickin High Commission didn't you? You planned it all along, Vicky Godown, the dancing, everything. You prick."

"I've dealt with these types before. Back in London once or twice. I knew that royal pain in the ass wasn't going to give us anything. And you know that in cases like this, every second counts, right?"

"Hey, take it easy. I happen to find Lord Hainesborough quite charming." Susan flipped through the documents Dutch had downloaded from his camera using the printer from the hotel office. "You copied the whole file. I can't believe you. Lord Hainesborough is our client you know? He's not the enemy."

"Here's the thing about clients, Ice. I like to know what they say, and know what I know. Know what I mean?"

"I'm completely lost," Ted chimed in.

"Lost is the right word. As in this file needs to get lost. These are confidential documents. If we get caught with these, it could cost me the agency, to say nothing of a couple of years in jail," Susan replied as she stuffed the file into her purse.

"Ice, before you get all carried away, let's just go over the file. We can then destroy it, burn it, like it never existed. Okay?"

"All right, but don't ever do this again. And if you do, let me know in advance, so I can have you arrested." Susan stood to leave, then reconsidered and grabbed two rum punches. She then led Dutch out of the bar.

"One of those drinks is for me, right Ice?" Dutch asked as they fought the strong breeze coming off the beach as they walked up the stairs toward the hallway. Susan took the folder from her purse as they approached her room. She casually flipped through the documents.

"I'll think about it." Dutch threw his arm in front of Susan, almost knocking her aside, as they reached her room. "Hey, I was just kidding, you can have the frickin drink."

Dutch pressed his index finger to his pursed lips and pointed to the curtained window in Susan's room. The shadow of someone in her room passed across the curtain.

"Shit, someone's in my room. What kind of hotel are they running here?" The shadow vanished, Dutch giving Susan a look of exasperation.

"Hell Ice, why didn't you just blow a foghorn?" Dutch snatched Susan's room key and unlocked the door. He and Susan entered just in time to spot the intruder jump from her balcony to the grounds below. Susan dropped her purse and the file folder by the open front door before chasing Dutch out onto the balcony.

"Do you see him?" Susan asked as they squinted out at the beach. A small glint of white suddenly darted across the length of the beach toward the fence that separated the hotel from the newly built condos next door.

"There he is. Come on, we can cut him off." Dutch grabbed Susan by the arm and the two of them ran out of the room and down the hallway. They reached the parking lot out front where they crouched down next to Ted's gaudy colored tour bus.

"There," Susan shouted, pointing at a shadowy figure in front of them. The figure moved along the other side of the dividing fence by the condos. Dutch took a step back and then ran and jumped, his left leg failing to clear the wire fence. He flipped over into a roll, landing with a thud on his back. Susan sprinted toward the street and around the end of the fence, followed by Dutch. The intruder jumped into a jeep and squealed out of the condo parking lot as Dutch and Susan helplessly looked on.

"Son of a bitch," Dutch cursed under his breath.

"We lost him," Susan sighed. Dutch looked about the hotel parking lot, his eyes lighting up.

"Not yet we haven't. Follow me." Dutch grabbed Susan by the arm and raced over to Ted's tour bus. "Get in," he ordered.

"The bus? You're going to take Ted's bus?"

"You got a better idea?" Susan shrugged and they jumped into the bus. Dutch turned the keys in the ignition and the bus lurched out of the parking lot onto Highway 7. "Hold on," Dutch shouted. "I'm gonna drive this bus like I stole it."

"You are stealing it!" Susan stood next to Dutch, her hands firmly grasping the door pole at the top of the stairs. The tour bus wheezed as Dutch pushed through the gears, the bus picking up speed as they pursued the jeep. The tightly packed rows of houses sped by, becoming a blur as the bus careened down the narrow winding road.

"Do you see him?" Dutch shouted over the whine of the engine.

Susan strained to look ahead as Dutch narrowly missed one of the many public buses that ferried people from town to town. "There, there he is. Right in front of us!"

Dutch grinded the bus into fourth and floored the gas pedal causing the bus to run up and bump the back of the jeep.

"Real subtle."

"I want him to know we're right on him. Maybe he'll panic, make a mistake, wreck the jeep." Dutch swerved to miss a pedestrian who had stepped out onto the road.

"And maybe you'll wreck. Take it easy Dutch, I mean it."

"Okay, okay. But if he gets away, it's your fault. Not mine."

"He's not going to get away. Just stay on him, but don't hit him."

Dutch downshifted, the gears crying out as the bus backed off. The jeep also slowed as they approached Bridgetown, the highway breaking into several smaller roads with bridges. The jeep suddenly lurched forward as it took a quick left turn.

"There, stay on him," Susan ordered, her hand clutching Dutch's arm. Dutch manhandled the steering wheel, the bus leaning as they took the sharp left turn.

"We've got him now," Dutch announced as he increased their speed.

"We do?"

"Yeah, this road curves back around, under the Highway 7 bridge and then meets up with McGregor Street. We can cut him off there." Susan took in Dutch's information, her mind finally registering the flaw in his logic.

"Dutch, wait a minute."

"Not now Ice. We've got him."

"You've got to stop Dutch."

"Stop my arse. We're not going to stop. I've got that bastard! I got him," Dutch growled like a bulldog with its bone. Susan looked ahead at the quickly approaching bridge, the bus closing in on the jeep as both increased their speed.

"Stop the bus, Dutch," Susan shouted as she tugged at Dutch's arm, Dutch only increasing his speed. Susan ducked down as they sped under the bridge, the bus shrieking with the sound of metal scrapping against hard rock. The bus wheezed and moaned as it came to a dead stop, its metal frame firmly wedged under the low bridge. Susan and Dutch lay on the floor of the bus in a heap.

Susan slugged Dutch in the shoulder. "I told you to frickin stop, you idiot."

The sound of an arriving police siren greeted the two as they picked themselves up from the floor. Dutch poked his head out of the driver's side window as the policeman squeezed himself in between the bus and the bridge wall. The policeman rapped his nightstick against the bus.

"What exactly do you think you are you doing?" the policeman angrily shouted.

"Oh officer, I'm glad you're here," Dutch replied after thinking for a moment. "I'm trying to deliver this bridge here and got lost. You wouldn't happen to know where High Street is, would you?"

CHAPTER 8

By the time Susan and Dutch finished with the police, including a handful of tickets and an earful of grief, it was after midnight. Susan was so tired that even her anger at Dutch had gone to bed, with Susan not far behind.

"Amazing how that bus wedged itself in there, huh?" Dutch stoically stated as they walked down Princess Alice Highway toward the port.

"Shut up," was all Susan could say as she trudged behind Dutch.

"I guess you can sleep on the boat tonight. Too late to get a cab back to the hotel."

"The hotel? Do you really think that I can stay at the hotel after what you did to Ted's tour bus? I'll be lucky if they don't burn my clothes." Susan kicked at a clump of limestone as they approached Dutch's catamaran. "And I'm taking your stateroom."

Susan boarded the boat with a groan and then summarily went down below, slamming the door of the stateroom behind her. Dutch shrugged and then lowered himself down the steps to the other two cabins only to be met by Crane Luk's snoring.

"I need a drink," Dutch mumbled as he grabbed a pillow from the closet and plodded back up to the galley.

The incessant ringing of a cell phone was the next thing that pricked Dutch's tired conscience. He opened his bleary eyes and groped about, not sure of how long he had slept or what time in the morning it was. He finally came upon the source of the noise. Dutch flipped the phone open and mumbled, only to be greeted by the ferocious shouts of Ted on the other line. He held the phone away from his ear and then buried it under the cushions of the dining bench that he slept upon.

"Another satisfied customer?" Susan asked as she entered from the galley, a pan full of scrambled eggs in her hands. She was wearing a pair of Dutch's old workout shorts, the tails of one of Dutch's worn dress shirts tied into a knot at her waist. Susan's long legs and silky smooth stomach met perfectly at her narrow hips.

"Why didn't you answer it?" Dutch groused.

"And rob you of the pleasure? No way."

"Look, it's your client too. Hey, are those eggs?" Dutch pushed himself up and stretched. He rubbed his eyes open and looked about the cabin as if for the first time, Ted's muffled diatribe continuing as a backdrop. "Did you use beer when you scrambled those?"

"No beer in the eggs," Crane shouted from the galley. "I always have to say that. No beer in the food." Luk appeared with plates of toast and kippers, along with several coffees on a serving tray. "You're lucky you're not dead, or worse."

"I guess you heard, huh?" Dutch said.

"Heard? It's all over town. You're the laughing stock of the marina. I am so embarrassed. Ashamed, that's what I am."

"God," Dutch muttered in lament. "It was Susan's idea."

"It was not my idea," Susan said in her defense. "You were the one who refused to stop."

Dutch grabbed a handful of scrambled eggs out of the pan and shoved them into his mouth. "In the heat of the moment, does it really matter who said, or did what? Things were just moving so fast. Although I'm pretty sure you came up with the bus."

"You're an idiot," Susan replied as she slapped Dutch's hand away from another try at the eggs. Dutch rustled his hands through his locks of mussed hair and took a deep breath, slowly letting it out with a sigh.

"I guess we'll have to get you another hotel room."

"You think?"

"Just as well, now that someone is on to you. It's got to have something to do with this case. But I can't imagine what. Maybe the kidnapper, or one of their accomplices?"

"You better go apologize to Ted," Crane said, shaking his spatula at Dutch. "He and his brother are good friends, and they know everyone here."

"That reminds me," Dutch replied as he dug his now silent cell phone out of the couch. "Thanks Crane."

"You calling Ted?" Crane asked. Dutch deflected his question with a wave of his hand; Crane angrily muttering under his breath as he returned to the galley. Susan followed, serving herself and Crane breakfast at the counter.

"Hello, is Harris Beerli there? Tell him it's the police." Susan and Luk peered over at Dutch from their plates of food, Crane shaking his head in disapproval.

"It's a crime to impersonate the police, Dutch," Susan shouted out as Dutch returned another dismissive wave.

"Harris, it's Dutch. No, don't hang up. Don't worry, I won't sue you for knocking me unconscious. Okay, then we're even. Look, I need a favor." Dutch stared at his phone with a grimace. "Crap, he hung up on me. Can you believe it?" Both Susan and Luk nodded in agreement as they continued with their breakfast.

"Okay, well at least we have the photos I took of Lord Hainesborough's file." Dutch went below and searched about the desk of the map room just off the den. "Crane, where is the camera?"

"I plugged it in up here," Crane replied without looking up from his food.

Dutch entered the kitchen and flicked on the camera. He began pushing the view button on the camera as he searched the photos on the screen. A quizzical look swept over Dutch's face as he continued to go through the photos on the camera's display. "Crane, did you by any chance use the camera?"

"Why you ask?" he replied without looking at Dutch.

"Tell me you didn't, Crane? Tell me you didn't take all these pictures of buildings around town?"

Crane looked down like a puppy caught chewing his master's best shoe. "You never tell me anything. How did I know those pictures were important? Besides, you printed them."

"What's going on?" Susan asked. Susan rose and took the camera, scanning through the photos of building after building. "Where are the photos of the papers from the Lord Hainesborough file?"

"Exactly," Dutch shouted. "Crane here erased them when he took his photos of buildings."

"Buildings? Why buildings?" Susan asked.

"It's always buildings. Building after building. Every island. Files full of them. Tell her Crane. Go ahead. Tell her your idea. Tell her why you keep taking these damn pictures of buildings all over the Caribbean." Crane looked away, his eyes full of regret.

Susan went over to Crane and put a comforting arm around him as Dutch fumed. "It's okay Crane, you can tell me. Don't listen to Dutch. What is it? You can tell me. It's all right."

"It's worse than that," Dutch replied. "Go ahead Crane, tell her."

"It's for a business I want to do," Crane finally offered. "Something huge. Really big. The next big thing."

"Well, that sounds like nothing to be ashamed of." Susan gave Dutch a dirty look.

"For Christ's sake," Dutch lamented as he poured himself a coffee.

"Shut up Dutch. You know, it's not always about you. Now go ahead Crane. What is it that you're trying to do?"

"Well, you know how everyone likes bacon?" Crane replied, a sense of excitement in his voice.

"Yes, go on," Susan counseled with a kind smile.

"So I have this idea. Dutch and I, we open a shop where we sell everything for bacon. All types of bacon. Bacon sandwich, like BLT, bacon press, bacon hats."

Susan's smile slowly dissolved as Crane continued. "So I am taking pictures of best places for the store. To find the perfect spot, the perfect island for the store. To become the king of bacon."

"Tell Susan what you want to call the store," Dutch added with a devilish smile as he sipped his coffee.

"Makin Bacon," Crane proudly announced. Susan looked stone-faced at Crane and then at Dutch who worked overtime to swallow a laugh.

"Yeah, Makin Bacon," Dutch said as he walked down the steps toward his stateroom to take a shower. "Don't forget about your voice recorder."

A look of realization came over Crane. He rushed to the chart desk and grabbed a small voice recorder, turning it on. "Note to self," Crane spoke into the recorder. "Get my own camera."

It was almost noon by the time Dutch, Susan and Crane cleaned up breakfast and themselves. Dutch had secured a room for Susan at the Little Arches Hotel in Christ Church. About a twenty minute drive up the coast from Bridgetown, it was one of the nicest boutique hotels on the island. Dutch stayed there for two weeks several years ago recovering from a nasty knife wound he had acquired in Kingstown. The two-story Little Arches Hotel sat across from the Barbadian version of what they called Miami Beach, which is easily the second best stretch of white sand on the island. Filled with flowering plants and an excellent open air rooftop restaurant, it deserved the slightly higher rates, both for its ambiance and privacy. Close to the St. Lawrence Gap restaurants and nightclubs, the Little Arches Hotel on Miami Beach was the perfect spot to put Susan under an alias.

Dutch sat in the car drumming his hands on the steering wheel to the song on the radio as he waited for Susan outside of the Caribbean Court Hotel. He occasionally glanced toward the lobby door like a weary cat.

The doors to the lobby suddenly swung open and Susan stormed out, dragging her luggage behind her. Dutch popped the trunk, Susan tossing her luggage in and slamming down the lid. She opened the passenger door and looked in.

"Those frickin bastards! They're trying to charge me twelve grand for the damage to that piece of shit bus!" Susan sat down in a huff, slamming the car door shut. They both looked to the parking lot across the street where the bus sat, its roof crumpled in like a recycled soda can. Dutch swallowed a laugh.

"The nerve of them," Dutch agreed.

"They said that they'd try to get it from you. Good luck with that."

"That's for sure," Dutch replied. Susan silently stewed as she stared out the window. So far, this case had cost her a fortune and they hadn't gotten a single solid clue regarding Lady Melody's whereabouts. On his way to Susan's new hotel Dutch drove past St. Lawrence Gap, a small village on the ocean that consisted of several streets crowded with dance clubs, trendy restaurants and party bars that went on until the early hours of the morning.

"Why do they call it the Gap?" Susan asked as they drove by the town's sign.

"This was the area where the old sailing ships would put up to get their hulls scraped and repaired. It has a short but accessible canal, or gap, that the ships could maneuver into at high tide to get the work done."

"Huh, I thought it might refer to the gap in your paycheck to pay for the damage to that bus."

"Real funny Ice. By the way, did the hotel maids find any of the paperwork from the Consulate?"

"No, damn it. They all blew away during that stupid chase of yours!"

"My chase?"

"Yes, your chase. Stupid chase."

Dutch shrugged and cracked a small smile. "Looks like I'll just have to do some more night work."

"My ass. You're not doing any more break-ins, period. You're in enough trouble with that bus stunt. The local police are just itching to put you and me both in jail."

"So what do you suggest?"

"I'll go over in the morning and butter up Wilfred Engleton. I'm sure I can get him to give me the info." Susan's confidence showed in her cocky smirk. She opened the door and pulled her luggage out of the trunk. Susan dragged her bag up the stairs toward the lobby as Dutch looked over the sugar white sands of Miami Beach across the narrow roadway. She gazed over her shoulder back at Dutch who looked on. "Don't you worry, I've got it covered," she said. Her luggage slipped out of her hand and bobbed back down the stairs heading straight for Dutch's open car door. Dutch quickly shut the door, the luggage rolling by the car and out into the street.

"That was close," Dutch said with a smile of satisfaction just as a dory truck came down the road and smashed into Susan's luggage, dragging it under its chassis, sparks flying. Susan dropped her ass onto the stairs like a tired donkey, her head in her hands. She looked out over the ocean, wondering what she could have possibly done to deserve Dutch, as well as what special hell still awaited them.

CHAPTER 9

Dutch was determined to begin at the beginning, which he told Crane in no uncertain terms, was where he always started from. So after Harris Beerli hung up on him three times, Dutch decided that a personal visit was in order. Crane refused to go, choosing instead to sulk in his stateroom over his diminished status among those in the marina. Susan also refused to take Dutch's calls while she went about replacing her luggage and much of her wardrobe after the truck destroyed her luggage and sent most of her clothes blowing about Miami Beach. If Dutch had been the sensitive kind, he might have felt a sense of rejection.

Dutch walked into the Bridge Bar and Grill, not sure if Harris Beerli would welcome him with a smile or a shotgun. The truth was a little of both. Harris shot Dutch a look that could kill as Dutch approached through the crowded tourists who had arrived from the cruise ship for karaoke night.

"Look, before you go off on me, I just want to apologize," Dutch started.

Harris looked at Dutch as if he had just puked up a baby. "You ... you're apologizing? What, have you now taken up smoking crack in favor of booze?"

"No, seriously, I feel real bad about getting hammered, and smashing up your place. Look, the truth is, I really need your help. This young girl has gone missing and if we don't find her soon, well, you know the odds."

Harris studied Dutch as if he might be a fake Van Gogh. "And what if I say no?"

Dutch looked about the crowd eagerly signing up for their chances at being a karaoke star. "No problem, seeing how I'm in the mood for a little karaoke singing tonight myself."

"Oh no, anything but that." Harris massaged his chin. "My jaw still hurts from your last singing debut on my stage. I'll help, but no singing. Deal?"

"Deal." Dutch cautiously surveyed the nearby patrons at the bar, in particular a short balding man as white as snow, who smiled back at him. Dutch leaned in close to Harris. "I need you to reach out to anyone in the know at Club Xtreme, in Worthing. It seems that's where the girl went missing last. If you can arrange a meeting for me, that's all I need."

"That I can do. How do I get in touch?"

Dutch withdrew a cell phone from his back pocket. He looked it over and then handed it to Harris. "I just bought this cheap throw away on my way over. Can you figure out what my phone number is?"

Harris punched some buttons and then squinted at the screen. "It's a cheap Kyocera cell phone. What'd you pay, fifty bucks?" Dutch nodded as Harris wrote down the number on a piece of paper and stuffed it into his pocket. He handed the phone back to Dutch. "Your number is on the screen there. I'd suggest you also write it down when you get back to the boat."

Dutch nodded and stuck the phone in his back pocket. He grabbed a beer from the tray of a passing waitress as he headed for the door. Dutch took a long sip from the beer just as the short bald man with the pallid skin bumped into him, causing Dutch's cell phone to drop from his pocket and skid across the floor.

"I am so sorry," the bald man said as he stooped across the floor and reached for Dutch's phone. The man handed Dutch his phone with the timidity of a beaten cat. "My name's Menton, Menton Moore."

"Thanks, Menton is it?"

"Yes, that's right. Menton, Menton Moore." Menton followed behind Dutch as he strode for the door. "My mother, God bless her soul, thought it would be a great name. Menton Moore she would sing, Menton Moore."

Dutch held up a hand. "I get it. Very lyrical, for sure." Dutch hit the sidewalk, Menton Moore keeping step with him at his side.

"I couldn't help but overhear you at the bar. Are you a detective or something?"

Dutch kept walking without breaking a stride. "Yeah, something like that."

"Well, I'm looking for a detective to hire. Are you available?"

Dutch looked over Menton Moore in his plain dark slacks, hard-toed shoes and cheap white dress shirt. "Detectives are pretty expensive."

"More than twenty thousand?"

Dutch stopped walking and looked into Menton's eyes for the first time. "You talking dollars?" Menton nodded in the affirmative. "What exactly do you need done for twenty thousand dollars?"

"I need you to find something."

"Find something, huh. What?"

Menton took out a folded piece of paper and carefully opened it, holding it up for Dutch to view. "It's a sword. A golden sword. It belonged to one of my ancestors."

"What, somebody steal it from you?" Dutch studied the photo. It was a sword made entirely out of gold. So much so that it seemed to jump out of the page. Down the sword's fuller, the wide groove that runs down the sword's blade, were exquisite jewels, the cross guard also bejeweled in the same manner. The pommel, the knob at the end of the sword's grip, was covered in the most perfect of diamonds.

"Not exactly. It was somehow misappropriated. Over time. You see, my great, great grandfather was given this sword for bravery. I've been able to trace its whereabouts to this island. Now, I just need a good detective to locate it for me."

"Do you mean locate it, or steal it?"

"No, no, not steal it. Of course not. I would never ask that. I just need you to find out who has it. Once I know that, I will go to the proper authorities. Follow the proper channels."

"And the twenty thousand?"

"I've got it in cash. I saved it up so I could find this important relic of my family's past."

Dutch wrapped his arm around Menton's shoulders in a friendly embrace.

"Why don't we go back to my boat and we can discuss the details of this wonderful opportunity?"

"So you're going to write up a case file?"

"Yeah, that's it. We'll go write up a case file. Right after we go over that twenty thousand dollar thing once more."

Susan spent a good two hours getting her appearance just right. She finally gave her image in the mirror a thumbs up before catching a cab into Bridgetown. She was determined to recover the file on Lord Hainesborough that she had allowed to blow away. If for no other reason than to show Dutch that she had more talent as a detective than he ever had. She was the owner of CDC, and by everyone's estimation, a damn good one. But for some reason, when it came to Dutch, she was right back wearing her retainer, watching the dynamic Dutch take on the world along with her father.

In the cab, Susan rehearsed in her mind every line she would use to bring Mr. Engleton under her spell. He had seemed somewhat asexual to Susan at the Hilton party, but Susan felt confident that she could sway him to do her bidding. Although Susan had an immediate and obvious physical effect of attraction on men, she knew that her strong personality turned most men off. She was determined to let her softer side show through with Engleton, positive that this persona along with the skin-tight dress that she wore would assure success.

As the cab meandered down the H1 Highway toward the British Consulate, thoughts of Susan's father again crept into her mind. A teary smile escaped as she recalled the last time they had spoken. Her father had slipped into reminiscing about his time with Dutch when they were in the Special Forces in Vietnam, and how glad he was that Dutch had recently resurfaced in Miami. Then he also told her how proud he was of her and her work at the agency. She could almost feel his presence beside her, his warm smile radiating inside the cab.

The cab came to a halt outside the British High Commission, jarring Susan out of her past. She paid the cabbie and hurried inside. The cold blast of air conditioning boosted her confidence as well as the outline of her breasts. The receptionist led Susan up the stairs to Mr. Engleton's office.

"Please, come in and sit Ms. Berg," Mr. Engleton welcomed with a gesture. "Things are a bit unsettled here today. Seems some island local tried to break in last night."

"That's terrible," Susan feigned concern.

"Afraid he was trying to steal items from Lord Hainesborough's collection. Just in case, we're packing it all up and the Lord is going to personally have it all sent back to England. With his daughter's disappearance, I'm afraid the Lord has lost his interest. I don't blame him, for sure. But it is a shame. The collection is really quite spectacular."

Susan took a seat on a small couch, crossing her legs with the grandest of style. She took out a silver cigarette case and smiled broadly at the man behind his desk.

"Do you mind if I smoke?"

"Well, uh, I am somewhat allergic."

"To me Mr. Engleton, or the smoke?" Susan asked with her sultriest smile. Mr. Engleton gave her a quizzical look.

"I'm not sure what you mean?"

Susan patted the cushion next to her on the couch. "Come, sit next to me, will you Mr. Engleton?" Mr. Engleton considered her request as Susan took a cigarette from the case. She tapped the end of the smoke on the case without taking her eyes off him. "Tell me, it's just too formal to call you Mr. Engleton. What do your friends call you?" Susan patted the seat next to her again as she placed the cigarette in her mouth, the end horribly bent from her overzealous packing on the case. Mr. Engleton stood and cautiously approached her.

"Wilfred actually. Willy for short." Susan withdrew a lighter from her purse and tried to light her smoke, glancing cross-eyed as she tried to maneuver the flame to the bent tip.

"Willy, yum, how naughty," she said as her cigarette finally glowed. Susan puffed hard to work the bent cigarette as Willy approached her. Willy reached down and straightened it before primly sitting down next to her. He waved away the smoke that lazily billowed from Susan's clumsy puffs.

"Now, how can I be of help Ms. Berg?" he asked. Susan began to cough, the smoke now enveloping both of them in a stinking haze.

"I was hoping we could talk a bit about you," Susan replied as her coughing turned violent.

"May I?" Willy said as he offered her a small plant from an end table, Susan smashing the cigarette out in its terra firma. "You were saying?"

"Must be a reject," Susan said, referring to the still smoldering butt. Susan put a hand on Willy's knee. "It just occurred to me that at the party, I never got a chance to get to know you. Such an important man as you, so interesting, with your position here. And you so kind, so understanding."

Willy abruptly stood up taking Susan by surprise. "Ms. Berg, I think it's quite clear why you're here, what you are trying to do."

"It is?"

"You are, as they say, coming on to me, aren't you?"

"Well I ..." Susan stumbled.

"And I like it!" Willy blurted out. Instantly he lunged onto Susan like a flying squirrel landing on its nut. He pawed at her as she struggled under him on the couch, his lips covering her face with wet kisses. "I knew you wanted me Ms. Berg, from the first time we met. Take me, I'm yours."

"Mr. Engleton," Susan shouted out as she wrestled him off the couch, the two rolling about the office floor. "Willy, control yourself." Willy pinned Susan's hands to the carpet, his full weight squirming on top of her.

"Can you feel my passion growing Ms. Berg, you naughty girl you."

"Nothing worth mentioning," Susan groaned as she struggled under him. Willy pawed at her clothes as he buried his face into the nape of her neck. Susan planted her knees and hands under his wriggling body and pushed with all her might. Willy flew off of Susan and sailed through the air, his head leading his collision into the wall directly behind them. He slumped to the floor in an unconscious heap.

Susan crawled over to Engleton and checked his vitals, pushing up his eyelids to verify his state. She struggled up from the floor and adjusted her clothes as she gazed about the office, her eyes stopping on the filing cabinet. Susan opened the filling cabinet and quickly located the file on Lord Hainesborough. She stuffed it under her shirt and then quickly left the office, locking the door behind her. Susan scurried down the stairs and past the receptionist on her way out.

"Was Mr. Engleton able to give you what you need, Ms. Berg?" the receptionist called out. Susan stopped at the door.

"He was a little short," Susan replied as she walked out.

CHAPTER 10

Dutch had just finished mixing up a tall batch of rum runners in the blender for himself and Menton Moore in his boat's galley when he heard footsteps on the fore deck.

"You expecting company?" Menton asked as he took a cold rum runner from Dutch. Dutch peered out of the cabin.

"It's just my first mate, Crane." Crane entered the cabin, his arms full of grocery bags.

"You owe me sixty dollars," Crane said as he went straight into the galley.

Dutch motioned to the bridge deck. "Menton, why don't we go and finish discussing our business?"

"What business?" Crane asked.

"Nothing Crane, nothing at all." Dutch hurried Menton up the four short steps onto the bridge. He closed the louvered doors behind him, flicking the locking latch closed. Dutch motioned for Menton to take a seat on the cushioned bench. "So Menton, you were saying that this sword, this gold sword, is currently on this island."

"Yes, that's right. I am sure it is with one of the older families on the island, most likely in their private collection."

"Let's say I did find this sword, Menton. I just want to be clear, you don't expect me to steal it, do you?"

"No, nothing like that. All I want is for you to locate it. My attorney and I will take it from there."

"Good, because that would be extra," Dutch said with a half serious smile.

Menton responded with a polite laugh. "No, nothing illegal. That wouldn't do." The latched louvered doors shook as Dutch's cell phone rang. Dutch sighed in resignation and dug the phone out of his pocket, making note of the caller ID.

"Yes, Marcel, yes. Tonight? At the club. Okay. Thanks ole buddy." Dutch hung up and returned the phone to his pocket.

"Did you lock this?" came Crane's voice from behind the latched louvered doors.

"Pay no attention." Dutch sat down next to Menton. "Now about the fee?"

"Yes, the fee. I've never done anything like this before, hiring a detective. What is typical for this sort of thing?" The louvered doors shook again, this time with more determination.

Dutch stood and discreetly kicked back on the doors. "Usually most detectives would want the whole fee up front," Dutch said with a contrite smile. "But I like you Menton. So let's say half now, and half when I find the sword. How's that?" The doors now shook violently, Dutch kicking back with full force.

"I believe your man is locked in," Menton said, pointing at the doors.

"Pay no mind," Dutch assured. "So, do we have a deal?"

"Yes, okay, that seems fair. Half now, and half when you find the sword."

"Perfect."

"When can you get started?"

"When can you get the money?" Dutch replied.

"Right now. I'll just call my bank back home and have it transferred to the branch here." Menton patted his pockets as if looking for something. "Darn it, I seem to have forgotten my phone."

Dutch dug into his pocket and withdrew his cell phone. "No problem, you can use mine." He handed his phone to Menton, who briefly looked it over.

"Yes, that would be fine. Is there somewhere I could make a private call?"

"Of course. Not a problem. I'll just go below." Dutch unlatched the louvered doors, which spilled open, Crane landing face first on the deck. Dutch gestured the act of drinking alcohol as he rolled his eyes. He collected Crane from off the floor who angrily babbled in Vietnamese, and stuffed him back down the stairs as he followed him below. He shut the doors behind him.

Susan walked down the dock with a spring in her step with her head held high. She not only felt accomplished about having secured the files on Lord Hainesborough which she clutched in her hand, but also vindicated. Nothing pushed her button more than when Dutch played his sanctimonious game on her. And nothing pleased her more than when she could do the same to him. As she approached Dutch's boat, she noticed a man unknown to her hunched over the table on the bridge. He looked to be feverishly at work, doing something to something.

"Hey you," Susan shouted. The man looked up as if caught pooping in the woods. Susan boarded the boat, her Glock 26 gun drawn, as the man stood with his hands up, a cell phone on the table. "What the hell are you doing here?"

"I'm here on business," the man uttered, his voice wavering. The doors swung open and Dutch emerged. He immediately positioned himself between the man and Susan.

"Susan, so good of you to come by." Dutch firmly took Susan by the arm. "I've got something really important to show you, in the galley." He led her down the steps into the galley below, quickly closing and latching the louvered doors behind her. Dutch turned and gracefully smiled at Menton. "Detective business. You all set?"

Menton nodded. "Yes, I've taken care of everything. I will go straight from here to the bank and get the deposit. Is that woman okay?"

"Her? Oh sure, she's okay. A little high strung, You know how women are." The louvered doors shook violently.

"Dutch, what the frick is going on!" Susan shouted from behind the doors, mixed with Crane's angry words in Vietnamese.

Dutch shrugged. "You know women." Dutch quickly escorted Menton off the boat and onto the docks. "So how about I meet you later, say about eight? Do you know where Club Xtreme is?"

"No, but I'm sure I can find it."

"Good, I'll see you there. Eight o'clock. Don't forget." Menton nodded as Dutch sent him on this way. The louvered doors crashed open causing Menton to scurry off down the docks. Dutch jumped back on the boat, Susan and Crane welcoming him with glares.

"What the hell was that all about?" Susan demanded.

"What the hell?" Crane repeated.

"It was nothing. Just a personal matter. A man thing, if you know what I mean," Dutch said.

"Family jewels huh?" Susan replied. "I heard that sort of thing happens to guys when they get old. Was he a doctor?"

"Let's just say he can fix what's ailing me. Nothing too serious, thank God." Dutch took the file from Susan's hand. "Hey, you got the files on Lord Hainesborough. Good work Ice."

Susan stood speechless, not sure of which way to go, but sure that Dutch had maneuvered the conversation away from the direction of her suspicions.

"Yes, it seems to be all there," she said proudly displaying the folder's contents. "I haven't really had the time to go over anything."

Dutch plucked at the errant strands of Susan's mussed hair. "What happened Ice? You have to fight off Mr. Engleton for them?" Susan slapped Dutch's hand away from her hair. She flattened her hair as best she could.

"No, Willy, I mean Mr. Engleton, was all too happy to give me the files. I just used my charm and reasoning with him. Nothing more."

"That's great Ice. Really, great." Dutch looked at his watch as if surprised by the time. "I've got to get ready to go, so maybe you and Crane can go over the files."

"Go where?" Susan asked.

"Where you going?" Crane added.

"I've got some good news too. Harris Beerli got me a lead on the girl. He called around and found me a bartender at Club Xtreme who might know something about our missing Lady Melody."

"And I'm supposed to stay here?" Susan fumed.

"I'd love for you to come, but I don't want to spook him. You know what they say, one's company, two's a crowd."

"How about three?" Crane said.

"Not this time. I need you to keep watch in case the person who was in Ice's hotel room comes snooping around."

Susan grimaced. "Why is it that even when the things you say make sense, I still can't help but believe I'm being taken?"

"It's his style," Crane thoughtfully said.

"Yeah, that must be it," Dutch agreed as he disappeared down the steps toward his stateroom to take a shower. Dutch always imagined that his plans would work out just as he imagined, but rarely is life so kind.

CHAPTER 11

Dutch had to pay the cabbie an extra ten dollars to hurry to Club Xtreme in Worthing, located on the South Coast off Highway 7. The Barbados dollar is divided into 100 cents, just like the US dollar, its rate of exchange fixed to the US dollar. Tourists often use either US or Barbadian dollars. A stone's throw from the restaurants and bars in St. Lawrence Gap, the outside of the Club Xtreme appeared mundane and typical. The club was the hottest dance spot on the island, but at eight in the evening, the parking lot was empty, the front door held open by a small rock. Dutch paid the cabby and entered the club. He stopped to allow his eyes to adjust to the darkness. Dutch always took his time when entering an unfamiliar place, no matter how uneventful the planned meeting seemed. Like a recovering alcoholic, Dutch's motto was "easy does it".

The club was cavernous with lights, speakers and metal objects that seemed to grow out of the ceiling. At one end was a huge dance floor offset by several bars, their neon lights glowing like a desert oasis in the dark. A strong hand on his shoulder startled Dutch. Dutch spun around, his fist clenched and drawn. The tall and lanky black man with long dreads raised his hands, palms flat open. A gaggle of gold chains hung around his neck.

"Hey, easy man. You the guy Harris called me about?" the man asked in a convivial English accent.

Dutch relaxed his stance. "You the bartender?"

"Bartender, bouncer, bottle washer. You name it, I do it. In this place, you gotta do it all, know what I mean?"

"Sure do. Been there, done that. Can I buy you a drink?" Dutch offered.

"No, I'm not really the drinking kind."

"Harris mention why I wanted to come by?"

The man wearily looked about. He motioned for Dutch to follow him. The man led Dutch toward the back of the club and out an emergency exit. Dutch found himself standing in a narrow alleyway behind the club.

"Can't be too careful in there. Never know who's listening. Know what I mean?"

"Sure. So you remember the girl, the one that's gone missing?"

"Remember her, hell, how could you forget her. Beautiful, like a blonde princess or something. She came in here for two weeks straight man. Almost drove us all wild."

"Maybe she did? Drive someone wild, I mean."

"Nah, not likely. We get all we want, right? No, I'm thinking it was this local white bread. He was crazy about her. Here every night. Wouldn't let her out of his sight."

"You got a name for this guy?"

"Sure, his name is Carrington, Reggie Carrington. Not that it'll do you much good."

"What do you mean by that?" Dutch asked, momentarily befuddled.

"Because that dude behind you is gonna bop you good." Dutch turned just in time to see a gruff face swing a two by four, the wood making a resounding cracking noise as it met with Dutch's skull.

The sense of stifling heat was the next sensation Dutch experienced. As if he were in a sauna, or hell. He struggled to open his eyes, a dull throb aching from his head down to his toes. The sound of island reggae drifted through the darkness adding to Dutch's confusion. Dutch struggled for several minutes and finally managed to place his hands under himself and push up, only to be met by a metal barrier. It was then that the roar of the engine made Dutch realize that he was in the trunk of a car. He rolled himself onto his side and took several deep breaths. Dutch struggled to recall the face of the man who had bludgeoned him and whether he had ever met him before. Convinced that he hadn't, Dutch decided that it must have something to do with Lady Melody's disappearance. He made a mental note to go back to Club Xtreme and kick the crap out of that bouncer the minute he got out of the trunk. The sound of a metallic object sliding about the trunk as the car bounced about the rough road caught Dutch's attention. He groped about, hoping to find a weapon of sorts, only to recover his cheap cell phone. Dutch managed to turn it on, the back light from the phone's LCD display casting a dim hue inside the trunk. Dutch punched in Susan's cell phone number and said a prayer. The number rang several times before Susan answered.

"Susan, listen up. I'm in the trunk of a car. No, not a bar, a car. I've been kidnapped, shanghaied. Yes, it must have something to do with the case. No, not race, the case, damn it." The car began to slow down, Dutch lowering his voice as he continued. "I think we're stopping. Look, I'll put the phone on speaker and try to describe where we are. Call the cops and get them over here. I have a bad feeling about this." Dutch punched the button for the speaker option and then placed the phone near the rear well of the trunk.

The car stopped, the sound of car doors and footsteps all around. The trunk opened, a flood of light and air momentarily stunning Dutch. Dutch rose up only to be greeted by the menacing grin of the captain of the Kazar fishing boat. He grabbed Dutch by the shirt collar and pulled him out of the trunk. Dutch looked about his surroundings as two burley men approached from a boat dock.

"So with whom do I have the pleasure?" Dutch asked.

"I think I'm the one to be asking the questions, sailor," the Captain said.

"I would have been happy to answer them back at the club. You didn't have to knock me out and haul me to this deserted boat dock," Dutch said as loud as seemed reasonable.

"What, are you deaf?" the Captain asked.

"I'm just saying, why bring me to this old boat dock, which seems to be on the north end of the island?" Dutch shouted.

"It's not the north end you fool, we're at one of the old rum refinery docks. And stop shouting, for Christ's sake."

"Okay, I will," Dutch shouted out. "The old rum refinery docks. Nice. What do you want from me anyways?"

"My God man, invest in a hearing aid, will you?" The Captain nodded to the two burley men who took Dutch by the arm and led him away. Behind a small wooden shack at the end of the dock, Dutch could see the sun which was just beginning to dip into the ocean's horizon.

"I hope we're not going in there?" Dutch asked, the two men just smiling. "Look, I'm happy to tell you anything you want. Really. No secrets here." One of the men opened the door to the shack and shoved Dutch inside. The Captain stepped inside, leaving the door open behind him.

"Look, I was just telling your boys here, I'm happy to discuss whatever you'd like," Dutch repeated.

"You would, would you? And what is it that you think I want to know?" the Captain replied.

Dutch moved toward the Captain. "Oh, I don't know, but I'm sure we can work something out." Dutch pushed the two men aside and made a break past the Captain, the Captain skillfully tripping him onto the wooden floor.

"Tie him up boys. I think he needs a little softening up before we talk further." The Captain pointed to a wooden chair, the two thugs manhandling Dutch into the chair and securely tying him down with a length of towrope.

"Look, I am no hero. And for sure, I don't have a dime to my name. But I'm always happy to chat. No problems. And I do it a lot better when I can move around, know what I mean?"

"Which one of you wants the honors?" the Captain asked. Both men raised their hands like anxious children vying for a hall pass. "All right Morgan, you can have it this time." The other man cussed under his breath and left the shack with the Captain. "Come get us when he's good and ready," the Captain mentioned as he closed the door behind him.

"Morgan, right? Look Morgan, this really isn't necessary." Morgan's sadistic smile told a different story. Morgan reared back and punched Dutch in the stomach, immediately jumping back as if he had been shocked. He curiously looked at Dutch who winced in pain.

"You're a pretty tough old bird. Most puke when I hit them that hard."

Dutch managed a small smile. "I've had a lot of practice."

"Let's try the face," Morgan replied, his clenched fist landing a right cross on Dutch's jaw. Dutch's head violently jerked back as a white object flew from his open mouth and into the air. Both men stopped and stared as the object seemed to float through the air before falling to the ground.

"Crap, that's my molar bridge. It cost me a fortune! Get it." Morgan began hopping about as the bridge spun around the floor like a top. "You know how much those dentists charge, the crooks."

"Damn straight. Guys like us always have to pay. We never get insurance."

"You got that right. There it is, over by the door. Careful now, don't step on it."

Morgan bent down and gingerly retrieved the bridge, holding it between his two fingers like a dainty teacup. "I got it," Morgan beamed as he faced Dutch. Dutch's jaw dropped open in awe as the background behind Morgan suddenly ignited like the entrance to hell.

"Morgan, the shack, it's on fire, behind you."

"Don't try to trick me old man."

"Seriously, come untie me. Seriously, turn around." Morgan studied Dutch for a moment. He reached his arm out behind him without taking his eyes off of Dutch. "I don't feel nothing. Nice trick."

"Really? Because your sleeve is on fire." Morgan glanced at his shirtsleeve which was burning at the cuff. Morgan dropped Dutch's bridge and swung his arm about in the air which only fueled the fire. Morgan turned toward the door, the front side of the shack now ablaze in yellow and red flames that whipped out at both of them.

"Untie me Morgan and I'll get us both out of here." Morgan wildly ran a circle around Dutch and without hesitation ran straight toward the fiery door of the shack. He burst through the door and onto the dock, which was completely engulfed in flames. Dutch winced as Morgan was consumed by the fire, his body falling to the burning dock, slowly twitching in the throes of death like a gassed cockroach.

With the flames only several feet away, Dutch managed to stand up. He took two steps back and jumped as high as he could, landing full force onto the floor. The wooden chair, as well as his coccyx, both gave way, leaving Dutch howling out in pain. He pushed himself to his feet and took stock of his situation, all four walls of the shack now ablaze. Dutch studied the floor near the door, the fire now burning through some of the boards. With his hands still tied behind his back, Dutch took two steps forward and jumped again, landing full force on the burning floor boards. The boards momentarily groaned and then gave way, dropping Dutch like a hanged man through the floor and into the water below. He struggled to keep his balance in the five feet of ocean, saying a silent prayer for the low tide. In the near distance, the wail of police sirens filled the air. To his right, Dutch spied the Captain and his henchman maneuvering an old Boston Whaler at full throttle through the light chop of the bay.

"You owe me a molar," Dutch shouted out as he carefully made his way toward the shore, the dock ablaze, its wooden embers sizzling as they hit the water. As he approached the beach, Susan Berg appeared along with Crane Luk. Crane hurried into the water and helped Dutch to the shore, untying his hands.

"The cavalry arrives," Dutch said with a smile, a trickle of blood running from his swollen mouth.

"It took us forever to find the dock," Susan said, a look of remorse on her face.

"So you heard me then?"

"Very good Dutch, very good," Crane replied. "Ms. Susan threatened the police to get them here. She was very concerned."

"Really Ice? You did that for me?"

Susan momentarily blushed and then shrugged. "I figured we might get a lead on the girl. Maybe next time you'll make a point to not go commando on us."

They began to walk toward the roadway through the police that swarmed about the area. "Nice touch, starting the fire on the dock, even if it did almost fry me."

"We didn't start the fire," Susan said. "I thought you did."

"No, it wasn't me." Dutch looked about as if the answer were written on the air. "By the way, you may want to let the cops know there's a dead guy on the dock."

Susan looked stunned. "Did you kill him?"

"No, he killed himself." Dutch stopped and dug around in the open trunk of the car he had arrived in. He retrieved his cell phone and shoved it into his pocket. "Oh, and you owe me a bridge."

Susan wondered who owed her an explanation about how that fire got started, and by whom.

CHAPTER 12

Dutch sat at the meager table and glumly smiled at the police chief. The chief tapped a pencil on the table with the intensity of an acid rock drummer.

"So Mr. Holland, let me understand this. You went to Club Xtreme to meet a client?"

"A possible client."

"Yes, a possible client, whose name you cannot reveal due to confidentiality."

"Yes, confidentiality. Very hush hush." Dutch put his finger to his lips.

"And you went out to the alley because of?" the chief stopped short.

"I heard a noise."

"A noise?"

"Not any noise. A strange noise. Like something I have never heard before."

"And what did this noise sound like?"

"It was weird, very strange. Kind of like a scream. No, more like a howl. Like an animal. Oww!" Dutch howled.

"A howl, like an animal. Oww," the Chief mimicked.

"No, not like that noise, more like Uhwowl."

"Uhwowl," the Chief howled.

"Yes, that's it," Dutch replied. "Let's do it together."

"I am not going to do it together Mr. Holland."

"Come on, it'll be fun ... Uhwowl."

"Mr. Holland, please. And the next thing you know you're stuffed in a trunk, taken to this dock, which is then set on fire, killing one of your captors."

"Yeah, that's about it. Oh, and I lost my bridge when he punched me in the mouth. Any of you guys find a bridge, it's mine. Okay?"

The police chief shook his head in dismay and then abruptly stood up. "I've got no further questions. Your friends can join you now while I finish the paperwork to release you. But let me remind you, if you are not honest with us, we can't be accountable for any further events that befall you."

"One question chief, if you don't mind," Dutch said.

"Yes, what is it?"

"Seeing how I've been through an ordeal, do you think your department could dredge under the dock for my dental bridge?"

"No!" The chief stormed out of the room leaving the door to the small interrogation room open. Dutch stood and scanned the walls and roof of the room as Susan and Crane entered.

"You are a lucky one Dutch," Crane began.

"Tell that to my jaw," Dutch replied as they all sat down.

"Can we talk?" Susan asked.

"I don't think the room is bugged. Otherwise, I don't think the police chief would have howled."

"Howled?" Susan asked.

"Never mind. Ice, were you able to get anything on the car?"

"No, it was stolen according to your buddy, the sergeant."

"Who set you up? The contact at the club?"

"Yeah, some tall skinny bouncer with dreadlocks. Shouldn't be too hard to find him. He wore enough gold chains to slow down a race horse. Not sure of his connection to the dude who nabbed me, but I can guess that it probably has to do with drugs."

"Drugs?" Crane asked.

"Sure. The contact said he does a little of everything at the club. Last time I checked, that usually doesn't pay enough to afford the gold chains he had around his neck."

"Did the sarg have any idea who it might have been? You told him I thought it was a sailor, right?"

"No idea, since there are thousands on this island that meet that description. And who started the fire? You think it was the guy who captured you?"

"No, that wouldn't make sense. Why would he risk burning up his own guy? Besides, he wanted information. And I'm pretty sure it had to do with Lady Melody. Very weird."

"What makes you say that?" Susan asked.

"Because I've never seen him or his two thugs. So it wasn't someone with a past axe to grind. No, he wanted to know what I knew. So it must have had something to do with Lady Melody."

"Do you want me to try and run them down?" Susan offered.

"I don't think it will do much good. They high-tailed it in a skiff. But the good news is we now have a lead. We can run it down tomorrow."

"What do we do now?" Crane asked.

"It's too late to do anything tonight. Besides, I'm beat. Let's get a good night's sleep and we'll figure something out. Maybe try to run down that dreadlocked bartender who set me up. He mentioned that Lady Melody had a boy who was all over her. Name of Reggie Carrington. I'm sure that's the kid the chaperone was talking about. Even if he's not involved, he might know something. Ice, why don't you stay on the boat tonight, save you the forty minute ride to your hotel?"

"Thanks, but I have a date."

"A date?" Dutch replied with a look of surprise. "You and Mr. Engleton, I presume?"

"No, it's not Mr. Engleton. But yes, a date. I do have a life outside of babysitting you and Crane. Jealous?"

"No, just amazed that you've been on the island for just three days and you have a date already." Dutch winked at Crane. "Good to see you still know how to work it."

"On that remark, I'll take my leave. I trust you two can get back to the boat without ending up back here." Susan strode out of the room leaving Dutch and Crane in her wake. She quickly exited the police station and hailed a cab.

"Where to?" the cabbie asked.

"Club Xtreme, and step on it." Susan had decided in the police station that waiting until tomorrow would give everyone involved in Dutch's kidnapping time to become scarce. With Club Xtreme on the way to her hotel, she made up her mind to find out who had tried to kill Dutch. It was one thing for her to want to kill Dutch, but nobody else had that right. Not her team.

It was after midnight when she arrived at the club. The nightclub was just getting started, with a constant stream of cars jockeying for position in the parking lot, the sound of island dance music and pulsating lights streaming from inside the club. The crowd was made up of twenty something sunburned tourists, local revelers and a smattering of drug dealers.

Susan merged with the crowd of partiers who filed into the club, paying her twenty dollar entrance fee at the door. She pushed her way about the club as loud hip hop and trance music played, squinting through the bright lights as she sought out her target. At one corner of the bar, she spotted the bartender with long dreadlocks who glibly chatted with several tourists, his wad of gold chains glimmering in the spotlights. She positioned herself in his line of sight, and with her most seductive smile, she motioned him to her. Immediately, he excused himself from his company and approached with a confident swagger.

"Sweet lady, you looking for some sugar tonight?" he asked.

"It depends what type of sugar you're talking about."

The man leaned in close to Susan. "You can have either the kind that goes up your nose or the kind you wake up in bed with the next morning. Your choice."

"Afraid I'm not here for either. There was a problem with the detective," Susan said in confidence. "He wants to see you. Out back."

"Now?" the man asked. Susan confidently nodded, her expression leaving no room for discussion. "Shit man, I got business to do, you know?" He motioned his departure to one of the bartenders. The man threw back his dreadlocks and headed for the alley door, Susan closely following behind. They exited the club and entered the narrow alleyway, the loud music from the club filling the air. The bartender looked about.

"Where's the Captain?" he asked.

"He's not here, but I am."

"Wait a minute," Susan's ruse finally dawning on him. "What the hell? You a cop or something?"

"Exactly, and what I need from you is some information."

The bartender looked Susan over and then broke out in a belly laugh. "You're no Barbadian cop. You're too fine. They could never afford you. I'd say you better be planning on giving me either money or sex, because that's the only thing that will get you what you want baby."

Susan withdrew her Glock 26 from her purse and pointed it at the bartender's head. "How about my gun? Will this do?"

The bartender again laughed wholeheartedly. "A pretty lady like you? Have you ever even fired a gun, much less shot someone? I don't think so." He stepped toward Susan, a look of menace on his face.

Susan pointed the revolver downward and expertly squeezed off a shot, the bullet going through the bartender's right foot. "I guess there's a first time for everything," Susan coolly said.

The bartender looked down at his foot in momentary shock as the color of red spread out over his white tennis shoe. He fell to the ground holding his foot as the pain reached his brain. "Oh God, you shot me!"

Susan bent down and put the gun to the bartender's temple, her teeth gritted with the same determination that showed in her eyes. "Look dumb fuck, I'm just getting started. Now you're going to tell me who screwed with my detective, or you'll take it to your grave. You got me, stiff dick?"

The man nodded, tears in his eyes. "It was the Captain."

"The Captain?"

"Yeah, I owed him. I was short on a couple of eight balls of white. He brings it in, along with other things."

"Where do I find him?"

"I don't know. Serious. He has a place on the north side. By the caves. Just ask anyone in Archer Bay, they'll know."

"What did he want with my man?"

"Shit, I don't know. It's not my business. Maybe something about that girl your buddy was asking me about. I don't know. Man, I need a hospital. Shit."

"You told my man that a local boy, Reginald Carrington, was dogging Lady Melody. Where do I find him?"

"I don't know," the bartender wailed. "He's just around the club. He could live anywhere, for Christ's sake." Susan grabbed the bartender's free hand and shoved it under her skirt, the man's eyes wide in shock. She then rubbed it over her arm before standing up.

"What the hell?"

"Insurance, asshole. You know what they'll do to you if they think you tried to rape a white tourist?" The bartender nodded. Susan smiled like the grim reaper, sending a visible shiver over the bartender. "I'll tell the bouncer you're back here. Just hope he doesn't have anything against a rapist."

"You're a devil woman," the man muttered as he writhed about on the ground in pain.

Susan stopped for a moment and considered his statement. "Yes, yes I am," she replied with a smile of satisfaction. "Thanks for noticing." And Susan now knew a few places where she could raise a little hell.

CHAPTER 13

Susan was more than curious when she got the message on her cell phone to meet Dutch at Queens Park located on Constitution Road in downtown Bridgetown. Queens Park, the only park in Bridgetown, has a large Baobab tree that is over fifty feet around and stands as the focal point. The tree, many believe, came from Africa by the slaves who were brought to the island to work the sugar plantations.

After her conversation with the man at the nightclub, Susan went straight to her hotel and slept like a baby. Getting justice, even a little bit, always resulted in a good night's sleep for Susan. When her father was murdered, she didn't sleep for three days until Dutch knocked on her door and announced that he had "taken care of it." That night she fell asleep on the couch cradled in Dutch's arms, only to awaken twelve hours later in her own bed upstairs. She never had the nerve to ask Dutch how she got there or who had changed her into her bed clothes.

Susan spent a good part of the morning studying the files on Lord Hainesborough, hoping to go over them with Dutch. Susan hadn't found anything of significance. Just a background of Lord Hainesborough's heritage and family, his home address and some standard background information on Lady Melody. She couldn't imagine what Dutch could be up to, wanting to meet her at the park. Perhaps a clandestine hook-up with an unknown source that would require a good sum of money to tell what they knew? Or an angry husband whose wife Dutch had finagled? Probably the latter, she thought. Susan got her answer the minute she stepped out of the cab. In the middle of the park sat Dutch and Crane on a picnic blanket, like two school girls having a tea party. She grinned all the way across the park.

"How nice of you boys. A picnic."

Dutch gave Susan a tired look. "It was Crane's idea."

Crane smoothed a place on the blanket for Susan. "Here, next to me Ms. Susan. I've made a nice meal. So much better to get off the boat, don't you think?"

Susan sat down smiling over Dutch's obvious torture. "An excellent idea Crane. You and Dutch should do this more often." Dutch gave Susan a dirty look.

"Yes, it's the least he could do, embarrassing me to all in the marina," Crane replied.

"I already told you Crane," Dutch protested. "It was just a mistake, okay? Can we get over it already?"

"What mistake?" Susan asked.

"Crane's still miffed about the bus thing."

"Oh, right. Well, what are you serving Crane?" Dutch dolefully shook his head as Crane came to life. Crane opened up a plastic container.

"For appetizers, we have bacon infused deviled eggs." Susan took one and popped it into her mouth, Dutch looking on with sweet expectation. Her eyes watered, her cheeks turning fire engine red as sweat beaded on her forehead.

"Hot, they're hot. Really hot," Susan managed as she choked down the deviled egg. Susan grabbed Dutch's beer and chugged it.

"Made the Viet way, with red chili powder. Good, yes?"

Susan fanned her mouth, Dutch grabbing back his beer. "Very interesting Crane."

"Crane, why don't you tell Susan the rest of the menu?"

"Yes, of course. Well, here we have BTL sandwiches."

"BTL sandwiches?"

"Yes, bacon, tomato and lettuce." Crane handed a sandwich to Susan. Susan began to take a bite and then stopped, noticing Dutch's devilish grin.

"Crane, what exactly is in this BTL sandwich?"

"Just the usual, bacon, tomato, lettuce and a light spread of garlic mayo on freshly baked French bread."

"Sounds delicious Crane," Susan assured. Susan took a bite, her expression once again blaring five alarms.

"Oh, and chili powder, of course," Crane added. Susan grabbed Dutch's beer and drank it dry. She tossed the empty aside and dug through the picnic basket for another beer, which she popped open and guzzled. Crane took from his pocket his voice recorder. "More chili powder next time," he said into the recorder. "And finally we have bacon wrapped chicken livers," Crane continued.

"Let me guess," Susan breathlessly managed, "with chili pepper."

"Yes, of course," Crane replied.

"Starting to see a pattern Ice?" Dutch said.

Susan gave Dutch a look that could kill. "Dutch, aren't you going to have anything to eat?" Susan asked with retribution in mind. Dutch dug about in the picnic basket and withdrew a sandwich. He took a large bite of the sandwich as Susan looked on with expectation.

"Isn't it hot to you?" Susan finally asked.

"Nope. I have Crane make mine without the chili stuff," Dutch replied as he happily munched away. Susan mentally spat in Dutch's eye and then downed the remainder of her beer.

"So what did the files tell you about our client, Lord Hainesborough?" Dutch asked.

Susan handed Dutch a photo of Lady Melody. "Besides the picture, not too much to write home about. The usual stuff, pretty boring. Other than the Lord's wife, whom there's really nothing on, other than her name. Seems like everyone just forgot about her."

"Yeah, that's how it goes. Rich or poor, famous or infamous. You can't take it with you and you can't stay relevant. That's for sure."

" Must have been pretty tough on him and our Lady Melody, I imagine. Other than that, not too much."

"How about the girl's chaperone, anything on her?"

"Nothing really. Works as the PE teacher at her school, and doubles as the chaperone on their trips. Appears very up and up. Got her address on the island. Based on her interview, she seemed pretty upset by it all."

"Well, it was on her watch." Dutch offered Susan a sandwich, dispelling her look of dread with a wink of assurance as Crane looked on. Susan took a tentative bite, her fear of fire relieved. "Let's make a point of speaking with her today."

"What's with that truck?" Crane said as he pointed across the park. Susan and Dutch followed Crane's direction just in time to see an old truck bounce across the sidewalk onto the park grounds, just narrowly missing a row of shrubbery.

"Wow, the driver must be in trouble, or drunk," Susan observed as they all stood and began to walk in the direction of the truck. "Maybe they need our help?" The truck continued across the park in their direction. Dutch stopped and squinted into the midday sun at the truck's occupants.

"Oh shit," Dutch muttered. "Ice, Crane, you better scatter."

"Scatter?" Crane replied.

"It's that asshole from last night. The thugs who grabbed me. Shit, run!" Susan and Crane ran in different directions as the truck barreled down on them. Dutch ran over to the picnic blanket and took the blanket in his hands. Dutch held the blanket out like a bullfighter, waving it at the truck. "Over here, asshole! Here I am jerk wad."

The truck turned in Dutch's direction, the dirty grin of the Captain behind the wheel beaming through the windshield. As the truck bore down on him Dutch turned and ran, the blanket furling behind him like an oversized cape. He abruptly stopped and held up the blanket with the truck no more than twenty feet away. The Captain hit the gas, Dutch throwing the blanket up into the air at the last minute. The blanket landed on the truck, covering the windshield, as Dutch jumped out of the way, the large Baobab tree just several feet behind him. The truck smashed into the tree at full speed, the crash looking like a highway safety test. Susan and Crane ran over to Dutch and helped him from the ground, the truck billowing smoke from a twisted mass of metal.

"Anyone have a gun?" Dutch asked.

"I never would have thought a day in the park would require a frickin gun. Oh, right, I'm with you, I should have known," Susan replied. The figure of a person wriggled from the wreckage, the bloody face of the Captain fixing on them. He held a gun in his trembling hand and fired in their direction. The three all turned and ran at full speed from the park.

"Back to the boat. We've got weapons there," Dutch shouted out.

"My picnic basket. We forgot the picnic basket," Crane remembered. "We've got to get the basket." Crane stopped and began to run back to the park.

"Is he crazy?" Susan asked as she and Dutch watched Crane run serpentine through the park.

"Crazy as a rat. Fast as one too," Dutch observed. The Captain, still caught in the wreckage of the truck, took pot shots at Crane as he grabbed the picnic basket and wove his way out of the park. Crane ran past Susan and Dutch at full speed, the two following Crane, who did not stop until he jumped onto the safety of the boat one full mile from the park.

Crane immediately entered the cabin and emerged holding no less than two Glocks, three semi-automatics and two shotguns in his arms. Susan and Dutch couldn't help but giggle as Crane feverishly began loading ammo into the weapons at the galley table. Dutch put a comforting hand on Crane's shoulder.

"Crane, it's okay. He's not coming here for us. He knows we've got weapons. I'm sure that dude is half way round the island by now. Really, it's okay buddy."

"Not taking a chance. You see what he did to my picnic. We will kill him, right?"

"Not so sure that punishment fits the crime my friend. But we will hunt him down, for sure. But right now, why don't we go see that chaperone. What do you think Crane?"

Crane took out his voice recorder from his pocket as he gripped a shotgun tightly in his arms. "Bring a gun to the next picnic," he said into the recorder. "No, you two go, with guns. I will be here." Crane handed Dutch two Glocks and a box of ammo.

"You guard the boat Crane. Ice and I will be back in about two hours. Okay?" "Let's go Ice." Dutch set the guns back down and led Susan off the boat.

"Shouldn't we stay with Crane? I mean, he's pretty wired Dutch."

"No, when he's this way, the best thing we can do is give him space. He kind of gets post traumatic, know what I mean?"

"I just have to ask. How did you and Crane ever become such a dysfunctional duo?"

"It was Vietnam. Crane was an intelligence officer. He was on patrol with me. We were training a group of Vietnamese in counter intelligence, which in Nam was an oxymoron for sure. Then the Tet Offensive went off, in a big way. By the time he and I got to his village, the Viet Cong had murdered his whole family, the bastards. It took me a lot of money and a lot of connections to get him out of there and back to the U.S., but I did it. We've been together ever since. I'd like to nuke those fuckers."

"The Viet Cong?"

"Them and the assholes who sent us over there." Susan silently followed Dutch down the dock, trying to imagine what it must have been like for Crane, finding his whole family wiped out. Much like the way she felt when her father was murdered, but so much worse. Dutch suddenly turned around and grabbed her by the shoulders.

"Ice, maybe we should bring some guns. After the park, you never know what might happen."

"With a high school chaperone?" Susan spotted a bald head behind Dutch's shoulder approaching down the dock. "Does this have anything to do with him?" she asked, pointing to the short bald man. Dutch glanced over his shoulder at the man.

"Oh, him? No, nothing to do with him."

"Mr. Holland. It's me, Menton Moore," the man hollered out. Menton approached Dutch and Susan, extending a hand toward Susan. "Hi, I'm Menton, Menton Moore."

"Yes, I heard," Susan replied as she shook his hand. "Susan Berg."

"I just came by to see Dutch. Dutch, I missed you at the club last night. I just wanted to come by and give you the deposit money for my case."

"Money?" Susan asked as she stared down Dutch.

"Yes, I hired Mr. Holland. Quite exciting. I've never hired a detective before."

"You still haven't," Susan replied as she planted an elbow into Dutch's side.

"Excuse me?" Menton asked.

"Oh nothing. So Dutch, Mr. Moore is our client, is he?" Dutch looked into the horizon as he worked overtime on an answer.

"Well, not really," is all Dutch could come up with.

"Nothing nefarious," Menton added. "He's just helping me run down an ancient sword that belongs to my family. I'm sure the twenty thousand he's charging me is a pittance compared to what he usually gets." Menton held out a cashier's check. "I had it made out for half, just like you said."

"Ten thousand," Susan said, her eyes burning a hole through Dutch.

"It must have skipped my mind, what with all the excitement around here lately," Dutch replied.

"I was just worried when you failed to meet me at the nightclub last night. Is everything all right?"

"Oh, you were going to meet Mr. Moore at the club last night. I see. Well Mr. Moore, I am sure Dutch here will make a point of going over your case with me. You see, he works for me." Menton looked at Dutch and Susan with surprise.

"Oh, you mean you work for her. Oh, I see. Well I hope I wasn't out of line going directly to Dutch."

"No Mr. Moore, everything is just fine now," Susan assured as she landed another elbow into Dutch's side. "Thank you for giving us this case." Susan took the check from Menton. "I'll just take the deposit and give you a receipt. How's that?"

"Hey you," came a loud voice from down the dock. At the far end stood Crane, a shotgun in one hand and a pistol in the other. "What are you doing down there?" Crane began to stride toward them, his guns drawn and pointed in their direction. Menton Moore began to retreat, a look of dread on his face.

"I think I'll be going now. I can get the receipt later. Please let me know about any progress you are making. Nice to meet you, Ms. Berg." Menton Moore hurried down the dock as Dutch waved Crane back to the boat. "I'll call you later to go over the details," Menton shouted from the parking lot.

"Dutch, you'll just have to tell me all about our new client on the way to see the chaperone," Susan said as they watched Menton Moore jump into a cab and squeal out of the parking lot.

"Yeah, super," Dutch replied. Alone in a car, with an angry Ice Berg, was like being locked in a closet with a pissed off hive of killer bees. The trip to Dante's Inferno held more promise.

CHAPTER 14

Before jumping into the water from the capsizing boat, Reg had the foresight to grab the Captain's gun. Before swimming with Lady Melody toward the shore, he grabbed two of the small white packages, the rest bobbing about in the water. He wasn't sure what they were, but the thought of them providing a source of income had crossed his mind.

Like two drowned cats, Reg and Melody finally made it to the shore. Without a word, Reg and Melody dutifully trudged down the beach until they met up with the Leeward Roadway. Because St. Vincent is so mountainous, there was only one roadway that snaked its way around two thirds of the islands perimeter. The lack of viable roads through the dense volcanic mountains and consistent rains made St. Vincent one of the pot growing capitals of the Caribbean.

"So where to now?" Melody asked, too exhausted to care as long as there was a shower and a bed at the end of the answer to her question.

"I've already arranged for a room not far from here. Just for tonight." Reg dug into his front pocket and withdrew a wad of bills, secured by a rubber band. He proudly held it out to Melody. "I saved all of this. Mostly from doing yard work."

Melody couldn't help but crack a small smile, having never met a boy who had to work for his money. Especially by tending people's gardens. "I imagine you have reserved two rooms?"

The thought caught Reg off guard, Melody's question being the first time he had even considered it. "Oh, well, I really didn't think. I mean, well, yes, of course, I will get two rooms. Adjacent of course."

Melody smiled again, in a way that made Reg's stomach do flips and his heart melt. "I guess I can trust you. We can get just one room, as long as the room has separate beds."

"Separate beds. Sure. Of course, separate beds. I wouldn't think of not having separate beds."

By the time they reached the Tranquility Beach Hotel situated on the ocean in Indian Bay, their clothes had dried, although the salt that remained made them feel as stiff as cardboard. Reg motioned Melody up the stairs to the office.

"Well look what the dory boat dragged in," the owner, Lucelle Providence, beamed with a smile as big as a rainbow. A St. Vincent native, Lucelle had owned the hotel for more years than she would admit. She proudly managed one of the best hotel bargains in the Grenadines, with clean adequate rooms overlooking the best white sand beach on the island. Reg had always stayed there when accompanying his father on legal business to the capital of Kingstown. Lucelle raised an eyebrow as she looked Melody over. "I see you are on some other type of business perhaps?" she said to Reg.

"Oh, no. This is my cousin. Melody. My father will be joining us later in the week."

"I see," Lucelle said, not entirely convinced. Never one to reveal a lie or curtail young love, Lucelle handed Reg a key. Regardless, her next call would be to Reg's father in Barbados.

"Thanks Lucelle," Reg said. He took Melody by the arm and led her out. They walked the narrow stairwell up to the top floor. Reg opened the door to room number eight, motioning Melody inside. Melody crossed the room and walked out onto the balcony. She looked over the panoramic view of the ocean and the sugar sand beach below.

"This is beautiful Reg," she said. For Melody, regardless of the circumstance, this was an adventure that was far beyond anything she had ever done. Everything seemed so much more real, magnified. Every scent, every touch, every word seemed to explode into her senses.

Reg puffed up his chest. "Sure, I knew you'd like it. My dad and I always get this room. We're regulars, you know."

"What are we going to do about these clothes?"

"I thought you could take a shower and I'll see if Ms. Providence can get us a change of clothes." Melody and Reg studied each other for a moment. "You're not going to run, are you?" he asked.

Melody shook her head. "No, I won't run."

"Just in case, go into the bathroom and throw your clothes out to me."

Melody hesitated and then went into the bathroom. Moments later her clothes flew out onto the floor. Reg checked the size tags on the clothes, daintily holding Melody's bra and underwear by two fingers as he did. Reg had a lot to arrange and little time to do it. He headed straight for the main Leeward Highway and flagged down a taxi.

"Where to?" the driver asked.

"Kingstown, and step on it."

CHAPTER 15

"I really don't see what the big deal is," Dutch said as he maneuvered the Toyota rental car down the narrow H2 Highway toward Paynes Bay. From the passenger seat, Susan shot him a look that could stifle a madman with indifference. "Honestly, I was going to tell you. Really."

"Sure you were," Susan finally replied. "I'll have to introduce you to yourself sometime."

"Come on Ice. I already said I'd split the money with you. What more do you want from me?"

"I'll tell you what I want. I want you to seriously help this Menton Moron."

"Menton Moore."

"Whatever. I want you to make a real effort to find this silver sword."

"Golden sword. It's a golden sword."

"Whatever. I can't believe you took the case in the first place. You know how impossible it's going to be to find a sword from the sixteenth century?"

"Eighteenth century."

"What do you mean?"

"If you're talking about something that happened in the 1700's, it's referred to as being one number later. In this case, the eighteenth century."

Susan punched Dutch in the shoulder. "Wow, that explanation feels like it took a century. Whatever! I'm just saying, you're going to have to do some research."

"Research?"

"Yes, research. At a library. Do you know what that is? It's a place with books Dutch. Books, with writing and reading."

"Very funny Ice. Okay, I hear you loud and clear. As soon as I can, I'll get over to the historical archives and check it out."

"Yeah, like tomorrow."

Dutch pulled the car into the parking lot of the Beach View Hotel, a luxury apartment rental. Set right on sugar sands with views of the crystal blue ocean, the Beach View Hotel was situated in the heart of Paynes Bay where all of the proper English vacationed. "Nice digs for a chaperone," Dutch observed. "Wonder who she's doing to afford this place?"

"It was in the files," Susan replied as she led Dutch toward the hotel. "The prep school is paying for her stay. She said she'd meet us by the pool when I rang her."

They walked through the lobby past the multi-story buildings which opened onto an oversized pool. Susan scanned the sparsely populated pool area for the chaperone. "Now who do you think would be our chaperone?" she said to Dutch.

Dutch pointed to a fifty year old pudgy woman in a large sun hat, her parchment white skin slathered in zinc oxide. "I'm guessing that's her."

Susan and Dutch approached the woman. Susan extended a hand. "Ms. Daniels?"

The woman rose and took Susan's hand. "Yes, yes, Ms. Berg, I presume?" Dutch and Susan sat down in the lounge chairs next to her.

"And I'm Dr. Watson," Dutch said with a boyish smile.

"What?" Ms. Daniels replied without a clue.

"Never mind him," Susan said. "Thank you for agreeing to meet with us to discuss Lady Melody. It must have been a terrible thing to endure."

Ms. Daniels shook her head in dismay, a look of true sorrow on her face. She fervently wrung her hands together. "I feel so terrible. So responsible. I know that Lord Hainesborough and Mr. Engleton said it was not my fault. But no matter, it was on my watch. Frankly, I don't know what to do. These girls nowadays."

Ms. Daniels made a flowing gesture towards several young girls that lounged about the pool. "They have minds of their own. The internet, text phones, all of that. I'm starting to reevaluate my career choice, that's for certain."

Susan took Ms. Daniels' hand in sympathy. "I understand how you feel, I really do. Perhaps you can tell us, was there anything unusual, out of the ordinary, that you observed?"

"Observed?"

"About Lady Melody?"

"No, nothing really. She was liked by all the girls, very friendly. But ... " Ms. Daniels' thought trailed off.

"What is it Ms. Daniels? Anything you tell us will be held in confidence, I can assure you," Susan prodded.

"Well, I have nothing more than my thirty years of experience to count on, you understand. But I always felt as though there was a sadness within Lady Melody."

"A sadness?" Dutch said.

"Yes, deep down. Something just wasn't right. I don't know, maybe she was just shy. Reserved, perhaps. But always polite, and of course very beautiful. Well kept, unlike many of these girls nowadays."

"So she kept to herself?" Susan added.

"No, she always made a point of being convivial. Friendly. It was something else, something deep down. A type of sorrow in her soul."

"Did she have any boyfriends that you knew of?" Susan asked.

"Well, not that I know of. Of course, with twelve girls to watch over, it was hard to keep a constant eye on them. I had heard some mumblings about a boy."

"Did the name of Reginald Carrington ever come up?" Susan asked.

"No, not that I can recall. But you never know with these girls. Hungry hearts at this age. I wish I could help you more, but I'm afraid it's just all beyond me."

Susan patted her shoulder. "Don't blame yourself. There's no way you could have known this would happen." Susan handed Ms. Daniels her business card. "Please call me if you think of anything else." Susan motioned to Dutch to take their leave. Dutch followed Susan to the parking lot before she stopped short. Next to their car stood a beautiful teenage girl in a string bikini.

"I'll handle this Ice," Dutch said with bravado as he moved past Susan. Susan grabbed him by his collar and pulled him back.

"I don't think so Tonto."

"I saw you two speaking to Ms. Daniels about Melody," the girl said as Susan and Dutch approached.

"Yes, yes we were. Are you a friend of Lady Melody?" Susan asked.

The young girl anxiously giggled. "Lady Melody. It's weird to hear her called that. We just call her Mel."

"Did you know her well?" Dutch said.

"As well as anyone could. Mel is, well, very guarded about her personal life. If you know what I mean? But she was seeing a boy, I know that much."

"Did she tell you that?" Susan questioned.

"Not exactly. I saw them together a couple of times. On the beach, at the nightclub. They were always careful not to be seen, but I saw them. Reg was his name. Reginald Carrington"

"Did she say anything about him to you?"

"In little ways. I could tell that she really liked him. Just by the way she acted. She seemed to be happy for a change. Really happy. She said a couple of times that she wished she could stay here forever."

"Were they intimate?" Susan asked in a sensitive tone.

"You mean were they sleeping together?" Susan nodded. "Mel was easier to make than a peanut butter sandwich, if you know what I mean. Which was weird, because she was always so quiet."

"It's always the quiet ones," Dutch chimed in, much to Susan's displeasure.

Susan handed the girl her business card. "Please call me if you think of anything else." The girl nodded and then quickly went back into the hotel lobby. Susan turned to Dutch. "So what do you think?"

"I would definitely hit that," Dutch said as he got into the car.

Susan sat down in the car and slugged Dutch in the shoulder. "I didn't mean that, you perv. I mean, was Lady Melody in love with this kid, Reg Carrington, or not?"

Dutch started up the car and headed down the road. "I'm not sure if it really matters, girls at that age. They fall as fast as a rabbit in heat. But I do think we had better find this Reg Carrington, or his family, or someone who's close to him. And soon. Any ideas?"

"Yes. I think we'll both pay a visit to the library. You for your sword fiasco and me for Mr. Carrington."

"It really hurts when you badmouth this sword case," Dutch glibly replied. "But to show you that I've got no hard feelings, I'm going to take you to dinner."

"Dinner? You? Do you mean you're going to pay for dinner or just take me to dinner?"

"Good point Ice. No, I'm going to take you to dinner. You'll have to pay for yourself."

"I thought as much." The two drove in silence for a moment.

"You think you could also spot me a twenty for my meal?" Dutch finally asked.

"No."

The Coach House restaurant was one of the gems on the West Coast. Nestled on the beach in Paynes Bay, the Coach House served a variety of island inspired dishes in an open air casual setting with fantastic views of the ocean. Because of the reasonable prices and the thought that he could get Susan to pay, Dutch had invited Ms. Godown to join them, unbeknownst to Susan.

"Dutchy. Dutchy," Vicky Godown shouted out as Dutch and Susan appeared in the bar of the restaurant.

"You've got to be kidding me," Susan whispered to Dutch.

"I thought you two had become friends," Dutch replied with as much sincerity as he could fake.

"Funny. Just for that, you're paying for dinner."

Vicky hugged Dutch as they walked to a table. Upon reaching the table, she continued her hug with Susan. "I so missed you two. What has it been, two days? My how time flies," Vicky said.

"Especially when you're having fun," Susan glumly added.

"Are we having fun?" Vicky wondered.

"No," Susan answered.

Vicky let out a belly laugh drawing the attention of everyone in the restaurant.

"I swear Susan, you just kill me."

"Don't tempt me," Susan muttered under her breath.

Vicky took Dutch by the arm and hugged him again. "I've missed you so much," Vicky said. "I'm so glad we are going to have some time together."

"Planning a holiday?" Susan asked Dutch.

"Oh, nothing like that. I have a few days off, that's all," Vicky replied. A waiter brought over two bottles of wine and presented them to Vicky. "They look like wine to me," Vicky said to no one in particular. The waiter poured the red and then retreated.

"Don't they take your order here?" Susan asked.

"I already ordered for the table. Dutch told me how much you like seafood, so I ordered their Mahi Mahi. It's fantastic."

"Great," Susan said with a smirk.

Dutch gave Vicky a comforting hug. "I'm sure it will be great. Vicky used to work as a waitress here, didn't you Vicky?"

"Oh, nothing that complicated. I was the hostess. It was so fun. Meeting everyone. I smiled a lot." Susan rolled her eyes and then downed her wine. She held out her empty glass, Dutch immediately refilling it. "So, tell me about your case Dutchy. How is it going?"

"It's going well," Dutch replied. "Vicky, you wouldn't happen to know anyone with the last name of Carrington would you?"

"Yes, yes I do. In fact, I think I once met a man by that name. Hum, let me think."

"Was he young or old?" Susan asked, now interested for the first time in what Vicky had to say.

"I can't recall."

"Do you remember where you met him? Where he lived?" Susan continued.

"I'm not sure. But I do recognize that name. Oh, wait a minute, I've got it."

"What? What is it?" Susan pleaded.

"Wasn't that the name of the family on that show, Dynasty? Yes, that's it. I so loved that show. It was so, oh I don't know, regal. Don't you think?"

Susan buried her face in her hands as Dutch laughed with glee. Dutch leaned over and gave Vicky a kiss. "You are the best, baby."

Vicky smiled broadly, not quite sure of why. Susan looked out on the beach dotted with lounge chairs right outside the picture window where they sat. The sun had begun its descent into the ocean's horizon, like a golden gumdrop slowly melting into a pot of blue. "This really is beautiful," Susan remarked.

"It is," Dutch agreed. "Vicky, how about we take a walk around the grounds? Do you mind Susan?"

"It would be a relief," Susan replied. Dutch helped Vicky from her chair and the two left the restaurant with Dutch's hand firmly placed on her rear.

The waiter paused as he passed the table. "Your company has left you?"

"Afraid so. There's an extra twenty for you if you can keep them away until sunset."

"I'm afraid that would not be fair. The sun will set in about five minutes. But don't worry, we will turn on the spotlights after dark so you can see our beautiful shoreline."

Susan shrugged and poured herself another glass of wine. She ran through the particulars of the case in her head as she doodled on a napkin. After all was said and done, she wasn't really sure if Lady Melody was straitlaced or loose as a goose. She imagined that like most people, she was somewhere in between. It seemed as though everything pointed to the young man, Reginald Carrington, as her kidnapper. If they were dating, could Lady Melody have called it off causing Reggie to go haywire? And what about the Captain who captured Dutch? Did he want to question Dutch or kill him, or maybe both? Nothing much made sense, other than the excellent Cabernet that she had just about finished off.

The commotion of her fellow diners in the restaurant shook Susan from her thoughts. She glanced about the room, some of the diners pointing toward the picture window while others looked away with expressions of shock. Susan followed the direction of their attention toward the large picture window to the beach below, which had just been illuminated by the restaurant's spotlights.

There for all to see, as if posing for a travel magazine, was a perfect view of Dutch spread out on one of the lounge chairs, his bare ass squirming about on top of an equally naked Vicky Godown. At first, Susan thought she must have entered a dream state and was still back at her hotel in bed. She pinched her thigh to make sure, the sting dispelling that favored notion. Susan finally managed to stand up and rap on the window to get Dutch's attention. Dutch looked up and sheepishly smiled, Vicky waving to her from below him like the parade queen on the main float. Susan silently left the room, holding as stoic an expression as she could manage. One more restaurant she could never return to, courtesy of Dutch Holland. The future was slowly dimming, not only for her at the restaurant, but for Lady Melody as well.

CHAPTER 16

As Dutch drove to Susan's hotel the next morning, he wondered how angry Susan would be at him. Susan hadn't said a word on the drive back to his boat from the restaurant. He felt sure that he should be full of regret for his naked debut at the Coach House restaurant, but somehow he just couldn't work up the emotion. He wondered if it meant that he had become a bit of an exhibitionist or if it was just that he didn't give a damn anymore. Either way, Dutch felt no shame. He couldn't even spell remorse.

Dutch pulled the rental car into the lushly landscaped parking lot of the Little Arches Hotel. He got out of the car and stretched, having convinced himself that Susan would have forgotten all about his inopportune unveiling at the restaurant.

"Dutch, up here," Susan called from the balcony of the hotel's restaurant above. "It's about time you got here."

"The traffic was terrible. You getting breakfast?"

"Just finishing up," Susan replied.

"Hey, could you grab me a coffee?" Dutch asked. Susan disappeared for a moment and then re-emerged on the balcony, a large Styrofoam coffee cup in hand. Dutch gave her a thumbs up sign. "Great."

Susan let the cup drop from her hand. It landed with a gigantic splatter just inches from Dutch, causing him to dance about the flood of hot coffee.

"Sorry," Susan shouted down with no sincerity. Dutch realized that he was looking at a very long day. No coffee and no mercy.

After twenty minutes of driving in silence, the car finally passed the Bush House on the nearby outskirts of Bridgetown. Now called the Washington House, it was the home where George Washington spent two months in 1751, his only trip ever outside of the United States. Having contracted smallpox during his visit here, Washington was nursed back to health by a local physician. The exhibits in the Washington House were an accurate representation of how life was in the eighteenth century. The gruesome artifacts such as the spiked collars for use on slaves always seemed a contradiction to the person who stood for the freedom of a whole nation. Time softens all reality, Dutch thought. He hoped the same would be true for Susan.

"Now don't get all talkative and antsy here," Susan finally spoke as they pulled into the library parking lot of the Barbados Museum at the Garrison, St. Michael. Just because this used to be a fort, it doesn't mean you can go all commando. It's the museum for the historical society, so keep it down."

"Mums the word," Dutch replied as they entered the museum grounds. Once the barracks for the British forces, the thick plaster walls with heavy wood doors still held an impressive aura. The two walked through the courtyard shrouded by centuries old banyan trees. Susan and Dutch entered the small office which held a small desk surrounded by many volumes of historical works about Barbados and the Caribbean. A big, bold and beautiful Barbadian woman greeted them with a warm smile.

"Welcome to the museum," she said with a proper English accent.

"We need to look into your historical records," Susan curtly replied.

"Well those would be up the stairs, in the anteroom," the woman replied. Susan unceremoniously motioned for Dutch to follow her up the stairs. The woman held out her arm, blocking their ascent. "Not so fast dear. It's a five dollar fee to use the study room."

"Five dollars? Really?" Susan objected.

"Air conditioning isn't free you know," the woman replied. "We run on donations and entrance fees, dear."

"Look, all we want to do is look at some old records. How can that cost five dollars each?" Susan protested. "I'm not going to pay that."

"Here, it's on me," Dutch said with a smile as he handed the woman a twenty dollar bill. "And you can keep the rest as a donation, okay?"

"Yes, that's very nice of you," the woman said, returning a smile. She withdrew her arm and Susan ascended the stairs in a huff followed by Dutch. The woman put her arm out in front of Dutch. "If you need some help, with anything, feel free to let me know."

"Well, now that you mention it, I could use some help with a little project I'm working on. I'm sure you must have a wealth of knowledge regarding research and such."

"It would be my pleasure." The woman led Dutch up the stairs to the second floor landing. She opened the door to the small records room. Susan was already scanning the numerous volumes of records that lined the shelves. "Now what are you looking for?" she asked Dutch. Susan gave Dutch and the woman a look of disdain.

"I'm looking for some information on a golden sword. From the eighteenth century," Dutch said. "I do have a dude's name. Charles Hollingsworth."

"Well, let's start with the historical registry of births and deaths," the woman said as she thumbed past the spines of several titles on the shelves. "Here we go, this is just what I was looking for." She brought down a large volume that looked as old as the island itself. The woman hummed a merry tune as she thumbed through the pages of the book.

"Do you mind?" Susan spat.

"Honey, you've got to enjoy what you're doing in life. You've just got to," the woman replied with a smile.

"Well enjoy it a little quieter, will you?"

The woman shrugged and continued her tune as Dutch looked on with a smile. "Oh darling, here it is," she announced, Susan shaking her head in antipathy. Dutch leaned over the woman, who gently caressed his face. "You've got the softest skin for a man."

"For God's sake, can you take it outside? I'm trying to concentrate here," Susan screamed. Dutch motioned toward the door, taking the book with him as he led the woman outside onto the landing.

"She's a nasty one, isn't she?" the woman said.

"And she's got a bad disposition too," Dutch replied. The woman slapped Dutch's chest, collapsing onto his shoulder in laughter.

"You are a funny one. I like you. If there's ever anything I can do for you, you just let me know."

"I will keep that in mind. Now about the book?"

"Yes, well I found something very interesting," the woman replied. "It seems that there was a Captain Charles Hollingsworth. Not sure what his background was in England. Most of the people who came to the islands in the 1700's were ne'er-do-wells. Either broke, no royal standing, or both. Anyway, he did a good job of ousting some pesky pirates that were bothering the folks. My bet is that he probably paid the pirates off."

"Really, people did that?"

"Sure they did. It's always about the money you sweet thing. Anyway, the folks were so happy that they actually gave him a golden sword as a token of their appreciation. According to the records, it was encrusted with jewels too."

"What happened to him?"

"I don't know. It doesn't say. This is the only official record of the government from that time. If you want to know more, you'll have to look into the church records. Births, deaths, marriages, all that."

"And where would I find those?"

"At the Barbados Archives, located in the lazaretto in the city of Black Rock. St. Michael parish. Ask for Judy. Tell her Sugar sent you."

"Sugar, huh. A name as sweet as yourself."

Sugar blushed and then kissed Dutch on the cheek just as Susan burst through the door. "Don't you ever take a break?" Susan said to Dutch.

"Well, thanks to Ms. Sugar, I've got a great lead on our golden sword. How did you do?"

Susan threw up her hands. "I don't have shit. First of all I can't read half of that stuff. It's all written in old English. Secondly, the room smells like old people. I've got a headache from ear to ear. I don't think this Reginald Carrington actually lived here. Probably a drifter."

"You two are looking for the Carringtons?" Sugar asked. "Why didn't you say so? They live in my town."

"Your town?" Susan replied.

"Yes, right in Speightstown. They live on Bowell Road. Father and son. I think the father was a lawyer. Retired now. Something like that."

"You are the best." Dutch gave Sugar a hug, who reciprocated by grabbing Dutch's butt. Dutch followed Susan down the stairs, Susan mumbling under her breath all the way to the car. Dutch made a point to hum a merry tune.

As they drove through Bridgetown on their way to the historical archives, Dutch pointed to a side road. "Turn here, will you? I've decided to buy you lunch."

"You, buy me lunch?"

"Well, it's the least I can do after last night."

"Least being the primary word." Susan turned down the road which stopped dead end at the Bridge Bar and Grill. Dutch motioned Susan out of the car and the two entered the establishment.

Harris Beerli immediately noticed them from his position behind the bar. "Oh God, what now?" he said as the two sat down on the bar stools.

"Harris, I'm just wondering, why would you send me to someone who was planning to kick my ass? I mean, do you hate me that much?" Dutch asked.

"First of all, yes, I hate you that much. Secondly, I did not set you up. You asked for a contact at the Club Xtreme and I gave it to you. Christ, the guy wasn't my brother or something. It was just a name. Nothing more."

Dutch withdrew a snub nosed 45 from his ankle holster and placed it on the bar. Susan and Harris literally pulled back in shock. "So you're saying I shouldn't shoot you in the groin, right here, right now?" his face as hard as a sock full of nickels.

Harris leaned over to Dutch in earnest to plead his case. "Look, I would have never been a party to that. You know me. Besides, you got your revenge already."

"What do you mean?" Dutch replied.

"Sending Black Dahlia here to plug that poor man," Harris said pointing to Susan. Susan looked away, as if the comment would disappear by her doing so.

Dutch did a second take of Susan. "You mean she went over there and shot the guy? On my account?" Dutch said, almost chocking up with emotional gratitude.

"That and worse. I'm not exactly sure what happened, but that dude not only left the club, he left the island. You ask her what she did."

Susan turned back to Dutch and shrugged. "It was nothing. He's making stuff up. All I did was convince him to tell me the truth. Nothing more. And it wasn't on your account. That's for sure!"

"You shot him. You shot him for me, didn't you?" Dutch replied, like a proud parent.

Susan dismissed Dutch with a wave of her hand. "Shut up."

Harris Beerli looked down at the revolver on the bar. "So what's it going to take for me to make it up to you?"

Dutch rubbed his jaw, still sore from the punch he had received from the Captain's thug. "I think two of your best burgers will do it," he said with a friendly smile, Susan's deed on his behalf having softened his resolve.

"You got it. Coming right up," Harris said as he scurried away to the kitchen.

"You shot him for me. You really shot him," Dutch repeated with a smile from ear to ear.

"God, would you shut up!" Susan said as she reached over the bar and grabbed a bottle of beer.

By the time Susan and Dutch had finished lunch and located Reg Carrington's house on Bowell Road in Speightstown, the sun was beginning to set. It cast a slight glow on the white washed house surrounded by the pink streaked sky. The house was an extremely plain white washed house made of wood. Susan stepped out of the car and admired the sunset.

"It really is beautiful here, isn't it?"

"Like a gorgeous lover with aids."

Susan gave Dutch a sour look. "And what does that mean?"

"I was reading in that historical record. Back then, half of the folks who lived here either died from some tropical disease or heat exhaustion. If the parasites in the water didn't kill them first. It was a tough place to live in olden times."

"Sure, but that was then. I'm talking about now." A shot rang out from the white washed house, striking the car's side view mirror, almost on cue. Dutch lunged for Susan and tackled her to the ground.

"You were saying," he said.

Susan withdrew her pistol from her purse as she scanned the house. Dutch placed his hand on the gun and forced Susan to lower it.

"Just hold up a second Ice." Dutch slowly rose from the ground, his hands up in the air. He slowly approached the front of the house. "Mr. Carrington, I don't know who you think we are, but we're not who you might think."

"What?" came a man's voice from within the house.

"What?" Susan echoed.

"What I'm saying, is we are not with the police, or anyone. We're detectives trying to help your son." A lace curtain slightly parted, a pair of steely eyes making a run over Dutch and Susan, Susan now approaching the house as well. Dutch took note of the front door, which showed the evidence of an attempted forced entry, the shoe marks still planted on the white paint. "I'm not sure who was here before, but I would guess it was an old guy. Am I right?" There was a moment of tense silence.

"You talking about the Captain?" the man shouted back.

"If he was an ugly old sailor type, then yes I am."

"That son of a bitch. Tried to break into my place. Lucky I was able to get to my gun."

"I hope you shot him in the balls," Dutch replied, Susan wincing at the thought. The front door opened to reveal a tall and stately looking gentleman in his sixties. He held a Winchester Model 71 in his hands, its sight still trained on Dutch and Susan.

"Do you mind if we come in?" Susan asked. Mr. Carrington kept his aim on both of them, providing the answer well enough. "Can we at least ask you some questions?" Susan continued.

"Go ahead."

"It seems Mr. Carrington that your son may have kidnapped a girl."

"Things can seem a lot of different ways. It doesn't mean they're so," he stoically replied.

"We are just trying to find the girl and return her to her father. Nothing more. Do you have any idea where they might be?" Susan continued.

"If you don't know where you're going, any road will take you there," he answered.

"Who the hell are you, the Caribbean Forest Gump?" Susan angrily replied as she took a menacing step toward him. Dutch held her back as Mr. Carrington tensed his grip on the rifle.

"Look, let's all calm down. Mr. Carrington, we're just trying to help your son, find him before the Captain does. Believe me, we mean him no harm. I can assure you from personal experience the same is not true for the Captain."

"I'll buy that," the old man replied. "The truth be told, I really don't know where he is. I told that bastard Captain the same thing. He didn't believe me and I guess you won't either."

Dutch held up his hands in capitulation. "Yes, we believe you."

"No we don't," Susan mumbled.

"Look, if you remember anything or just need someone to talk to, would you call my cell phone?" Dutch continued.

Mr. Carrington nodded. "Just leave it on the porch on your way out," he said as he abruptly shut the door.

Susan walked out to the street and scanned the sky, her hands on her hips. "Great, just great. We're right back where we started. Nowhere. What do you suggest now?"

"Two things. We leave him my phone number and we call Crane and Vicky to meet us for dinner." Dutch motioned toward Susan's purse for paper and a pen as he dialed Crane on his cell phone.

"Frick!" Susan muttered as she grabbed her purse. The leads on this case were coming slower than an Amish drag race. She decided right then and there that it was going to be up to her to speed things up.

CHAPTER 17

The night before, both Reg and Lady Melody had slept like logs. Between the harrowing boat ride, the long swim and the equally long walk to the hotel, both were exhausted despite their young age. Reg woke up before Lady Melody. He gazed at her asleep on the other bed, both wearing oversized tee shirts. While in Kingstown, Reg had purchased for Melody, as well as for himself, two sets of tee shirts and shorts along with bathing suits. In the morning light, Reg thought Melody looked like a perfect angel. He noticed how even her fingernails down to her perfect dainty toes were a vision of beauty. How even the slow rhythm of her breath, her bosom moving up and down, was perfection. He wanted to reach out to her, to caress her face, to kiss her wonderfully full lips. But he didn't have the courage. No, she was too good for him, or for any man, he thought. When Melody awoke around noon, Reggie had breakfast ready as well as the plan for the day. The two had a breakfast of pre-packaged muffins and juice before they set out for a swim in the ocean and a walk on the beach. He had to guess at the bathing suit size, which ended up being a bit too large for Melody's shapely body. Reg made a point of keeping his eyes off of her to the best of his ability when they swam, afraid that any inadvertent slippage of her bathing suit would send him into a pubescent frenzy.

"So what is your plan from here Reg?" Melody asked as they walked the white sand beach.

Reggie shielded the sun from his eyes as he looked at her. "If I told you, I'd have to kill you," he said with a chuckle. "Don't worry," he said, sensing Melody's apprehension. "It will all be okay. I promise. I would never let anything or anyone ever harm you. Ever! Do you believe me?"

Lady Melody looked deep into Reggie's eyes. "Yes," she replied. "I don't want anyone else to get hurt either. I'm so tired of all that. Know what I mean?"

Reggie knew all too well what she meant. Melody turned away from him as she looked out over the endless ocean, as mysterious and unpredictable as their fate.

The rest of the day and evening were spent in the room, flipping channels on the small TV between bits of pointless banter.

"Can we at least go out for some dinner?" Melody finally asked.

"No. We'll have to have dinner in. There's a restaurant down the street. It's quite good. My dad and I always eat there. Great grilled flying fish. Have you ever had it?"

"I guess I will now," she replied. "I'm really starving. How about we get it now?"

Reg checked his watch, the sun just beginning to set over the ocean outside their balcony. "Okay, but you know the drill."

Melody glumly nodded and headed for the bathroom. "I've got to take a shower anyways," she said as a bit of rationalization. Moments later her clothes came out of the bathroom. Reg scooped them up and collected all of the other clothes from the room. He stuffed them into a plastic laundry bag that hung in the closet and then left the room, securely locking it before he headed to the restaurant.

On his way down the stairs, Reg was greeted by Washington, Lucelle Providence's dog. The dog nudged up to Reg giving him a welcoming growl, having become familiar with Reg's smell from his previous stays. "Shh," Reg said as he patted him, putting his finger to his lips. "We don't want to disturb Lucelle."

"You won't disturb me Reg," Lucelle said, standing at the bottom of the stairs. "Where are you heading out to?"

"Oh, just to get some dinner Lucelle. Maybe down the road a bit to the Grandview restaurant."

"That's way too far for you to walk, even if you are younger than my shoes," Lucelle joked. "Here, you come with me. I'm just finishing up some country stew. Fresh fish and vegetables."
Lucelle motioned Reg to follow as she walked down the hallway and entered her apartment. Reg followed, cursing himself for being so honest about his destination. He checked his watch as he stashed the bag of clothes behind the ice machine outside the door to the office, nervous about the appointment he had made while in Kingstown earlier in the day.

Lucelle stood at her stove, a large stew pot brewing on the burner. The small apartment unit was furnished with an odd assortment of hippie memorabilia and sailor related items. Washington continuously sniffed the air like a smell detective as Lucelle ladled large servings of the stew into two oversized bowls. "You can carry these up the stairs, can't you?"

"Yes, thank you," Reg politely replied.

Lucelle chuckled to herself. "You'll have to forgive me Reg. I can't help but think of you as the ten-year old that I first met. Do you still remember that?"

Reg warmly smiled. "I do Lucelle. You have always been so good to my father and me. This always feels like home."

"Is that why you came here with her?" she said as casually as she could manage.

"Her? Oh, no, I mean yes. Uh, I'm not sure what you mean."

Lucelle laughed out loud. She warmly stroked Reg's cheek. "I'm afraid that I'm doing it again. That's the problem with old ladies like me. We're just too nosy."

"No Lucelle, you're not too nosy, and you're definitely not too old." Reg took the bowls and carefully steadied them as he left. From the moment Reggie had made Lucelle's acquaintance as a young child, there had been a mother and son connection. It was more than the result of his motherless situation, or the fact that Lucelle never had a child. It was almost a past life thing, with both immediately knowing inside that there was a deeper connection. It took Reggie several tension-filled minutes to maneuver the bowls up the stairs without spilling them. He carefully set them down when he reached the apartment, withdrew the key and opened the door. Reg almost fell backwards as he beheld the back of Melody, completely naked as she looked out over the ocean from the balcony. He dropped both bowls. Melody turned toward the sound and let out a short scream of surprise. Both stood motionless for a moment as Reg took in the sight of Lady Melody, her full breasts and hour glass waist leading to a heavenly pair of shapely legs. Melody ran into the bathroom and slammed the door.

"I'm sorry. I didn't realize," Reg stammered. "I got stew from Ms. Providence downstairs. I'll go get more." Reg picked up the bowls and quietly left as he tried to push the image of Melody out of his mind and come up with an explanation as to why he dropped the stew. After another ten minutes of polite conversation with Lucelle, Reg was back upstairs with their dinner, this time knocking before he entered.

Lady Melody primly sat on the edge of the bed draped in a bath towel. "I cleaned up the last dinner," she said with a smile.

"Sorry. I didn't know," Reg stammered as he set the bowls down on the dresser. "I mean, that you would be, uh ... "

"Naked?" Melody said with a coy smile.

Reggie nodded, his face blushing as he tossed Melody the bag of clothes. "You should probably put some clothes on. I'll go into the bathroom and wait." Reg went into the bathroom and shut the door. He checked his watch, the time of his appointment drawing near. Reg pulled the two packages he had rescued from the boat from behind the toilet tank where he had stashed them, as well as the Captain's gun. He shoved the revolver into the back of his pants and set the packages on top of the toilet tank. Reg began to wash his hands, more out of anxiety than cleanliness.

"I hope it wasn't too much of a shock to see me naked?" Melody shouted out to Reg.

Reg stopped washing his hands and stood motionless. "No, no it wasn't. I mean, I've seen things before," he finally replied, cursing himself the minute he said it.

"I don't think any boy has ever seen me that way. I hope I wasn't, you know, gross or anything."

Reg turned off the water, his hands shaking. "No," he replied, his voice cracking. "No, nothing gross. I mean, no, you look great." Reg again silently cursed his reply.

"So, you think I'm pretty?"

"Oh, sure, yes, of course you are. I'm sure you've been told that tons of times." Reg reached for the hand towel on the rack above the commode.

"So what did you think of my breasts? I think they're a bit smallish."

The comment made Reg falter, dropping the towel which knocked one of the packages onto the toilet seat where it burst, its white powder falling into the toilet. "Shit," Reg said as he scrambled to rescue it, to no avail.

"What was that you said?"

"Nothing. I meant to say that your breasts are fine. I mean, they look great." Reg frantically scanned the bathroom. He grabbed the complementary tube that held a tampon, removed its contents, and carefully scraped as much of the white powder from the toilet seat into the tube as he could. Reg put the tube into his pocket and stuffed the remaining package down the front of his pants. He used a towel to wipe away any remaining powder and then left the bathroom.

"Where are you going?" Melody asked as Reg headed for the front door.

"I've got to meet some friends of mine. I'll be right outside the balcony on the beach below."

"Okay," Melody said as she headed for the bathroom, unbuttoning her pants.

"No, that's okay. You don't have to do that. I mean, I don't want to come in and catch you like that again. I mean, well ... I'll trust you not to leave, if you promise."

"I promise."

Reg smiled. He took Melody by the hand and led her to the balcony. Melody stood by the balcony railing. The full moon cast rays of light across the lazy ocean. Melody looked into Reg's eyes. She slightly lifted her chin and closed her eyes in preparation for a kiss. The sound of the glass door to the balcony closing broke her spell, Reg stranding Lady Melody on the balcony by locking the glass doors from the inside.

"Hey," Melody shouted, pounding on the glass doors as Reggie left the room and locked the front door behind him.

Reg hurried down to the beach, uncertain if his brief meeting with the two men in Kingstown would assure their appearance. He found his two partners in crime already waiting in the shadows of the palm trees. The two men, one black and one white, both in their twenties, stepped out into the moonlight. Both had the hard looks of the street, dressed in well worn tee shirts and shorts, their hygiene as ragged as their clothes.

"Men," Reg acknowledged as he glanced toward the third floor balcony of his room to see Melody silently looking on as she sat sulking in one of the chairs.

"All right, so when you told us you had some good stuff, I hope you meant it. We're busy with things to do, you know," the black man said.

"I'm sure this will be what you want," Reg said, fishing the tampon tube out of his pocket and handing it to the black man. The black man handed it to his partner who looked it over.

"Is this a female thing?" the white man said. "You know, a Tampax?"

"Not really," Reg said as casually as he could manage. "I use it for samples. I mean, who would check something like that?"

Both men nodded in agreement. "Smart," said the black man. The white man poured the powder onto the back of his partner's hand as well as his own. They both snorted the substance, leaning their heads back as they savored the drug.

"That's some good coke," the black man said.

"The real deal," the white man agreed. "So how much do you have?"

Reg turned from the men and pulled the package out from the front of his pants as the two men looked on.

"I'm starting to see a pattern here," the white man said.

"I've got this one package," Reg said as he held it up for the men to see. The two men looked at the package and then at each other. The white man took a step closer and peered at the design on the package.

"I don't know what you're trying to pull kid, but that's the Captain's cocaine."

"That's his mark," the black man said. "No way we're taking the Captain's stuff. We're not stupid."

"No. No, you see, he gave it to me."

The two men looked at each other and then both pulled pistols from their belts.

"I don't know who put you up to this, but the Captain don't give nothing to no one," the white man said.

"I'm thinking we might just take this coke and give it back to the Captain," the black man said to his partner. "That would get us in good with him."

"That's a good idea," the white man said. The two pointed their guns squarely at Reg. "Now you can hand that over to us kid or we can take it off of your dead body. What's it going to be?" Reggie's mind raced as his nerves shook him to his core. This definitely wasn't in his plan. And he sure didn't expect to give Melody a front row seat to him pleading for his life.

The shrill sound of Melody screaming from the balcony above caused both men to look in her direction. Reg used the distraction to pull out his pistol.

"Nobody move or I'll shoot the coke. I swear I will," Reg said.

The men returned their attention to Reg who pointed the gun at the package of cocaine in his other hand. They then looked back up at Melody who had stepped back into the shadows of the balcony, and then at each other, and then back to Reggie. "I think he means it," the black man said.

"Now settle down kid. We don't want to see anyone get hurt here. Just put the gun down."

"I mean it. I'll blow it away," Reg said, cocking the gun.

The two men looked at Reg, then at each other, and then back at Reg. "I don't think he'll do it," the white man said.

"I don't know. He seems pretty crazy. And what's with the girl up there?"

"Go ahead kid, shoot it. I dare you," the white man said. Reg looked up for Melody and then back at the two men. The white man took a step toward Reg, causing Reg to fire the gun. The bullet burst the package of cocaine, the coke blowing up in the air as the bullet continued on, striking the white man in the shoulder of his gun arm. The white man's gun went off, the shot hitting the black man in his right butt cheek. Both men fell to the sand as the white coke clouded the air. Reg threw the package down and ran for the hotel, not stopping until he was in the hotel room. He opened the glass door of the balcony, Melody spilling into the room.

"Are you stark raving mad!" Melody shouted.

" I know. That didn't go well," Reg shouted back. He ran about the room stuffing their clothes into the bag. "We've got to get out of here. Now." Reg grabbed Melody by the hand and dragged her to the front door. He swung the door open. Lucelle Providence was standing in the doorway.

"Reg. Lady Melody," Lucelle said. "I spoke to your father. Follow me. Now."

"Lucelle, I can explain," Reggie protested, pointing toward the beach. Lucelle's reply was a stern look that almost caused both Reggie and Melody to break into tears.

CHAPTER 18

No matter how at odds two people can be, having things in common are the ties that bind. The love of a fine meal in a perfect setting was that tie for Susan and Dutch.

A six-time winner of the Barbados Gold Award and only one of five restaurants chosen to be a Caribbean member of the prestigious Relais & Chateux organization, the Terrace Restaurant located just outside of Speightstown was a jewel they both treasured. As Susan sat with Dutch, Crane, and Vicky at a table overlooking the tranquil ocean bay, she couldn't help but consider how moments like this should be treasured. It brought back memories of the times she and her father would spend at Joe's Stone Crab in Miami Beach, his favorite place. Talking about this case or that client while savoring stone crab claws and lobster bisque soup. Executive Chef Brian Porteus, a classically French trained chef, with his own fisherman "Barker" that brought him fresh fish every day, served the table a meal of grilled lobster tails with creamed spinach and a lemon butter sauce on the side. Everyone partook of his specialty except for Crane, who demanded the grilled chicken supreme with bacon garnish served with bacon and onion potato cakes. Having helped the chef with a few minor issues in the past, Dutch felt as though he had the right to ask for what he wanted. And the chef, always the perfect host, obliged.

To prevent Dutch and Vicky from repeating their last dinner unveiling, Susan made sure they had a constant supply of fine wine on the table. She was sure that her strategy would appeal to both of their Bacchus appetites. She poured the last of the third bottle into everyone's glasses and forced herself up from her chair, by this time everyone feeling inebriated. Crane leant her a steadying hand as she raised her glass, bowing and then lifting her head through the fog of fine wine. "To me, for putting up with you three dear, dear people."

"Hear, hear," Dutch replied at they all clinked glasses and downed the last of the wine.

Susan slumped back into her seat and gazed about the restaurant taking in the breathtaking view of the pristine ocean as she paid the check. "What shall we do now?"

"We could go scout for locations for the Makin Bacon store," Crane suggested.

"Really Crane, the Makin Bacon store again? I am not going to traipse about while you take pictures of vacant lots," Dutch replied.

"I know. Let's go down to the Port St. Charles Marina," Vicky said. "It's such a nice walk and we can look at all the pretty boats there."

"It's yachts dear, not boats," Susan slurred. "And yes, that's a fine idea." Susan pointed a drunken finger at all three. "The walk will do you good. You all need to sober up." Dutch hoisted Susan from her chair and led the group out of the restaurant. Like a line of deck hands that had discovered the rum barrel, they walked down the road and out to the marina giggling and talking to themselves about nothing in particular, as drunken deck hands do.

Susan and Crane walked together as Dutch and Vicky cuddled behind. "Crane, you've known Dutch a long time?"

"Yes, too long I think sometimes."

"So what is the deal with him? I mean, most of the time he can be such a dick, know what I mean?" Crane dutifully nodded. "But then, sometimes, there's a part of him that's so different."

Susan stumbled in her inebriated stupor, Crane catching her by the arm. "In my village they say you are born either good or mean. Dutch was born good and mean."

Susan considered Crane's comment as they walked along. "And what do you think I was born as?" Susan asked of Crane as they reached the marina.

"I think you have a soft heart with a steel gun Ms. Susan," Crane replied with a smile.

"Good answer," Susan replied as Crane once again caught her as she stumbled.

The Port St. Charles Marina was man-made, but made only for the rich men who could afford a rich yacht. No matter what one's social or economic class in life, you couldn't help but behold with awe and joy the beauty that these vessels possessed. In the form of a giant letter J, the marina was the berth for only the best that other people's money could buy. Dutch stopped the group on the dock in front of a brand new Bertram 630. They all admired the sleek lines of the fishing yacht, Susan peering into the windows at the four staterooms glutinous in cherry wood.

"I hate whoever owns this boat," Susan said.

"It's whom, not who," Vicky replied with a warm smile. Susan laughed out loud as she stumbled over to the seawall and sat down. She made a majestic wave of her arms.

"I wonder what it would be like to be this rich?" Susan looked across the marina and spotted two men walking down the docks toward an older 42 foot Carver. "Take those two losers for example," Susan said as she pointed at the two men on the dock across from them. "They look like bums, and yet here they are, owning a yacht, living the high life. What makes them so special?"

Dutch looked across the marina at the two men, illuminated by the stand pole lights that lined the docks. A look of disbelief came over his face. Dutch jumped about like a child on recess who had just discovered that he's sitting on an ant hill. He pointed at the two men.

"Holy crap," Dutch finally managed. "It's the Captain and that other dude who kidnapped me!"

"That's impossible. Are you sure?" Susan asked.

Without a reply, Dutch took off running down the dock toward the two men who had reached the yacht and began to board it. The

Captain was picking the lock on the stateroom door as Dutch turned the corner.

"Hey you! Asshole!" Dutch hollered out, his scream catching the attention of both men. Without hesitation, the henchman withdrew a pistol and fired at Dutch, the bullets splintering the wooden dock pilings next to Dutch's head. Dutch turned and quickly began running the other way as the Captain and his henchman opened fire on Dutch, their shots hitting the yachts and splintering the dock all around him. As he turned the corner, Dutch ran into Susan who had her pistol out and ready.

"Shoot them, shoot," Dutch screamed as he ran past Susan toward Vicky and Crane, who both stood dumbfounded.

Susan took cover behind the bow of a yacht and began firing in rapid succession at the Captain and his henchman, who were open targets on the aft deck of the yacht. The Captain and his henchman kicked the door of the boat cabin open, the boat's security alarm wailing as Susan moved toward them, taking cover behind the tied up yachts. The Carver suddenly started up and in an instant it pulled away from its berth. It roared out of the marina as Susan continued to fire at the boat. Susan rose and walked back toward Dutch, who had placed Vicky and Crane behind the cover of the seawall.

"This is the last time I go to dinner with you," Crane said with conviction.

It was an early morning following a late night. Dutch and Susan spent most of the night explaining to the police who had shot up the marina, and why. The cops considered taking them in for statements until they got the police chief on the line. His recollection of their last conversation ended with strict orders to do anything but bring Dutch to the station.

The faces that looked upon the breakfast of eggs and kippers that Vicky made for everyone could have modeled for death masks.

"Okay, everyone eat up," Vicky cheerfully chimed.

"Why?" Dutch moaned as he slumped over on the bench seat at the galley table.

"Because breakfast is the most important meal of the day," Vicky chirped.

"No, I mean why am I alive? My head hurts so bad."

Susan took a glass of water in her shaking hands and lapped at it like a dog. "I am so hung over."

"Whoever invented wine should be shot," Crane said.

"Whoever ordered all that wine last night should be shot," Dutch added.

"If I had any bullets left, I'd shoot myself and then I'd kill you both," Susan replied.

"You white people, always ordering wine. You suck," Crane said as he applied a cold compress to his forehead.

Vicky picked up a skillet from the counter and smacked it with a metal serving ladle, the sound vibrating their brain stems. "Everyone rise and shine. It's a brand new day. A beautiful day," she sang out.

Susan nudged Dutch. "I guess she's got a hollow leg to match her head, huh?" Dutch rose and took the skillet from Vicky and directed her toward his stateroom.

"Honey, why don't you go clean up down there. I've got some things I need to discuss with Susan. Things about the case."

"Okay baby."

"Good move," Susan said as they watched Vicky descend from view.

"She's pretty, but obnoxious," Crane added.

"Look, we have got to find this Captain. I've had it with this crap."

"This is three times. Three times he tries to kill you. Sooner or later, he's going to miss and kill me," Crane said.

"What do you suggest? He's got a boat now, so chances are we're not going to find him on the island," Susan pointed out.

Dutch thought for a moment and then took out a map from the desk drawer of the navigation station. He spread it out on the table and pointed to the northern tip of Barbados. "Susan, what was it that the dealer at Club Xtreme told you?"

"He said that the Captain had a place on the north end, near the sea caves. Around Archer Bay."

"And why would he live there? After all, it's out of the way."

"Because it's isolated and he likes his privacy?" Crane suggested.

"Yes, you're right. But it's something more. It's the closest point to the island of St. Vincent. Get it, St. Vincent?" Crane and Susan both looked at Dutch like deer in headlights. "Okay, let me ask you this?" Dutch continued. "What island grows the most pot in the Caribbean?"

"Jamaica," Crane shouted out.

"No, Puerto Rico," Susan said.

"This isn't frickin Jeopardy. No, it's St. Vincent. And what does the Captain bring into the islands?"

"Oh, I get it. So the Captain needs the boat he stole to get more pot. So we'll find him in St. Vincent," Susan concluded.

"No," Dutch flatly replied. "But good thinking. He'll first have to stock the boat. Which means he'll be somewhere on the north end, getting provisions. All we have to do is get our own boat and search the north side for the yacht they stole."

"Great, let's raise anchor and shove off," Susan said.

"No, we can't take the catamaran, the waters are way too rough on that end. We'd smash up on the rocks for sure. But I do know someone who has a power boat."

"No, you can't be serious," Crane said.

"Can't be serious about what?" Susan asked, the drift of the conversation easily floating past her.

CHAPTER 19

Susan spent two hours in her hotel room trying on different combinations of clothes. She was determined to affect a better outcome this time. She finally chose her most revealing bikini top along with a tight fitting sarong and her tallest pair of heels. Susan spotted Ted in the parking lot of the Caribbean Court Hotel as he worked on the inside roof of his bus. Susan repeated the personal affirmation that she could be very persuasive, even when not carrying a gun. Ted, wearing only surf trunks, looked up the minute she entered the bus, her Angel perfume from Thierry Mugler preceding her arrival.

"Hi Ted," she said as she slowly ran her finger across the top of a vinyl bench seat.

"Well if it isn't search and destroy," Ted said, half in jest.

"You know that wasn't my fault."

"Guilty by association. That's the thing with Dutch, you live by him, and you die by him. Believe me, I should know."

"Ted, remember you mentioned that you'd show me around the island sometime?"

Ted wiped his hands with a rag as he approached Susan. "Yes, I do remember saying that. But that was when I had a bus. Now all I have is a tin can on wheels."

"I'm really sorry about that. I really am. And I swear I'll make it up to you. I really will." Susan traced a bead of sweat down Ted's chiseled abs. "It's just that I have some time off, and well, you know so much about the island. If there were some other way for us to go sightseeing."

Ted surveyed the bus. "Jeez, I don't know. I've got a lot of work to do on the tour bus. Besides, you still owe me quite a bit of money Susan."

Susan pursed her lips into a little girl pout. "Ted, I was so looking forward to finally spending some quality time with you. Forget about the money. Of course I'll pay you Ted. But now that I have a bit of free time, I thought we could enjoy it together. My way of making up for your bus. Just you and me."

"How about if you rent a car?"

"No, that wouldn't do. I mean, that wouldn't be very romantic, would it?"

Ted cleared his throat and tugged at his surf trunks like a shy boy waiting for his first kiss. "Hey, how about by boat?"

"By boat?"

"Yeah, I've got a 25 foot Outrage. It's a Boston Whaler. Keith and I use it mostly for fishing, but it's a great boat to tour around in." Ted leaned in close to Susan. "We could go out for a moonlight ride."

Susan put her hand on Ted's thigh and gently squeezed. "Ted, you devil. I'm afraid we wouldn't get too much sightseeing done at night, would we?"

"Well, there are some other sights we could see."

Susan put her lips to Ted's ear. "I'd rather wait until we're at my hotel to unveil those," she whispered.

"Okay," Ted squeaked. "Can you be ready to go in an hour?"

"An hour? I can't wait." Susan gave Ted a full peck on the cheek and then turned and sauntered toward the bus door. She stopped at the doorway and turned around. "Oh, you know, I almost forgot. I've got to run something over to Speightstown. We may have to wait until later in the week."

"No. No, that won't be a problem. I could bring the boat over to the Port St. Charles Marina. I could pick you up there. Do you know where that is?"

Susan pertly smiled and winked at Ted. "I'm sure I can find it." She turned and did her best wavy hip impression as she left the bus. "God I'm good," she said under her breath as she sauntered off toward her car, the gravel parking lot causing her to stumble in her heels. Ted, his face plastered to the bus window, followed her every move.

Susan had been waiting for over an hour by the time Ted had motored to the Port St. Charles Marina. Dutch had driven her over in his rental car. He sat listening to Susan over a small VHF radio from the parking lot of the marina. Dutch kept turning Susan off to listen to a football game on the radio, causing Susan to storm over to the car and demand that he turn his walkie talkie back on. Very High Frequency radios, VHF for short, work in a range from 156 megahertz to 174 megahertz, and are used as maritime radios because they can transmit about 5 nautical miles, or 9 kilometers. Like any typical walkie talkie, they operate in a simplex mode in which only one person can speak at a time. And today, Susan was doing all the talking.

"Look Dutch, I don't want Ted to discover that we're using him, over," Susan said into the hand held radio.

"Ten four," Dutch replied in a bored monotone. "Over."

"So don't start talking on this thing. I'll keep it in my purse, and I'll call you if I spot the boat. Just stay up with us as we go along the coast. Over."

"Ten four, back door. Over."

"Very funny. Okay, here comes Ted."

"You forgot to say over. Over."

"Shut up. Over." Susan stuffed the radio into her purse. She felt the butterflies in her stomach as she walked down the dock toward Ted's boat. Susan liked Ted, but not in the way she was having to portray. It wasn't her habit to beat around the bush or deceive people she liked. "Damn Dutch and his stupid plans," she said to herself. Ted tied up alongside the dock and jumped out of the Boston Whaler. He made a sweeping gesture.

"My lady, your chariot awaits you."

"Ted, I'm so glad we're doing this. It sounds so exciting," Susan lied.

"I can assure you, I'm the best guide on the island." Ted looked about the docks and the yachts at berth. "Wow, it looks like this place got shot up or something. What's with that?"

"I haven't a clue," Susan lied again. Ted helped Susan into the boat and then cast off. Susan took her seat as Ted revved the boat out to sea.

"How about we start with the north side of the island Ted?"

"The north side? Geez, I don't know. That area has really rough seas. And sharks."

Susan stood up and placed her hand on Ted's lower back. "I like it rough Ted." Ted swallowed so hard his Adam's apple almost popped a seed.

"Okay." Ted turned the boat northward as they bounced from wave to wave along the coastline dotted with white sand beaches. Susan kept her eye on the coast road spotting Dutch's car through the occasional breaks of foliage.

"Are there any pretty coves and such along this coast?" Susan asked with as much innocence as she could muster.

"Yes, this coast is really amazing Susan. It's as if this island was perfectly created." Ted pointed to the rocky cliffs that began to rise from twenty to one hundred feet from the ocean. "The north side of the island faces directly out to the Atlantic. From this point there's nothing between us and Europe, except the ocean of course. That's why the islands in this area are called the Windward Islands. They are more windward since the trade winds blow from east to west. That's why Barbados was such a major port for the old sailing ships. The slave ships leaving from the African Gold Coast and Gulf of Guinea would first reach Barbados, which is also called the Lesser Antilles."

"Where did the name Lesser Antilles come from?"

"The word Antilles was what the charts of the world in medieval Europe called the unknown lands that were somewhere in the mid-ocean between the Canary Islands and India. After Columbus, his term of West Indies for the islands became known as the Antilles, and the Caribbean Sea and Gulf of Mexico were called the Sea of Antilles."

"It's amazing how things change over time."

"The only thing constant is change."

"Speaking of change, how about we move a little closer in?"

"I don't know, the waves can be pretty rough. These Boston Whalers claim to be unsinkable, but I sure don't want to be the first to find out."

Susan spotted a row of coves that looked promising as a possible hiding place for boats, in particular the Captain's boat. She pointed to the coves, partially obscured by a large outcropping of rock. "That looks interesting. How about we shoot in there real quick?"

"Okay, but hold on. It'll be pretty rough." Ted gunned the throttle, and the boat's bow lifted up into the air as they headed straight into the cove. Susan looked up at the tops of the cliff, Dutch's vehicle nowhere in sight. As the boat cleared the rock face, Susan spotted the yacht that the Captain had stolen in the second cove. It was tied up at a small floating dock, a narrow trail leading up the cliff from the boat.

"Let's tie up at the dock Ted. We can walk up that trail and look out over the ocean," Susan suggested.

"I don't know, there's already a boat there. It looks like it could be a private dock."

"They won't mind Ted. Heck, they'd probably love the company." Ted shrugged and turned the boat into the cove, pulling back on the throttle as the boat drifted toward the dock. Susan scanned the cliff tops for any sign of Dutch as they neared the dock. The galley door of the yacht opened and the Captain stepped out with a shotgun in his hands. Without a word of warning, the Captain aimed squarely at Ted and Susan and fired, the blast hitting the bow of the Boston Whaler like a splattering of paint.

"Holy shit!" Ted screamed as he jerked the throttle into reverse. "That guy is crazy." Ted looked about the boat, not sure what to do next.

Susan on the other hand suffered from no such indecision. She scrambled for her purse and withdrew her Glock 26. Susan pushed Ted to the floor and returned fire as she braced herself against the helm's steering column. Her aim landed shots all around the Captain's head, the Captain's only saving grace being the ocean swells that rocked the boat as well as her aim.

"You brought a gun onto the boat?" Ted incredulously screamed, his hands over his ears. The Captain dropped his shotgun and darted into the cabin.

"Stay down Ted, I've got this sucker," Susan shouted, her adrenalin running like charged lightning. She scrambled to the bow railing and took aim as she held onto the rails. Susan fired her full clip into the engine well as it roared into gear. Ted pulled himself up by the wheel as she surveyed his boat's position. He began to turn the boat around as the Captain's yacht exploded from the dock and headed straight for them. Susan held onto the railing as the swells slapped the side of boat.

"Stop turning the boat Ted. I can't get a shot off."

"Stop shooting so I can get us out of here for God's sake," Ted yelled back as he frantically struggled to turn the wheel against the incoming swells. Ted glanced up as the yacht bore down on them, its bow no less than twenty yards from their port side. "Hold on, they're going to ram us!" Susan grabbed the railing as Ted lunged toward the stern. In a heartbeat, the Captain's boat smashed into the port side of the Boston Whaler at full speed, the yacht's weight slicing through Ted's boat like a knife through butter. Susan and Ted both looked on in shock as the Captain's yacht limped away, the collision along with Susan's gunfire having caused it more damage than anyone could have imagined. A cloud of black smoke bellowed from the stern of the Captain's boat as it motored out of view.

"You okay?" Ted shouted out as the two halves of the Boston Whaler slowly drifted apart. Susan looked about her as if she were in a dream.

"We're not sinking. Why aren't we sinking?"

"I told you, these boats are unsinkable. I never thought I'd get to prove it though." The sound of a car horn pierced the air. Susan and Ted followed the sound to the top of the cliff where Dutch animatedly waved to them. Ted looked at Dutch and then studied Susan for a moment. "You!" Ted shouted pointing up toward Dutch and then at Susan. "Him! This! You've got to be kidding me! This, all of this, this was a setup, wasn't it? Some crazy case you and Dutch are on. Right?"

"What? I can't hear you," Susan shouted back, her thinly veiled pretense luffing in the wind.

"You heard me," Ted screamed as the two continued to float apart toward separate ends of the cove. "I can't believe it! You used me! Just for my boat. You two are unbelievable." Ted gestured, his fingers positioned in a "v" which he pointed to his eyes and then at Susan. "I hate you guys. You and Dutch."

"Just wait on the beach. I'll come get you," Dutch shouted from above.

"Don't bother," Ted shouted back. "I hate you."

Dutch and Susan silently sat as they stared down at their meal of fish cakes with rice and peas. The excellent food at Mannie's Suga Suga wasn't at issue, nor was the spectacular Mullins Beach setting. They were like two obnoxious drunks who had just sobered up after destroying their best friend's wedding. Susan and Dutch both felt regret for their actions, first for destroying Ted's tour bus and then his boat. Susan slowly shook her head in disbelief.

"It was hard to believe. It just split in half, like a cracked egg."

"Like a splintered board," Dutch added without looking up.

"More like a clay plate."

"Yeah, a clay plate. Wham, and it was all over. Still, it did float."

"Yes, it did do that. Ted wasn't kidding about that." Susan stared off into the ocean's horizon. "You think his insurance will cover it?"

"Depends," Dutch replied as he joined her gaze. "Probably, as long as he doesn't bring up the gun play. You think you hit anyone?"

Susan produced a short smirk. "I don't think so. Sure wish you could have returned some crossfire."

"Yeah, crossfire. That would have helped."

"I guess apologizing to Ted wouldn't do any good?"

"No, not really. Not now. Not after the bus and the boat. Maybe just the bus or the boat. But both, no, I don't think so."

"I need a drink."

"I need two." Dutch rose up from his chair, his sights set on the bar.

"Dutch Holland!" The man's voice came from the far end of the bar. Susan glanced over, Dutch looking like a thief caught in a spotlight. Menton Moore's bald head emerged from out of the crowd. "Dutch, what an unexpected pleasure. What are you doing out here?"

"Just drinking and thinking," Dutch replied. "And you?"

"Checking out the local color. Is that your boss over there?" Menton waved at Susan who remained clueless to his presence, absorbed in her guilt over Ted. Menton immediately went to her side, Dutch momentarily torn between the bar and the unplanned meeting. The bar easily won.

"Ms. Berg. Susan Berg, what a pleasure," Menton said as he stood in front of Susan.

"Mr. Moore, what a surprise," Susan replied, startled out of her self-pity.

"You look just lovely, as always, Ms. Berg. I was just telling Dutch that this was such a coincidence."

"Well it is a small island. I just want you to know that Dutch ..., Mr. Holland and I are going to spend all day tomorrow working on your case."

"You are? I would be so appreciative. I really would. I can't tell you how much it would mean to me. Really."

"No, it's our pleasure. After all, you hired us to do a job and that's just what we plan to do."

"Do what?" Dutch asked, announcing his arrival with four large Mai Tais in his hand.

"I was just telling Mr. Moore that you and I are spending all day tomorrow working on his case."

"We are? Oh yes, we are. Of course."

"How nice of you to get me a drink Dutch," Menton said as he took one of the drinks, Dutch handing one to Susan. "Who's the fourth one for?"

"Me," Dutch replied as he sat down. "So Susan, why don't you let Menton in on your plan?"

"My plan?"

"Yes, your plan for tomorrow. You know, to find the golden sword. I'm sure he'd like to know."

"Oh that." Susan's brain spun into action as she tried to devise a plan. "Actually, Mr. Moore probably isn't interested in the details. Right Mr. Moore? You just want results. Am I right?"

"Actually, I would love to hear how you detectives work. I find it fascinating, really," Menton replied with stars in his eyes.

"Oh, right, well in that case, I'd be happy to go over it with you." The sound of repeated chirps suddenly floated through the air. Menton patted his pants pockets and then withdrew a small cell phone. He held one finger up as he answered the phone. Menton listened intently as Susan shot Dutch a dirty look.

"No, don't do anything until I get there," Menton said into the phone and then abruptly hung up. "I'm so sorry, but I'm afraid something pressing has developed. I'm afraid I'll have to catch up with you later. How about tomorrow night, say for dinner in Bridgetown?"

"Jeez, I'm not sure Menton," Dutch replied. "We're going to be pretty busy working on your case, right Ice?"

"Yes, the case, very busy. But do give us a call. We can update you." Menton nodded and then rushed off, disappearing into the crowd at the bar. Susan kicked a spray of sand at Dutch. "Real cute."

Dutch grinned as he downed one of his drinks. "All kidding aside, do you have any thoughts about his case?"

"Actually, I do. You and I are going to spend the day searching the historical records at the Barbados Archives."

"Not the lazaretto in Black Rock?" Dutch wined like a spoiled child.

"Yes, the lazaretto. And we're not leaving until we get a clue. Besides, that crazy Captain is probably halfway to St. Vincent by now."

"I don't think so. Not with the way his engine was smoking. I'm betting he's holed up somewhere on this side of the island until he can find, or steal, another boat."

"So what do you suggest?"

"Well, we can wait for something to pop up, or make something pop," Dutch said as they both watched Menton rush to his car in the parking lot and quickly drive away.

"Let's do both," Susan said.

CHAPTER 20

It took some doing, but after complimenting Crane on his use of spices in his cooking, as well as agreeing that a chain of Makin Bacon stores was the way to go, Dutch had Crane's agreement to sit on the desk sergeant at the police station. It took nothing more than a phone call and a promise of dinner from Dutch to get Vicky Godown to watch the house of Reginald Carrington's father in Speightstown. However, it did take more than twenty minutes for Dutch to explain to Vicky what he meant by watching the house.

The city of Black Rock is nothing more than a short stop about fifteen minutes outside of Bridgetown. The lazaretto, a collection of whitewashed wooden buildings shadowed by large banyan trees on the outskirts of town, is located right off of the 2A Highway in St. Michael's parish. When it came to book research, those boring facts alone were enough to make Dutch whine like a dog getting a bath. Susan, familiar with her own young nephew's behavior, paid Dutch no mind.

"What does lazaretto mean anyways?" Susan asked as they approached their destination.

"In times past, it was a term for a hospital where people with contagious diseases were kept. More of a quarantine than a hospital really," Dutch recounted. "They would keep people with leprosy, cholera, whatever, until they died. Then they'd burn their bodies in an attempt to keep the outbreaks from spreading. More often than not, once you went into the lazaretto, you never came out."

"Well let's hope that's not the case with us." Dutch directed Susan around the back to the smaller building on the far side that housed the library. The gravel parking lot was shrouded by trees, making it seem even more desolate. "Nice spot," Susan mentioned as they got out of the car, "for a murder."

"Funny," Dutch replied. They were met by a welcome blast of cold air as they entered the small library.

The librarian, a short motherly type with graying hair pulled tightly back, greeted them from the back of the main room. "Good to see you," she said in a hushed tone that all librarians are required to have.

"Hi, I'm Dutch, and this is Susan. Susan Berg," Dutch replied in his usual booming voice. The librarian pressed her forefinger to pursed lips, a shushing noise escaping from her mouth. Susan gave Dutch's ribs a firm nudge as Dutch scanned the vacant room. "What? There's nobody here."

Susan approached the librarian who was viewing Dutch with suspicious disapproval. "My partner and I are here to do some research," she said in the tone of a confessional. "It's historical research."

"What exactly are you researching?"

"We're looking for a historical record. From the 1600's. It has to do with a golden sword of all things. It was given by Barbados to a ship's captain."

"Do you know the name of the ship's captain?"

"Yes, I believe we do."

The librarian solemnly nodded and motioned for them to follow as she moved to the back of the room. She withdrew a skeleton key from her pocket and ceremoniously inserted it into the lock of a large glass case, Susan and Dutch looking on in anticipation. The librarian slowly turned the key, the clank of the turning lock vibrating through the library.

"Nothing's gonna fly out of there and eat our faces is it?" Dutch said out loud.

"Shish," Susan and the librarian responded in unison.

"Shish yourselves, this is creepin' me out."

The librarian slowly opened the glass top and carefully withdrew a large hardcover ledger from the case. "Follow me," she said as she led them to one of the worktables that occupied the middle of the room. The librarian gingerly placed the book on the table, running her hand over the top cover as if to bless it.

"This is the only recorded ledger of all the deaths, births, and marriages in Barbados since the fifteenth century. In that time, since most of our citizens were slaves and could not write, it was the priests of the Catholic Church who kept all the records." The librarian gingerly opened the ledger and lightly ran her hand over the large pages, yellowed with time. "This is the actual book written in the 1600's, so please be careful as these pages are over five hundred years old." Dutch reached for the book, the librarian swiftly slapping his hand away with a look as hard as diamonds. "The lady will be using the book, if you don't mind."

Susan smirked at Dutch and sat down in front of the large ledger. Dutch took a seat beside her as the librarian hovered over them. Susan scanned the first page, the awe of the historical significance overtaking both of them. Susan traced her fingers over the page as if to confirm its existence. "So this is the actual writing from people in the 1600's. Wow, that's so unreal."

The librarian beamed with smug satisfaction. "Amazing, isn't it? All those lives and deaths, all in this book. One can only imagine the stories behind them. Is there something in particular you are seeking?"

"Yes, we're helping an old friend. He's looking for his lineage."

"If you have a name and a date, we can probably narrow it down."

"The date is around 1750. The name we are looking for is Hollingsworth. A Captain Hollingsworth. Some sort of pirate chaser. Not too sure about anything else."

"Let's see," the librarian said as she gingerly turned the pages of the book. She stopped on a page marked with the hand written dates of 1750 running down the far right column of the page. The librarian scanned the page and then stopped toward the bottom.

"There. There's something right here," she said pointing to an entry. "It looks like a marriage notation."

Dutch and Susan peered down at the entry. "It has the name Hollingsworth all right," Dutch announced.

"Who's Margaret, daughter of James Gambier?" Susan asked.

"Based on the way it's entered, that must be whom he married," the librarian surmised.

"So where do we go from here?"

"Well, now that we know the names exist and we have the surnames of the two families, we have to research their genealogies."

"How's that?" Dutch asked, already becoming impatient.

The librarian went over to a low row of books and ran her hand across the titles. She stopped and pulled out a short, fat volume. "This is the one that will tell us what we need to know." The librarian set it on the table and began to thumb through its pages. "This is the book of Genealogies of Barbados Families. The Barbados Museum and Historical Society researched and created this book, compiled by Mr. James C. Brandow." The librarian scanned the table of contents, then turned to the index in the back, and then back and forth between the contents and index repeatedly.

"Are you all right?" Dutch finally asked her. "You're not having a stroke are you?"

"This is strange. Very strange. It seems some pages have been torn out of this book." The librarian forcefully tapped her finger on the index pages. "See, right here. The pages where the letter "H" for Hollingsworth would be. Damn vandals." The librarian slammed the book closed just as Dutch's cell phone rang. The librarian shot Dutch a look that could kill the dead as she pointed to a hand written sign taped to the wall over her desk. "No cell phones."

"Sorry, I'll just be a second." Dutch flipped open his cell phone and listened.

"Who is it?" Susan asked as the librarian crossed the room to a large armoire.

"It's Crane. He's got a lead on the Captain." Dutch listened intently and made a writing motion in the air. Susan hustled over to the librarian's desk and returned with a paper and pencil. "Write this down," Dutch instructed. "Mullins Bay, about a mile up the beach. Okay, got it." Dutch hung up the phone as the librarian approached with an identical book in hand. "It looks like they found the Captain. We've got to go."

"Good thing I have another copy," the librarian announced as she thumbed through the book.

"I apologize but we really must go," Susan said. "Is there any way you could fax the pages to my hotel?"

"Well that's quite unusual."

"I assure you, it's a matter of most urgency," Susan replied. "If you could, we would be so appreciative. I'm staying at the Little Arches Hotel . Do you know it?"

"Yes, I will send them the fax at my earliest convenience."

"Thank you so much. You're a dear." Susan motioned Dutch out of the library. "So what do we have?" Susan asked as they motored down Highway 1 toward Mullins Bay.

"Crane said that he heard the dispatcher at the police station call in a homicide. When he saw a couple of the detectives leave, he overheard them say it had something to do with the Captain. We should be about ten minutes ahead of them since they're leaving from Bridgetown."

Dutch shifted the car into fourth gear and floored the gas. It wasn't long before they found the spot. A small fishing shack perched along a stretch of white sand on the side of the road. A lone police car with its lights still flashing marked the spot.

"How do you want to play this?" Susan asked as they walked toward the shack. A local policeman stood like a sentry in the doorway.

"I've got this," Dutch replied with bravado. Dutch strode up to the officer with a wave. "Hey, what are you doing in my boat house?" Dutch asked as if he owned the place.

The officer gave Dutch a look over and then pointed his finger into his chest. "I got news for you. This is old man Morgan's boat shack, unless you just bought it. And if you did, I'm gonna need to see the bill of sale. You got that? A bill of sale?" Dutch literally sputtered out loud like a rusty car running out of gas. Susan shoved Dutch out of the way, positioning herself within a tongue's reach of the officer's ear. She whispered some words to him and with a slight smile he motioned them in.

"What the hell did you say to him?"

"Me to know. You to find out," Susan replied as they strode into the boat shack. Specks of dust floated in the beams of light that streaked through the gaps in the wooden walls and roof. Against one wall was the Captain's goon, his arms curled up in front of him as he lay on one side. He looked as if he were asleep, except for the oozing bullet hole in his forehead. In the middle of the room was the Captain, slumped over in the chair to which he was bound. Susan pushed the Captain upright by his shoulder to reveal his face. Beaten to a pulp, he looked as if all the bones in his face had been sucked out of him.

"Shit," Dutch murmured as Susan studied him like he was some newly discovered species. "Doesn't that gross you out?" Dutch asked as he looked away.

"Not really," Susan casually replied. "I'm used to it after working for the public defender's office. You wouldn't believe what those drug lords would do to snitches. Looks like they used that pipe on him," she said, pointing to the bloody weapon that lay at the far end of the room.

"They? Why do you say they?" Dutch asked.

Susan pointed to the floor. "Look at the dust. There are at least two or more shoe prints there. With all the dust in here, they've got to be fairly new. Only one reason to torture someone like this."

"They wanted information," Dutch added.

"And they were willing to kill for it." Susan let go of the Captain who slumped back over. "We had better get out of here before the detectives arrive." The policeman stuck his head into the shack. He held out the name badge that was pinned to his shirt.

"Now make sure to get the name right. Carmichael, like Michael with a car."

"I will do that. Don't you worry," Susan said as they strode out of the shack. "And no need to mention we were here?"

"You've got that right Miss," the policeman agreed.

"A reporter?" Dutch burst out as they reached the car. "You told him we were reporters?"

"What else could I say after your lame story? You know this is a small island. Everyone knows everyone here."

"Maybe including who killed those two."

Susan and Dutch sat in silence as they drove back toward Bridgetown, their solemn mood a result of the brutal murders and the new questions they created.

"I just don't get it?" Dutch finally said as Susan concentrated on maneuvering the car down the dark roadway.

"Nothing makes frickin sense with this case. There's no way that kid did this."

"No, this was a two man job, for sure. Those dead guys were tough dudes. They wouldn't go down without a fight."

"Unless they were taken by surprise."

"Yeah." Dutch stared out the window and pondered the possibilities. "Maybe the kid's father? He didn't seem like someone to back down from a fight."

"No, I don't think he would have gone looking for them. He just didn't seem the type. Besides, who did he have to help him?"

"Speaking of Mr. Carrington, I wonder why we haven't heard from Vicky?" Dutch said as he took out his cell phone.

Susan began to speak and then thought better of it.

"What?" Dutch asked of her self censure.

"Nothing."

"Come on, I know you. You always say what's on your mind unless it's pretty bad. What were you going to say? Am I dying or something?"

"No, it's just, well, I don't get it. I mean, you and Vicky. She doesn't seem your type. I mean, if you had a type."

Dutch smiled like the devil after just collecting a soul. "I'm like clay, she's like water. Every time I'm around her, I get harder."

"I knew I shouldn't have said anything." Susan turned her concentration back to the road as Dutch dialed Vicky's cell.

"Vicky, what's going on there?" Dutch's expression turned serious as he intently listened. "No, don't follow him. It's too dangerous." Dutch screwed up his face as if Vicky's words were literally slapping him. "No, no don't do that. He may be dangerous, a killer. Look, stay right there and I'll get there right away. And don't get too close, whatever you do!" Dutch flipped off the phone and tossed it onto the dash. "Damn it."

"What is it?"

"It seems our Mr. Carrington is taking off. Vicky tailed him from his house in Speightstown to the Port St. Charles Marina."

"You think he's trying to leave Barbados because he killed the Captain?"

"Hell if I know. The crazy girl is calling from the cabin of the boat he's on."

"What?"

"She snuck onto the boat. I swear."

"What are we going to do?"

"We've got to find that boat."

"How? We don't even have a power boat."

"Head toward the airport. I've got an idea but we're going to have to move fast."

CHAPTER 21

Dutch had already spent twenty minutes and a thousand words on his cell phone by the time they reached the Grantley Adams Airport in the town of Seawill in Christ Church. Dutch was about to have a brain freeze, between keeping Vicky calm on the line and speaking to Horizon Helicopters at the airport.

"Look Mardrid, this is the thing," Dutch said to the owner of the helicopter service. "I can appreciate that you've got some issues with the helicopter. Yes, I realize how important the gauges are. But I've got a special lady and she's in big trouble. That's the bottom line. I don't need to remind you of what I did for your mother. And I don't care what the cost. Let's just be ready to get into the air to try and find her in five minutes. Okay?"

"Where are we at?" Susan asked.

"It wasn't easy but Mardrid is standing by with the chopper. Vicky was able to tell me that she's on a 46 foot Hatteras Sport Fisher."

"Does she know where it's heading?"

"She's somehow managed to stow away in the front storage locker in the front stateroom. The only thing she can see is the view out of the one porthole when she cracks open the door. She thinks they're headed west."

"If she's right, that means they're headed for St. Vincent."

"Exactly. The Captain's home base for picking up pot."

"You think he or his son were in business with the Captain? Running drugs?"

"I don't know Ice. All I know is we've got to get Vicky off of that boat. For all we know, that guy could be a killer," Dutch replied just as his phone's battery ran out. Dutch pounded the phone on the dash in frustration.

"How do you know Mardrid? I mean, can you trust him?" Susan said in an attempt to divert Dutch's temper from the phone.

"Sure enough. I've known him since he was a kid. I helped his mother out of a jam awhile back. Nothing I'd like to talk about."

"You kill someone for her?"

"Like I said, nothing I'd like to talk about."

Susan spun the car into the parking lot in front of the Barbados Concorde Experience Facility at the airport. A tourist attraction that actually contained one of the Concorde supersonic planes, it stood as a tribute to bad ideas that cost way too much. Leave it to the French. Dutch held out his hand. Susan placed her Glock handgun into it without hesitation. He jumped out of the car and ran over to the helicopter whose blades were already whirling. Susan watched as Dutch climbed in and the chopper lifted off from the tarmac.

"Thanks Mardrid," Dutch said as he put on a pair of headphones so he and Mardrid could converse over the sound of the rotors. Mardrid, a handsome Barbadian in his early thirties, just nodded as he kept his attention on the myriad dials that crowded the dashboard of the Robinson R-44 Raven helicopter.

"What's the heading of the boat?" Mardrid asked as the chopper reached its apex.

"Just head toward St. Vincent," Dutch replied. Mardrid finally looked over at Dutch, as if it hurt him to do so.

"St. Vincent. You know this bird doesn't have any fixed utility floats for the water?"

"Don't worry. We'll catch up to them before they get there for sure. Just head for the Port St. Charles Marina. We can try to pick up their heading from there." Mardrid banked the copter as if sliding on ice. Dutch instinctively held onto his seat as they coasted over the island toward the Port St. Charles Marina. At a top speed of 130 miles per hour, the Robinson R-44 Raven chopper was over the crescent shaped marina in a matter of minutes.

"I don't think we should be going over the water."

"What? You can't swim?"

"Funny. It's just that I didn't fuel up. I thought we were just going around the island."

"Look Mardrid, this lady, my lady, could be on a boat with a double murderer. And all I know is that I couldn't live with myself if I let something happen to her."

Mardrid gave an audible sigh of resignation. "By that, you mean like my mom."

"No, I didn't mean that. I wasn't even thinking that. But now that you mentioned it, yes, just like your mom."

Mardrid chewed on Dutch's words like a tough steak. He aimlessly looked over the dials on the console and then lingered on the view of the horizon. "My mom, I mean, were you two ever an item?"

"No, no we weren't. She was just a really nice lady who needed some help."

"My Dad. He was very mixed up."

Dutch studied Mardrid and then joined his watch of the horizon. "Yes, I guess you could say that," Dutch finally said. Dutch waited through the following silence, wondering if Mardrid ever did know the real story.

"Did you know my Dad?" Mardrid asked.

"No, no I didn't. I just know that your mother was scared to death of him. Scared of what he might do to you."

"I guess."

Dutch put a light hand on Mardrid's shoulder. "I lost my dad when I was young too. Just about the age you were. Probably the worst time for someone, in between being a boy and a man. But I can tell you, I'm real proud of you Mardrid. I mean, if I ever had a son, he couldn't do better than you." Dutch noticed a tear run down Mardrid's cheek from behind his aviator's sunglasses. "Hey, have you ever shot a gun from one of these things?" Dutch added in an effort to change the mood.

"A gun?"

Dutch pulled out Susan's Glock and pointed it out the window. "Yeah, I was just wondering. How much would I have to lead a target?"

"Come on Dutch, put that away. You know what that gun could do to this bird if it accidently went off?"

"Don't worry. If I shoot it, it won't be an accident."

"This guy we're chasing. He's one bad dude, huh?"

"I think so, but I hope not. What's the best way to find this boat?"

"We could do one of two things. I can either take a flight path moving back and forth in an attempt to find them underway. Or we can go to where we think they're headed, and fly in a straight line back and forth, hoping they will come to us and cross our path. What do you think?" Dutch calculated the odds of Vicky staying quiet enough for them not to find her aboard.

"We better try to find them first," Dutch said. Mardrid obliged and glided the chopper into a looping north to south pattern over the azure blue ocean below.

"How much time since they left?" Mardrid asked.

"They've got about a two hour lead on us."

"Well, if they are in that Hatteras, at 20 knots an hour, that means they've got another three hours before they reach St. Vincent." Mardrid glanced at his fuel gauge and then furrowed his brow as he did the calculations in his head. "It's gonna be close Dutch. Let's just hope we find them before that."

For the next three hours, Dutch and Mardrid scanned the ocean below as they searched for the boat. The feeling of helplessness increased with every fruitless pass as they traveled closer to St. Vincent. The primary island of the Grenadines with the capital city of Kingston, St. Vincent is part of a chain of islands made up of over 600 islets extending over 60 miles down to Grenada. With volcanic mountains that are densely forested due to consistent rainfall, its terrain and poverty make it an ideal island for growing some of the best marijuana in the Caribbean. The Bay of Kingston and nearby Calliaqua Bay finally came into view. Mardrid studied the fuel gauge as Dutch carefully scanned the St. Vincent Marina, nestled within the safety of Johnson Point.

"Bring it down toward the marina Mardrid."

"I think we had better land at Joshua International Airport and refuel Dutch."

"Just one last look before we get fuel at the airport. Down there, at the marina." Dutch pointed to the marina with its slew of motor yachts coming and going. Mardrid shook his head with regret and then dropped straight down to the marina below. Dutch searched the rows of boats, his eyes finally catching site of a 46 foot Hatteras Sport Fisher with a white object fluttering brightly from a porthole. "There, down there," Dutch ordered as he pointed to the boat. Mardrid maneuvered over the Hatteras as Dutch studied the object. "It's her bra," Dutch said.

"What?"

"Her bra. I'd know it anywhere. It's Vicky's bra. That's the boat." A sense of movement caught Dutch's attention at the end of the dock. He took up the pair of binoculars and focused in on the figure. "I'll be damned," Dutch said to himself out loud.

"What is it?"

"It's our target. Hang back a little and let's give Mr. Carrington a little rope." Mardrid obliged and lifted the helicopter to one thousand feet.

"What about the girl?"

"If Vicky's hanging her bra out of the boat, then I'm sure she's fine. Whatever you do, don't lose our target."

Dutch flipped open his cell phone and called one of the saved numbers in its memory. "Ice, it's Dutch. Call the St. Vincent Police and get them over to the St. Vincent Yacht Club ASAP. Tell them to look for the Hatteras in a slip on the north side. They'll know it by the large white bra hanging out of a portal. Yes, I said a bra, a brassiere. It's Vicky's. Have them put her on the first flight back to Barbados. Make sure they tell her to go to your hotel room and wait for us, for her own safety." Dutch hung up and returned to watching Carrington through the binoculars.

"He's headed to the parking lot. Move in just a bit closer." Mardrid moved the copter down toward the main building of the yacht club. "There, there he goes," Dutch shouted as he pointed to a nondescript blue sedan as it pulled out of the parking lot and onto the main road. "Stay with him now. But stay high. We don't want him to notice us."

With a nod, Mardrid moved through a low lying cloud. He positioned the chopper on the island side of the car as it raced down the Windward Highway toward the city of Prospect. "Hang back a little Mardrid. We don't want to blow it now." Mardrid lifted the chopper another thousand feet in seconds just as the car took a sharp turn down a dirt road toward the beach side. "Damn it, we're going to lose him. Go down Mardrid."

"Will you make up your mind? Up, down, what do you think this is, a yo-yo?" Mardrid dipped the copter as they strained to spot the car through the overhanging palm and bamboo trees. "There, there he is," Dutch shouted as he pointed to the car that had stopped in front of a small concrete bungalow.

"I'm not deaf you know," Mardrid replied. "Look, we know where he is. We're only one click from the airport. We really need to refuel."

"Sure, just one minute. Let's just get a bit closer. We need to know if the girl is in there. Then we can go to the airport, call the police, and let them handle it. Job done. Okay?"

"Look, I didn't want to worry you, but I'm not real sure about these gauges. Particularly the fuel gauge. I told you the digital controller was acting up. We really should fuel up."

"Just go down and hover right over the house, real low. If that doesn't bring them out of the house, nothing will."

"We really need to go get some fuel."

Dutch pointed a stern finger at Mardrid. "Do not make me call your mamma." Mardrid looked at the fuel gauge and then back at

Dutch. He was convinced that the gauge might be wrong but he was certain that Dutch would call his mother.

Mardrid pushed forward on the teetering bar cyclic control and the chopper went down like a rock, stopping just inches from the roof of the house. Dutch smiled with satisfaction as the wind from the rotors tore shingles from the roof and sent them whirling about like papers in a cyclone. Even Mardrid's concerns faded into delight as he revved the engine causing the windows of the small abode to shake.

It wasn't until the second bullet cracked Dutch's side window that they realized they were being shot at, the roar of the helicopter easily drowning out the sound of gun fire.

"Up Mardrid. Get us up." Mardrid pulled back on the cyclic control causing the bird to swiftly rise until a distinct sputtering sound interrupted their trajectory. "What's that?" Dutch asked, his look of concern over the bullets now one of dread.

"You know what it is," Mardrid screamed back, as full of anger as fear. "We're out of fucking fuel damn you!" Mardrid pushed down on the control hoping to land as the helicopter's main rotor blade slowed its rotation.

"Okay, just set her down," Dutch suggested as if the obvious would calm Mardrid.

"Helicopters don't glide Dutch."

"What do you mean?"

"They just crash!" Mardrid yelled, his words hanging in the air as the helicopter fell like a stone, the blare of the emergency signals filling their ears. The chopper impacted the middle of the roof in a split second, crashing straight through into the bungalow.

Like a bag of flour that had exploded, the air was thick with dust and debris, the glass of the chopper and parts of its metal skin stripped away. Dutch struggled to recover his senses, a deluge of warm liquid flowing over his face. He wiped his eyes and then reached for Mardrid who was slumped over in his seat. Dutch instinctively felt Mardrid's carotid artery for a pulse, relieved to find one. As the dust cleared, Dutch could make out three figures standing a distance away, like ghostly apparitions in the haze. He withdrew his gun, not certain if they were real or ghosts sent to collect him. Dutch again wiped at his eyes, not realizing it was his own blood that streamed from a gash across his forehead. He unbuckled his seatbelt and leaned forward, his arm shaking as he tried to aim the gun at the three figures. One of the three stepped forward, the face of Lady Melody clearly visible. Her expression became all that Dutch could see, as if superimposed on his mental viewing screen. Dutch momentarily looked into her eyes, and then there was nothing.

CHAPTER 22

Dutch struggled through a strange mix of dreams that flipped through his unconscious mind. Like a film festival showing twenty movies at the same time, the viewing screen in his mind constantly flickered through images and scenes from his past, present and future psyche. The only constant that came into view in every scene was Lady Melody's eyes. That look was always present, at times the featured image and in other dreams, just a momentary glance. But it was always there, saying a million words in just one momentary glimpse.

Suddenly, like a cold splash of water, Dutch was sitting straight up and gasping for air, his eyes wide open. Susan and Crane both shrieked, startled by Dutch's abrupt return to the real world.

"What the fuck?" all three said in unison.

"Doctor!" Crane shouted. Crane ran out of the room as Susan held up two fingers.

"How many fingers am I holding up?" she asked.

"I don't need a drunk test Ice."

"Do you remember how you got here?"

"Here? Where the hell is here?" Dutch felt for the bandage that was wrapped around his forehead, making him look like the flute player in the Spirit of '76 painting of the American Revolution.

"You're in the hospital. Someone called in the crash and they rushed you and Mardrid to the hospital. It was lucky that you were near Kingston when you crashed."

"How's Vicky? Did the police get her from the boat?"

"Yes, I just spoke to her. She's safe and sound in my hotel room back in Barbados. Undoubtedly running up my tab with room service," Susan replied.

"And Mardrid? How is Mardrid? Is he okay?"

"He's okay, but madder than a devil kicked out of heaven," Susan said.

Crane Luk entered the room dragging a doctor with him. Crane shoved the doctor in Dutch's direction. "Fix him," Crane ordered.

The doctor gave Crane a dirty look and then turned his attention toward Dutch. "You're awake. That's a good sign." The doctor took out a pen light and shone it into Dutch's eyes. "Look to the left."

"What, another drunk test? I've been knocked out, not on a three day binge."

"Now look to the right," the doctor instructed.

"Dutch, do what he says," Crane demanded as he peered in at the doctor's appraisal.

Dutch pushed the doctor and Crane away. "Would you two get out of my face?"

"What do you think Doc?" Susan asked.

"His reactions look fine. Basically, I think he's just too stubborn to die." The doctor shared a sarcastic look with everyone as Dutch stuck his tongue out at the doctor.

"The police said you and Mardrid crash landed into a house on the coast very near here. Were you headed for the airport?" Susan asked.

"Not exactly," Dutch said as he held his hand to his aching head. "We found her. Lady Melody. We found her Ice. I saw here."

"Lady Melody? You saw Lady Melody?"

"Yes."

"It's about time," Crane quipped.

"She was in the house?" Susan asked.

"She and both of the Carringtons, father and son."

"Holy crap. And you let them get away?"

"I was in a crashed helicopter for God's sake. By the way, how is the helicopter?"

"Glad you asked," Mardrid replied as he entered the hospital room.

"Mardrid, should you be up?" Susan asked.

"They gave me a quick going over. Seems like everything's okay. There's only one thing wrong," Mardrid said as he approached Dutch's bedside.

"What's that?" Crane asked.

"My fuckin' helicopter is destroyed!" Mardrid shouted as he attacked Dutch, his hands firmly grasping Dutch around the neck. "All because of you."

"Get him off me," Dutch managed to say as he tried to fight off Mardrid's stranglehold. Crane grabbed one of Mardrid's arms and pulled on it, his feet pushing against the bedside for leverage.

"I've seen this before. He's gone made Doc. Sedate him for God's sake," Susan shouted out as she tugged on Mardrid's other arm. "Let go of him Mardrid. It's not worth it."

"What she said," Dutch rasped. Susan took aim at Mardrid's hand and bit down hard, causing Mardrid to scream out in pain like a wounded animal. The doctor stuck a needle into Mardrid's ass and administered its contents, Mardrid immediately releasing his grip just as two orderlies entered the room. Mardrid stumbled away from the bed, the orderlies taking charge of him. Dutch rubbed his neck as the doctor and orderlies escorted Mardrid out of the hospital room.

"I'm telling your mother," Dutch shouted after them.

"Screw you," Mardrid groggily replied from the hallway.

Susan and Crane shook their heads in dismay. "That's the fourth time I've seen someone have that reaction to Dutch," Crane pointed out.

Dutch gave Crane a dirty look as he slowly climbed out of bed. "We've got to get out of here. Give me a hand, will ya?"

Susan stiff armed Dutch in the chest. "Hold on there Dutch, we're not going anywhere. You were in a serious crash, remember?"

"I'm fine Ice. Look, there's something that's not adding up. You didn't see her like I did."

"Who's her?"

"Lady Melody. It was in her eyes. If you'd seen her, you'd know what I mean." Crane took Dutch by the shoulder and helped him from the bed.

"What are you doing Crane? Put him back in bed," Susan ordered. "He's not going anywhere."

"I know him Ms. Susan. If he says he knows, then I know he knows. You know what I say?" Susan shook her head in dismay and then reluctantly supported Dutch's other shoulder.

"So where are we headed?" Susan asked as they carried Dutch out of the room and down the hospital corridor.

"Your hotel room," Dutch replied.

"Good. I could use a rest," Susan said.

It took three hours to get to the St. Vincent Airport, board a plane and fly back to Barbados. Dutch dozed in and out the whole way. By the time they reached Susan's hotel, Dutch had gotten a full hour of sleep in the back seat of the car. Throughout his dreams he kept seeing Lady Melody's gaze. He struggled to understand what she was trying to tell him, sometimes shouting out to her in his dreams, asking what she wanted.

"How are you feeling old man?" Susan asked as she shook Dutch awake in the parking lot of the Little Arches Hotel.

"Fine, I'm fine," Dutch groused, Susan and Crane helping him out of the car.

Dutch walked toward the hotel, waving off their help. "Really, I'm okay. The rest did me a world of good. Right now, we've got to figure some things out."

"Yes, I know. Lady Melody's gaze. So tell me again about what you saw in Lady Melody's eyes?" Susan asked.

"She didn't have the look of someone who was kidnapped. There wasn't a look of fear in her eyes."

"What was it then? Surprise? I mean, it's not every day that a helicopter comes crashing through your roof."

"No, it wasn't that either. It was more like a look of pleading."

"Pleading?"

"Yes, like she was asking me to *not* help her. Does that make sense?"

"No. Not for someone who was kidnapped."

"Exactly. She wasn't coming toward me as if she were trying to get my help. It was as if she were telling me to leave her alone."

"And you could tell all of this by looking into her eyes huh?" Susan asked with a note of skepticism. "Look into my eyes and tell me what they're saying? I'll tell you what they're saying. You're not making any sense." Dutch waved off Susan's comments. "Maybe you dreamed it. I mean, with the crash and all. You could've been unconscious. Maybe that was it?"

"He has looked into a lot of women's eyes," Crane said.

Dutch began to falter as they crossed the parking lot, Susan and Crane taking him by the shoulders. "Very funny," Dutch said. Dutch gestured toward the main office on the first floor of the Little Arches Hotel. "We need to stop in at the office. They've got something that should answer a lot of questions."

The hotel manager looked up in shock as they entered the office with Dutch on the shoulders of Susan and Crane, his bandaged head starting to show spots of bleeding. "Oh my God, has there been an accident?"

"He is an accident," Susan remarked.

"Did you get a fax from the Barbados Museum and Historical Society for Ms. Berg?" Dutch asked.

The manager rummaged through some papers and withdrew a single page.

"Yes, I have it here," she said, handing the fax to Dutch. "It looks very interesting. Doing some research on our past history?"

"You could say that," Dutch replied as he read the document. The color ran away from Dutch's face, a knot gurgling up from a pit deep within his stomach. "Quick, we've got to get up to your room Ice." Dutch struggled to follow Susan and Crane up the short flight of winding stairs to Susan's room.

"What's wrong Dutch?" Susan asked as she searched for the room key in her purse. Dutch pounded on the door.

"Vicky?" Dutch shouted. Susan shoved the key into the door and Dutch stormed in. "Vicky, are you here?" he shouted out.

Susan looked over a cart stacked high with empty dishes. "Well at least we know she's not starving to death."

"Maybe she's at the beach?" Crane suggested as he went out to the balcony and scanned the white sands of Enterprise Beach directly across the street. Dutch flipped open his cell phone and dialed her number.

"Vicky. Where the hell are you? Oh, the pool. Lunch? Yes, we'll be right there." Dutch motioned toward the door. "She's having lunch by the pool," Dutch sheepishly said.

"Eating, again?" Susan said as she motioned to the stacks of room service dishes. "Where does she put it all?"

Susan was still complaining about how much Vicky's room service orders were going to cost when they reached the rooftop table at the Luna Café. Vicky was surrounded by plates of appetizers and had a large frozen drink in her hand. Sitting in her string bikini with oversized Dior sunglasses, she looked like a celebrity on the French Riviera.

Vicky extended her arms, her lips pursed for a kiss. "Come to me poor baby," she said. Dutch leaned over and gave Vicky a passionate kiss causing Susan to roll her eyes and Crane to blush. "Isn't this the most perfect setting, here on the rooftop overlooking the beach, right next to the pool? I just had to have lunch here."

"For the third or fourth time today?" Susan cracked.

Dutch took a nibble of the calamari as he admired the view. He took a seat next to Vicky and motioned for everyone to listen in confidence. "I think we've all been chasing our tails on this case,"

Dutch said as he withdrew the fax from his pocket. "It seems we've been playing a game of cat and mouse without even knowing it."

"Let me guess who the rat is," Susan smirked as she took the fax from Dutch's hands.

"Read it out loud Ms. Susan?" Crane asked.

"Well, let's see," Susan said as she cleared her voice. Susan held out the page and read:

Captain Hollingsworth married Margaret, daughter of James Gambier, and sister of Vice-Admiral Jame Gambier, who became Governor and Commander-in-Chief of Newfoundland in 1802. Captain Hollingsworth was created a baronet in 1801. In 1805 he became an Admiral, 1st Lord of the Admiralty, a Privy Councillor, and was created Baron Barnam, with remainder to his only child Diana, the wife of Sir Gerard Noel-Noel. Lord Barnam's son-in-law was the heir of Henry Noel, Earl of Hainesborough, to which title he later succeeded. The Barnam barony became merged with the Hainesborough earldom, so that the present Earl of Hainesborough is also Lord Barnam. Lord Hainesborough still has in his possession the gold hilted sword studded with diamonds presented to his ancestor by the House of Assembly, Barbados.

The table stayed silent for several minutes as everyone considered the content of Susan's rendition. Then, like traders on the floor of the stock exchange, everyone began shouting out their opinions regarding the historical account.

Dutch finally stood up, one hand raised, the other to his aching head. "Everyone, shut up. Working with you all is like herding cats for God's sake." The table went silent like a class of dismissive children. "Okay, now one at a time, please."

"Well it's obvious that this Minton Moore somehow is involved with Lady Melody's disappearance," Susan said.

"Why do you say that?" Crane asked.

"Because he's got us looking for the golden sword. The same sword that according to the history is in the possession of Lord

Hainesborough. Maybe he kidnapped Lady Melody as a hostage? A way to barter for the golden sword?"

Dutch sat back and mulled over what Susan said as Vicky squirmed about in her chair as if her thoughts were about to explode. Dutch smiled and nodded in her direction.

"I don't think Susan's right. I mean, if he had kidnapped Lady Melody in order to trade her for the sword, why wouldn't Hainesy have told us that? After all, it's clear to me that he wants his daughter back."

"Hainesy?" Susan replied.

"Can I help it if he has a thing for me?" Vicky said more as a matter of fact than a question.

"Who doesn't?" Susan dolefully added.

"All right ladies. I think Vicky may be right. Why would both of them come to us if one of them was blackmailing the other? It doesn't make sense. It's not like Lord Hainesborough is trying to hide the fact that he has all these treasures. Remember, they were going to exhibit them at the High Commission."

"Until you broke in and scared them out of it," Susan pointed out.

"What are you, the Jiminy Cricket of the group?" Dutch replied.

"Are you forgetting that the page we just read had been torn out of the history book? Maybe Minton Moore or Lord Hainesborough did it so we wouldn't find out?" Crane recalled. Everyone silently chewed on the facts as well as the plates of appetizers.

Dutch suddenly slammed his hand onto the table startling the others into choking on their food. "It all comes down to Lady Melody. She's the key to all of this. Something's not right here. I don't know if it's the Captain and drugs or the golden sword and the other treasures. But we need to figure out her angle first."

"Let me guess. It's her eyes," Susan snidely said.

"Yes, that's exactly it. If we are going to help that poor girl, we've got to understand what her part in this is." Dutch stood up and looked into the horizon. He then turned back to the table. "I'm going to where all this crap started," he said with determination.

"Where's that?" Crane asked.

"London."

CHAPTER 23

The eight hour night owl flight from Barbados to London's Heathrow Airport gave Dutch time to think and sleep. Mostly sleep, which is just what he needed. The view of Lady Melody continued to haunt his dreams. It was as if the crash and her vision had become an ethereal fixation, the gash on his forehead the only reminder of the reality of the event.

Using his cell phone on the way to the airport in Barbados, Dutch managed to arrange for the flight and a meeting with his old friend, Mickey Farer, much to Susan's displeasure. Not over Dutch's meeting with Mickey but rather the flight that cost close to two thousand dollars. Dutch's ruse regarding the unfortunate death of his favorite stepfather didn't even help to reduce the fare, but it did get him a business class upgrade.

Dutch had met Mickey Farer just before the Tet Offensive. Dutch was serving in the Special Forces teaching Crane Luk and other Vietnamese to be snipers. Mickey was serving as a logistics adviser. In an effort by the English government to remain out of the Vietnam War, certain British forces were sent to Fort Dix, New Jersey where they resigned from the British Army and reenlisted in the US Army. Mickey was one such officer, a hard as nails brawler who immediately took a liking to Dutch. They had saved each other's lives more than once during their stint together in Nam, so their bond went beyond friendship as only those who have been in war can understand.

The damp air of London almost took Dutch aback upon his arrival at Heathrow Airport. Compared to Barbados, London's environment was like being on another planet. Dutch took a taxi to the Port of Tilbury, which lies on the north shore of the River Thames about 25 miles below the London Bridge. Although many of London's ports scattered up and down the Thames had been turned into trendy urban centers with housing and shopping, the Port of Tilbury is still a full- fledged working port. Dutch was never really sure what Mickey did there and he never asked. Their relationship was one based on "doing" rather than "knowing".

Dutch walked through the docks and finally spotted the late model Austin Martin with Mickey sitting on the hood, his large six four frame dwarfing the car. Although they had not seen each other in over four years, both men nodded as if they had just thrown darts at the local pub the night before.

"Kid," Mickey said in his Cockney accent reminiscent of when the Whitehall District was mostly English rather than immigrants of Afro-Caribbean descent. Dutch smiled broadly, which always made Mickey smirk in a way that no one could resist.

"Mick," Dutch replied.

"So what's up?"

Dutch glanced around the docks, the large cargo ships busy with freight handlers and cranes working overtime. "I've got to find someone Mick."

"Yeah, you said so when you called."

"The mother of Lady Melody, heir to Lord Hainesborough."

"Yeah, I got that too. What's this all about?"

"I'm not sure Mick. I mean, I think I might know something, but what exactly I couldn't say."

"Well, I sniffed about a bit. You know, like I do."

Dutch smiled again. "Yes, I do know how you do."

"Seems the mother is a ghost. I mean, I can't find hardly a whiff. It's as if the Lady Melody materialized out of thin air. You don't think she's . . ." Mickey's question trailed off.

"Think she's what?"

"Like the second coming or something?" Mickey always did have a bent toward the surreal, if not the melodramatic.

"No, I'm pretty sure she's not the second coming of Christ Mick. But I am sure that something's not right."

"Well there's two things I can always say about you Dutch."

"What's that Mick?"

"That your hunches are almost always right."

"What's the other thing?"

"Don't ever leave you alone with one's wife." Mickey smirked again.

"Funny Mick," Dutch deadpanned.

"But true mate."

"So, did you find anything out at all?"

"Well, you see I started thinking about this whole thing."

"That's a dangerous thing Mick, but go on."

"These royals like Lord Miles Hainesborough are the worst fuckin' parents there are, you see. They always have some nanny taking care of their kids, especially when they're young. And since I couldn't find the mother, it's a sure thing that's just what this bloke did."

"Go on."

"So, I made an inquiry to the Royal Nannies Service Company."

"What did you find out?"

"Nothing really. I mean, would you tell someone like me anything?"

"No."

"Exactly. So I had to make a nighttime visit after hours, so to speak."

"Brilliant."

"Exactly. Brilliant. Took a bit of scrounging about but I finally found the file on our lord."

"We are still talking about Lord Hainesborough?"

Mickey smirked again. "Funny."

"That's fantastic. What did you find out?"

"Seems our lord had one nanny who worked for him for the first twelve years of Lady Melody's life."

"That's odd don't you think?"

"What part?"

"That he had the same nanny for twelve years and then she quit."

"Not sure. I mean, people leave jobs for lots of reasons. Maybe she had a little slap and tickle with our lord?"

"We're still talking about Lord Hainesborough?"

"You're one sick bitch Dutch."

"I can't help it Mick. It just comes naturally."

"No matter what, I do have the old nanny's address." Mick reached into the pocket of his pea coat and casually handed a slip of paper to Dutch. "Ms. Landry. She lives over in the Dalston District, in Hackney. Cape House, on Dalston Lane."

"Cape House?"

Mick smiled broadly. "I forgot you're not British. It's a council house, you know, public housing. Kind of tough that area, but nothing you can't handle."

"Okay then. We're off."

"We?"

"I need someone to drive me, don't I?" Dutch smiled at Mickey in a way that Mickey could never resist.

Mickey playfully slugged Dutch in the shoulder, making Dutch stumble back. "You bum chum."

It took Dutch and Mickey about an hour to maneuver the streets of London and locate the Cape House. The time passed quickly as they reminisced about old and new times, including the details of the current case. Mickey's advice regarding the case was straight forward as usual. He suggested grabbing Reginald Carrington's lawyer father and beating the truth out of him. Effective, but a bit extreme Dutch mused, even for a lawyer. Besides, having chased him away during the helicopter crash, Dutch figured the Carringtons were dug in deeper than a mole hole.

The Cape House was a large apartment building providing public housing in the way that the British Empire always did, effective and minimal. Dutch and Mickey took the elevator up to the open air hallway on the fourth floor and counted down until they reached the nanny's apartment. Mickey pounded on the front door like the Gestapo at a Bris.

"Christ Mick, you're gonna wake the dead."

"She should know that we mean business, Dutch."

"Yeah, but let's not give her a heart attack." The front door to the next apartment opened, a short elderly black woman with white hair partially emerging.

"What are you two blokes pounding about here?" she shouted out in a Jamaican accent.

"We're looking for the lady who lives here," Dutch replied as the old lady looked them over.

"Who wants to know?" she asked, suspicion in her eyes.

"We're from the Tenant Services Authority," Mickey jumped in. "We have a check for Ms. Landry. You wouldn't know if she's home would you?" The elderly woman checked her watch and then carefully looked them over.

"She should be coming home any minute. I can't get around so much anymore. Ms. Landry popped over to the grocer for me." The Lady looked out toward the road that ran in front of the apartment building. "There she is now."

Dutch and Mickey looked out to see a middle aged woman with a tall, slight build waiting to cross on the other side of the street. She struggled with an overstuffed bag of groceries.

"Aren't you two wankers going to help her?" Dutch shrugged and then led Mickey down the hallway like two errant school boys. "And don't forget to tell her she owes me twenty quid when you give her the check."

Dutch and Mickey emerged from the stairwell just as Ms. Landry took her first steps to cross the road. Dutch waved to her, Ms. Landry straining to recognize them. "Ms. Landry," Dutch shouted out. Dutch and Mickey walked toward the roadway as Ms. Landry continued toward them. From his left, Dutch heard the sound of a car engine just as he saw the blur of a black car in the corner of his eye. The black sedan came out of nowhere and with accurate deliberation sideswiped Ms. Landry flipping her into the air like a circus act. The bag of groceries rained down onto the road as Ms. Landry hit the curb, her body making a slight bounce as it landed. Mickey withdrew a four inch barreled .44 Magnum from the pocket of his pea coat and pointed it at the rear of the tagless car as it turned the corner and disappeared from sight. Dutch ran over to Ms. Landry's side and propped up her head with his jacket. Blood ran from her mouth, her eyes wide with shock.

"Call an ambulance Mick," Dutch shouted out as he took the lady's pulse. "Ms. Landry, can you hear me?" The woman's whole body shook with tremors as she stared into Dutch's eyes.

"Who?" she managed.

"Don't worry. We've got an ambulance coming. It will be okay. We're here on Lady Melody's behalf."

"Melody? Is she safe?"

"I'm not sure. That's why we came to see you. Don't worry Ms. Landry. We can talk later. Save your strength." Ms. Landry took Dutch's hand and pressed a key into it.

"The clock. Look in the clock," she mumbled as her eyes rolled into the back of her head, blood now rushing from her mouth.

"She's got internal bleeding," Dutch shouted to Mickey who spoke on his cell phone. "Tell them to hurry Mick." A small crowd began to assemble around Dutch and the injured Ms. Landry like solemn sentinels. Mickey broke through the crowd and took a knee next to Dutch.

"The ambulance is on its way. How's she doing?"

"Not good Mick. That was no accident, you know."

"Sure thing. No tag. Out of nowhere. How could anyone know? Anything you can think of?"

"I got nothing." Dutch stood up and led Mickey to the edge of the crowd as the wailing sirens of an approaching ambulance filled the air. He opened his hand to reveal the key. "She gave me this Mick. It was as if she knew we came about Lady Melody. Weird."

"What's it to?"

"I'm thinking her apartment. She mentioned a clock."

"A clock?"

"Yeah." Dutch glanced back toward Ms. Landry and the crowd as the ambulance pulled up. "Nothing we can do for her now. It's probably best if we check her place out, before the police do. What do you think?"

"A bit morbid, right?"

"Yeah, a bit."

Dutch and Mickey were up the stairs and in Ms. Landry's apartment in less than two minutes. The apartment was decorated with cheap but well cared for furnishings, everything neat and tidy. Dutch approached a bureau where photos of Ms. Landry's life, including several of Lady Melody in her younger years, were neatly arranged.

"Looks like Ms. Landry really had feelings for our Lady Melody?"

"Let's find this clock and get out before the bobbies show up," Mickey advised. "I'll take the bedroom. You check around here."

"Okay, but no trying on her clothes," Dutch replied.

"Cheeky bastard. Have some consideration, will you." Mickey disappeared into the bedroom as Dutch looked about the small kitchen area that adjoined the living room. Dutch wondered if this was a harbinger of his end, a public housing apartment with nothing to show for his life but some photos on a bureau. Alone, bleeding out on a street, surrounded by strangers. Dutch pulled out a kitchen chair and sat down, the thought leaving him weak in the knees. He glanced about the room, no clock in sight. Mickey entered interrupting Dutch's pity party.

"What the hell, you balling up over the old lady?"

"No, not really. You ever wonder Mick how you'll end up? I mean, like Ms. Landry."

"Sure. I hope to get bonked to death. You?"

"Yeah, same here." The two remained silent for a moment, both considering the question. Neither able to really talk about how they felt.

"Hope she has big norks," Mickey finally said with a smirk.

"You are nothing if not an optimist my friend. No clock, I guess."

"Nothing but a little alarm clock. I smashed it to bits but didn't find anything." Dutch returned a look of dismay. "Don't worry, I left a fiver on the bed."

"No clocks in here either," Dutch replied. "Dutch went to the bureau and looked over the photos. "I really should start using a camera. I don't think I even have a picture of you."

"Don't go getting batty with me Dutch."

"You know what I mean," Dutch said as he looked over the photos that represented a person's lifetime. It was then that a particular photo caught his attention. It was one of Ms. Landry holding the hand of a nine year old Lady Melody with the Big Ben clock of Westminster Palace in the background. Dutch picked up the photo and removed the back panel. A slip of paper fell out and floated to the floor. Both Dutch and Mickey looked at the paper with baited breath, as if it were a lost treasure map. Mickey finally picked it up and read.

"Well, Ms. Landry did have some secrets after all."

"What does it say?"

"It just has a name, Margaret Moore, and an address."

"What do you think it means?" Dutch wondered out loud.

"It means we're going to Peckham."

Dutch and Mickey drove in silence as they each considered the case and Ms. Landry's fate. Despite Mickey giving his car a thorough going over for any trackers, as Mickey called them, Dutch kept a constant eye on the side view mirror, convinced that they were being followed. As they entered Peckham, the gloom of the streets increased tenfold.

"Damn Mick, you really know all the best places in London," Dutch said.

"Fucking Peckham is the worst of the worst Dutch. Most don't know that London is a lot tougher than even New York. And Peckham is as bad as it gets my friend."

Mickey took the turn onto Peckham Park Road off of old Kent Road and then onto Friary Road. He stopped along the roadside in front of a dilapidated brick mid-rise. "This is the address. Stay close Dutch. And don't say a word to anyone." Mickey led Dutch up the enclosed stairway to the second floor. They pushed through the debris in the dark enclosed hallway that smelled of nothing good until they arrived at Margaret Moore's door. Dutch beat Mickey to the door and politely knocked.

"Ms. Margaret Moore," Dutch called out.

"Tenant Services Authority," Mickey announced. "We have a check for you." Mickey smirked. "It worked last time," he said to Dutch as they waited. The door finally opened, a pair of bloodshot eyes looking out through the crack in the door.

"You got a check?" asked the lady.

"Yes, yes we do. Are you Margaret Moore?" Dutch asked.

The door opened, Dutch and Mickey both having to choke down their audible gasp at the sight of Margaret Moore. It was as if they were looking at a living survivor of a concentration camp, her emaciated body and shrunken eyes belonging more to the dead than to the living. She motioned them into the apartment as she shrank back into the darkness of the main room. The stench was putrid, like entering a mausoleum chamber that had a few freshly decaying members. Dutch and Mickey entered, both straining to adjust their eyesight in the darkness. There was nothing in the one room apartment other than a scarred coffee table and a dilapidated bean bag chair, which Margaret Moore collapsed upon. Various drug paraphernalia lay scattered about the room and on the coffee table.

"You got a check for me?" Ms. Moore repeated.

"Yes, but we first need to make sure you are Margaret Moore. Regulations, you know," Mickey said.

"If you don't mind, we need to ask you a few questions," Dutch added. Margaret Moore nodded as her eyes closed, her head going back as if the effort would kill her. "Do you happen to know a Ms. Landry?" Ms. Moore opened her eyes and looked at Dutch as if he had called up a ghost.

"Ms. Landry?" Margaret Moore continued to look at Dutch and Mickey with a blank stare. "Yes, I know her."

"How about a Lord Hainesborough?" Dutch continued. Margaret Moore's expression became as taught as wet leather drying in the hot sun. Her eyes opened wide, her mouth partially open as if she were straining to suck in air.

"Yes, I know that name. Why do you ask? Who are you?" she said as she tried to rise from the chair. Mickey placed his large hand on her shoulder keeping her in place. A frightened look came over her. She pointed a shaking finger at Dutch. "Who are you?" she shouted.

Dutch took out his wallet and held out several bills. "We're not here to hurt you. We just need some information." Dutch placed the bills on the coffee table. "This is for you, for your trouble. Just answer a few questions. Please?"

The woman gave Dutch and Mickey a momentary look of defiance which immediately vanished when she gazed at the money on the table. "Go on then."

"Do you know Lord Hainesborough?" Dutch repeated. Margaret Moore began to softly whimper, her hands covering her face.

"Yes, Yes. I know him, and I know the devil." Dutch and Mickey looked at each other and then at her, bewildered.

"What do you mean by that?" Mickey asked. The woman stared at both of them, her eyes wet with tears.

"Evil is not only in others, it's in ourselves. What we do to others we also do to ourselves. Look at me. Look what I've done to myself. What he has done to me."

Mickey picked up the money from the table and waved it at Margaret Moore.

"You're going to have to talk some sense to us if you want this money. Understand? You need to tell us about Lord Hainesborough and his daughter, Lady Melody." The woman began sobbing uncontrollably, her body literally shaking from her sorrow.

Dutch grimaced at Mickey, motioning him to the side. "I don't think the tough stuff is going to work here Mick," Dutch discreetly counseled. "Why don't you hang back a little and let me give it a try?"

Mickey acknowledged Dutch's advice with a shrug of his shoulders, taking a position by the front door as Dutch went to Margaret Moore's side. Dutch placed a sympathetic hand on the woman's shoulder. "Margaret, I realize how difficult this must be for you. But we are trying to help Lady Melody. Do you understand? We're not here to hurt her, or you. But we need your help. Can you help us? Please?"

Margaret Moore blinked the tears from her eyes, her shaking hands wiping over the boney skin of her face. "It's all my fault," she finally said in a whisper. "I made the deal with that devil. I just never knew. But I found out later. Much later, you see. Ms. Landry told me. She begged me to do something about it." Margaret Moore looked into space as if waiting for a sign from the heavens. "Look at me," she continued. "What's a junkie to do? Who would listen to me? Who would believe me?"

"Believe what? What was it that was so awful?" Ms. Moore continued to look away, unable to turn back to Dutch. Dutch gently squeezed her shoulder. "There's no wrong that can't be righted Margaret."

Margaret Moore violently shook her head as if the thought were crushing her soul.

"This can never be undone. Never."

Dutch placed his hand on her hand. "Margaret, listen to me. We can help you." The woman continued to look away, her sobs making the few words she spoke unintelligible. Dutch looked back at Mickey who wore an expression of pity. Mickey took a step toward Dutch just as the door behind him exploded open as if blown apart from its lock. Mickey turned toward the door as an arm emerged holding a revolver, Mickey immediately falling back against the front door. Dutch sprung toward the door that had pinned the man's arm holding the gun. Dutch grabbed the arm and pushed against it, the gun firing wildly as the appendage snapped in half like a dead tree branch. The intruder's howl of agony reverberated through the apartment. The gun dropped to the floor as the arm withdrew. Dutch kicked the gun aside as Mickey withdrew his weapon. He pushed Dutch back from the door.

"You okay?" Mickey asked. Dutch nodded. Mickey pulled the door open and rolled out into the hallway, his gun in the ready. He vanished down the hallway in hot pursuit as Dutch turned his attention back to Margaret Moore who lay splayed out on the bean bag chair. A pool of red slowly spread over the dirty shirt she wore. Dutch rushed to her side and took her pulse as he lifted her shirt to reveal a single entry wound just below her heart.

"Margaret. Hold on Margaret. I'll get an ambulance. Hold on." The woman squeezed Dutch's hand and mumbled some words. Dutch leaned in close, putting his ear to her voice. Margaret Moore managed to mutter the last words of her life just as Mickey came back into the apartment.

Mickey stopped dead still at the sight of Dutch, his face as drained as hospital sheets in a snowstorm. "What is it Dutch?" Dutch slowly rose as if the woman's words had shaken the foundation of time and space. "Is she dead?" Dutch solemnly nodded. "You should call the police," Mickey said.

"No. No cell phones."

"Okay Dutch. Sure," Mickey said with a note of puzzlement. "Whatever you say."

"We can call the police from the airport. I'll get a ticket there."

"The airport?"

"I've got to get back to Barbados. I've got to get back now."

CHAPTER 24

The flight back to Barbados felt like being strapped to an electric chair, but without the priest standing by. All the facts of the case seemed to bang into each other like out of control bumper cars crashing inside his head with no direction. Dutch tried to find a common thread, but all he could come up with was a needling fear that there was still something missing. He could clearly see all of the players, the Captain, Reg Carrington and his father, Lord Hainesborough, Menton Moore and Lady Melody, but he couldn't understand what role they all played. After his fifth scotch, Dutch finally nodded off into a restless sleep, for which he was grateful. This time, Lady Melody's gaze did not invade his dreams. Upon waking, Dutch considered the last words that Margaret Moore had spoken to him and what they might mean.

Upon arrival in Barbados, Dutch went straight to the pay phone in customs and called the Little Arches Hotel. He provided a carefully worded message to the desk clerk, instructing her to immediately deliver it to only Susan Berg as soon as possible. After clearing customs and retrieving his bag, Dutch scanned the line of cars waiting at the open air curbside of the airport. The sound of a horn followed by Susan's stern shout caught his attention, sending him darting between the cars.

"What's with all the cloak and dagger?" Susan asked as he approached.

"And how was your trip?" Dutch sarcastically replied.

"Get in," Susan curtly said. Within minutes Susan had revved the rental car through the traffic and out onto Tom Adams Highway.

"You a little tense?" Dutch finally asked as Susan grinded the gears.

"What the frick? No calls Not even a word while you're traipsing about London. And then I get some frickin note from the frickin desk clerk. Maybe you've forgotten, but you work for me."

Dutch held a hushed finger to his lips and then pointed about the inside of the car. "I didn't mean to leave you in the dark. It's just that I didn't have any way to call you." Susan furrowed her brow and then nodded in understanding. "Ice, just take Highway 6 back to the hotel. I'm really beat. Besides, I would have called you if there was anything to talk about. But I didn't find anything. It was a wasted trip." The two rode back to the hotel in furtive silence. The moment Susan and Dutch reached the Little Arches Hotel and stepped out of the car, Susan was upon Dutch like a starving dog on steak.

"What the hell is going on Dutch?"

Dutch cautiously looked about the hotel grounds. "Who all is here? I mean, in your room?"

"Vicky and Crane. And let me tell you, between her constant eating and Crane's non-stop chatter, I'm about to shoot them both."

"Have you noticed anyone tailing you, watching you?"

"No, should I?"

"I'm not sure," Dutch replied.

Susan grabbed Dutch by the arm for emphasis. "What's going on Dutch? What did you find out in London?"

"I was able to locate Lady Melody's mother."

"Her mother? You mean her mother's grave, right?"

"No, her mother. She was alive. At least until someone shot her."

"What the hell are you talking about?"

"He's full of crap Ice. Lord Hainesborough lied to us. Lady Melody's mother didn't die at birth. She's a down and out drug addict. At least she was. Someone was following me. Knew my every move. They tried to take me out. Take us all out."

"Who? Why?"

"That's what we've got to figure out. I've been working on it during the flight back."

"Not leaving me a message, not calling me? What's that all about?"

Dutch pulled out his cell phone as if to provide proof. "It's got to be my cell phone. They must have bugged it. That's the only way they could have known I was in London. They must realize we are getting close, but to what I'm not sure of."

Susan grabbed the phone out of Dutch's hand. "Well let's pitch it then."

Dutch grabbed her arm. "No, let's not do that. Not yet. If they don't know that we know, it may work to our advantage. You know?"

"Yeah, okay, whatever you said. But I don't see how they could have gotten to your phone to load the spy software. Can you recall when that could have happened?"

"I'm not sure. All they needed was about fifteen minutes to install the software on my phone. Then every time I made a call it would also call their phone. The software can also use the GPS in my phone to track me. They literally could have heard everything I said and knew everywhere I went. That's the only way they could have known I was in London."

"But why Dutch? It couldn't be Lord Hainesborough. Hell, he was the one who had us hired to find his daughter."

"I'm not sure. Lady Melody's mother told me just before she died that Lord Hainesborough had hired her to have his child. Literally paid her to get pregnant with his child and then to go away."

"Well, I've heard of stranger things. You know how those royals are."

"Let's get Crane and Vicky from your room and talk about it over lunch. At least that way we'll know we're not being bugged."

Dutch and Susan walked up the winding stairway and then stopped at the top of the stairs, the door to Susan's room standing wide open. Susan motioned Dutch to stay back as she withdrew her Glock, holding it in a firing position as she moved toward the door. Susan rolled into the room with Dutch close behind The room was vacant. Susan darted into the bathroom as Dutch looked out from the balcony.

"Nothing," Susan said as she reemerged from the bathroom. The muffled sounds of dull thumps caught their attention. Susan held up her hand and followed the sounds to the closet. She pointed the gun at the closet as Dutch threw open the door to reveal Crane bound and tied on the floor, a river of blood streaming from his head. With one motion, Dutch carried Crane to the bed as Susan unbound him.

"I am so sorry Dutch. I am so awful. I didn't see them. But they took her. They took her," Crane said between gasps for air.

"Took who Crane?" Dutch demanded, although he already knew the answer.

By the time Dutch drove to the Caribbean Court Hotel in Hastings, Crane's head wound had stopped bleeding thanks to Susan's quick stitching and ice pack. Dutch led the group down the outside stairs to the restaurant bar on the terrace below the office. Both Keith and Ted jumped to their feet at the first sight of Dutch, their clenched fists evidence of their feelings toward him and Susan.

"What the hell are you doing here Holland?" Keith asked.

Ted pointed at Susan, who arrived on Dutch's heels. "You've got some nerve coming here Susan," Ted added.

Dutch held up his hands in capitulation as Crane emerged still wearing his bloodied shirt, his hand holding the bag of ice to his head.

"You okay Crane?" Ted asked. Crane solemnly nodded.

"We've got some real trouble. They've taken Vicky," Dutch said.

"Vicky Godown? Who? Who's taken her?" Keith asked as he helped Crane to a chair.

"We're not sure. At least not yet. We need some time, and some help in figuring this out," Susan said. Everyone took a seat at the table as Winston brought over a round of Banks beers as if on cue.

"I wasn't expecting this. Ms. Vicky asked me to bring some food from the restaurant," Crane bemoaned.

"That figures," Susan said under her breath.

"They hit me from behind as I was going into the hotel room."

"Was there a note?" Keith asked.

"No, nothing," Dutch replied. "And I'm pretty sure whoever it is had my cell phone bugged. You have any idea how we can figure out who did that?"

Keith motioned toward the bar soliciting Winston's presence. Winston approached and took the cell phone, which disappeared into his large brown hands. "Can you take this into the office and look at the spyware on it?" Keith asked. Winston nodded and bounded up the stairs to the office.

"Bartender and super snoop?" Susan asked.

"Winston is a man of many talents," Keith replied. "So what do we do next?"

"Like any kidnapping. We wait for them to contact us," Dutch replied. "I'm not exactly sure why Vicky was taken, but I am sure that she'll be used as leverage."

"No doubt, but for what? I mean, we still don't know crap," Susan said.

"But whoever took her must think we do. It has to have something to do with my trip to London," Dutch replied.

"London? You went to London? England?" Ted asked.

"Yes," Dutch nodded. "But all I found out was that our Lord Hainesborough hired some drug addict to have his kid. Nothing worth risking a charge of kidnapping over. No, I think it has to do with something else. Maybe the helicopter crash?"

"Helicopter crash? You crashed a helicopter?" Ted almost shouted out.

"Afraid so. And we almost had Lady Melody," Dutch responded.

"Your boat doesn't look so bad now, does it?" Susan said.

"Boat? That was my boat too!" Keith replied, cutting off Ted. Susan shrugged and took a sip of her beer as Keith growled.

"Okay, let's not get hung up on that. Susan's got insurance so it'll pay for that," Dutch said.

"Insurance? You've got insurance?" Ted blurted out.

Susan rolled her eyes. "Good going Dutch."

"Well thanks for telling us," Keith said.

"You can't imagine how high my premiums are having Dutch on my payroll. That's why I didn't say anything. After this, I'm sure they'll cancel us," Susan lamented. Winston's arrival with the cell phone in hand granted Susan a welcome distraction. "So Winston, what did you find out?" she asked.

"Dutch was right. It's bugged. Works off your GPS function so they can see whereever you go, or at least where the cell phone goes," Winston replied.

"They can do that?" Ted asked.

"This software does even more. It actually calls the perpetrator's number so they can listen in on your calls."

"Were you able to find the number in the code?" Dutch asked.

Winston handed Dutch a slip of paper. "There it is. No way to know who owns the number though. Unless you've got someone at the cell phone company who can look up the records?"

"Actually I do," Ted replied. "My aunt works in the billing department of Bartel. They provide all the wireless services to the cell phone rental companies."

"Why don't we just call the number and see who answers?" suggested Crane.

"We can't," Susan said. "If we call the number the person who answers will realize we know about their phone tap. I don't think we want to give away that advantage."

"But it's Ms. Vicky we are talking about," Crane said in earnest. "I don't think we can wait. It's my fault she is gone."

"It's not your fault Crane," Dutch said as he put a comforting arm around Crane's shoulder. "Ted, I hate to ask, but if you could reach out to your aunt?"

"Already done," Ted said. Ted turned and bounded up the stairs to the office.

Susan dug her nails into Dutch's forearm. "Crap!" Dutch shouted out in reaction. "What's wrong with you?"

"It just came to me. I know who tapped your phone," Susan said.

The cell phone in Dutch's hand rang as if on cue.

CHAPTER 25

Susan, Dutch and Crane rode in furtive silence toward the cliffs above Crane Beach.

"What made you think it was Menton Moore who bugged my cell phone?" Dutch finally asked Susan who was sitting in the front seat next to him.

"I'm not sure," Susan replied. "It just came to me. He just looked so guilty when I saw him that first time on your boat. Remember, you were down below with Crane and Menton was at the top deck table messing with your phone. At first I thought it was because I had drawn my gun on him. But now, it all fits."

"You sure it was him who took Ms. Vicky?" Crane asked from the backseat.

"I'm not sure," Dutch replied. "All he said on the phone was that we had to meet. So far, we've got three possibilities. There's Reg Carrington and his father, Minton Moore, and finally Lord Hainesborough," Dutch said.

"And don't forget the Captain," Susan added.

"But he's dead," Crane said.

"Yes, but I'm thinking that perhaps he was working with the Carringtons bringing in drugs," Susan replied. "It would all make sense. Reg's dad retires to Barbados. With no job bringing in money, he hooks up with the Captain. Carrington finances the whole operation. Being a lawyer, he probably knows all of the ins and outs, as well as the criminals."

"But what would that have to do with Lady Melody and Lord Hainesborough?" Crane wondered.

"That's what we've got to find out," Susan replied. "That's the missing piece. I don't know. Maybe Lady Melody was into drugs? Maybe she owed the Captain a lot of money and they took her to force Lord Hainesborough to pay up?"

"I don't know Ice. I mean, Hainesborough obviously has plenty of money. Why wouldn't he just pay up? And he surely wouldn't bring the British High Commission into it and hire us to find her. No, something's not right" Dutch said.

"You may be right Dutch. Unless there's someone we don't know about. The Captain and all his men are dead," Susan pointed out. "I can't imagine why the Carringtons would kill all of their partners in crime. I think we should leave all of that on the back burner and concentrate on Menton Moore first."

"What's the plan?" Susan asked as they pulled into the parking lot which led to the landscape shrouded trails.

"You tell me and we'll both know," Dutch replied as they all got out of the car and surveyed their surroundings.

All three stood at the trail's end and looked out over the crescent strip of sugar sands that separated the clear azure waters from the lush cliffs above. Crane Beach, deriving its name from the large crane that was once used for loading ships, is considered one of the ten best beaches in the world. Overlooking the beach from one of the cliffs stood the Crane Beach Resort, a honeymoon favorite with its landscaped gardens where the young and in love watch the first sunrise on the island. There were enough thoughts racing through the heads of all of them to fill a library, but not one of them was sure about what to expect.

"Strange place to meet us, don't you think?" Susan asked as she looked about the area.

"He's a strange guy," Dutch replied.

"I hear that," Susan said as she withdrew her gun into the ready.

Dutch walked to the head of one of the trails and peered into the lush foliage. The ring of his cell phone made everyone jump. Dutch answered the phone and then looked toward the Crane Beach Resort in the distance. Dutch pointed toward the gardens that spread over the cliff top behind the resort as he listened to

Menton Moore's directions. "He's over there in the garden, by the bronze statue of the dancer."

Dutch led Susan and Crane along the roadside and around the perimeter of the resort to the gardens. In the distance they could spot the image of a man sitting on a bench by the statue of Grande Jete, a term for the leaping split in ballet which the statue portrayed. The man rose as they approached, waving them over. "Keep your eyes peeled and your safeties off," Dutch advised. Susan and Crane checked their weapons, stuffing them back into their belts as they approached.

"This is a beautiful spot, don't you think?" Menton said as if they had been talking for hours. He shook Dutch's hand as if they were meeting to discuss the weather.

"You called us here for more than the view I hope," Susan said.

"This is the first place I ever remember about Barbados. I came here with my wife, God rest her soul, and my sister. I thought it was paradise. Funny how life can be so circular."

"I have no idea what you're talking about Menton? How about you clue us in and then we can all take a walk together down memory lane," Susan said.

"Yes, exactly, memory lane. That's all I have now, memories."

Dutch sat down on the bench next to Menton as if in counsel. "Look Menton, I'm not sure, we're not sure, what you're going for here. Maybe you can clear some things up for us?"

"Like what you did with Ms. Vicky?" Crane shouted.

Menton looked at Crane like a deer in headlights. "Who?"

"Don't play dumb with us. We know you took her and we want her back," Crane demanded as he took a menacing step forward.

Menton shirked back, clutching Dutch's arm. "I'm sorry, but I don't know who or what you are talking about. I asked you here to come clean, to explain everything, and plead for your help."

Dutch held up his hands imploring calm. "Okay, let's all settle down and hear what Menton's got to say. Go ahead Menton."

"I'm afraid I was somewhat dishonest with you. You see, it wasn't the golden sword that I wanted you to find, but rather the person who owned it."

"Lord Hainesborough?" Dutch asked, Menton nodding in confirmation.

"You see, it all started some seventeen years ago. In London. My sister was working part time for a maid service while she went to school. That's when she met him."

"Hainesborough?" Susan added.

"Yes. Although I begged her not to do it, she thought it would be easy money. Deep down I think she really believed that something would come out of it. A relationship. A fairytale wedding. I don't know."

Dutch studied Menton carefully. He put a comforting hand on Menton's shoulder.

"She agreed to have his child, didn't she?" Dutch surmised.

"Yes."

"Her name was Margaret," Dutch said, the weight of the realization occurring to Susan and Crane as well.

"Oh God," Susan muttered as she slumped onto the bench on Menton's other side.

"You know?" Menton said.

"We do now Menton," Susan said as she took his hand in hers. "I'm sorry Menton, but she's been killed."

Menton looked at Susan as he tried to understand what she had just said. "How? When?" he finally managed.

"I went to London to investigate," Dutch said. "Someone followed me. Was tracking me. We think it was the same people who kidnapped our friend."

Menton buried his face into his hands and wept. "That's why I came here. To stop him. To find that bastard Lord Hainesborough and rescue my niece. To take my revenge. To kill that devil. For what he did to my sister and her daughter."

"What do you mean Menton? What did he do to your sister and Lady Melody?" Susan asked.

"To my sister, it was all too easy. He got her involved with people, bad people. It wasn't long before the heroin and guilt she carried around for having to give up her child finally ruined her life. Destroyed her, inside and out."

"And Lady Melody?" Dutch asked. "What guilt did your sister have?" Menton looked across the garden grounds as if the answer hung in the ocean breeze.

"There are some things that are worse than death. At least my sister is at peace now. No longer having to live with the burden that has plagued us both for so long."

"What burden Menton? What could be so awful?" Susan prodded.

"We both learned about it several years ago. From the housekeeper, Ms. Landry. She occasionally kept in touch with my sister, letting her know how Lady Melody was doing. It was about four years ago when we heard."

"Heard what Menton?" Susan asked.

"We weren't sure at first you see. We always thought it was best that Lady Melody grow up with all the rights, money and privileges that royalty could bring. I mean, what did I and my sister have to give her? I realize now we were just deluding ourselves. You see, Lord Hainesborough is the worst of the worst. He is molesting her Dutch."

Everyone sat silent as Menton's words pounded their senses. The sickening realization seemed awkwardly juxtaposed against the idyllic sound of waves lapping on the shore below. "Are you sure?" Dutch finally managed.

"Yes," Menton solemnly nodded. I managed to speak with her about a year back. He always has her under constant watch, but I was able to speak with her at her school. It was awkward. Very difficult to discuss with her. She just wants help. Wants to get away from that sick bastard."

"Is that why you bugged Dutch's cell phone?" Susan asked, once again soliciting a dumbfounded look from Menton.

"Again, I'm not sure what you're talking about. I'm just an accountant. I can barely figure out how to use a cell phone."

"When Susan first met you on my boat Menton. What were you doing with my cell phone?"

"Oh, that. I apologize for the intrusion. I was just so desperate to find Lord Hainesborough and get Lady Melody. I thought you might have his address or phone number in your contacts on your cell phone. I'm just at wit's end. I didn't know what else to do."

"So that's why you hired me to look for the golden sword?" Dutch asked.

"Yes. I knew Hainesborough was showing it here as part of his family collection. I thought if you looked for it, you would lead me to him. To his address. Then I could find Lady Melody. But when I learned about her being kidnapped, I decided to tail you to see if you could lead me to her."

"Let me guess. You learned about that when you broke into Susan's room?" Dutch asked. Menton again nodded with a look of embarrassed regret.

"Ah, the patch of white we saw running along the beach. That was your bald head!" Susan realized. "Okay, what do we do now?"

"We go get Ms. Vicky," Crane said.

"Yeah, that's what we do," Dutch agreed.

The how and where was still an open question that they had to find out. Someway, somehow.

Vicky wasn't sure where she was, much less what time it was when she came to. When she first opened her eyes, the blurry sight of a white ceiling was all she could see. At first, she thought it was all a dream. The two burly men breaking into the hotel room and putting a needle into her arm as Crane lay helpless and bleeding on the floor. And then nothing but a fast fade into darkness.

Vicky pushed herself up from the bed and tried to focus through the haze as she surveyed the room. From the blurry images, she could tell that it was a bedroom with large double doors at the far end. After several attempts, she managed to stand and get herself to a dresser which she used to support herself. Vicky pulled herself along the dresser until she was just several feet from the doors. She lunged for the doors, her legs giving way causing her to fall to the floor. Thankful for the plush carpet, Vicky crawled forward on all fours to the door. She placed her hands against the door and walked her way up to the handle which she finally managed to grab and turn, the door thankfully unlocked. Her weight caused the door to swing open, followed by her falling out into a long hallway. The faint sound of voices echoed in the air as she crawled down the hallway in the opposite direction. Finally arriving at a spiral staircase, Vicky slowly made her way down the stairs on her hands and knees, one step at a time. Seeming more difficult than a two hour Pilates class, she finally made it to the bottom of the stairs only to find herself in the kitchen. Vicky crawled to the first row of cabinets and pulled herself up to the countertop. Less than ten feet away was a door, the rays of sunlight streaming through its window confirming it as her way out.

Vicky wasn't sure where she was or why she was there, but felt certain that she had to escape. Summoning all of her strength, Vicky made her way toward the door using the countertop for support. She finally reached the end of the counter, only four feet separating her from freedom. With all of her might, Vicky pushed off from the counter and landed against the wall next to the door. She threw her arm out several times in an effort to reach the doorknob, her arm feeling as though it weighed twenty tons. On the fifth try she managed to take hold of the handle, pushing down on it with all the strength she could muster. The handle slowly moved and the door swung open as the ear splitting sound of a house alarm reverberated in her ears. Vicky crumpled to the floor in tears. She summoned all of her strength and began to crawl through the open doorway as the sound of men's voices approached.

"What the hell?" Lord Hainesborough yelled as he slapped the face of a burly guard. "You were supposed to make sure all the doors were locked. You idiot!"

"I'm sorry. She was so drugged up, I didn't think it would matter," the guard replied in his defense.

"Well obviously she is anything but that," Hainesborough said as he shut the door in Vicky's face. "Shoot her up again. And this time make sure she stays down and out."

The guard bent down and inserted a needle into Vicky's posterior, the warm sensation of the drug flowing through her veins causing her vision and consciousness to slip from view.

CHAPTER 26

Dutch, Susan and Crane furiously ransacked Dutch's boat, turning over every item and turning out every piece of clothing.

"Keep looking. It has to be here. Somewhere," Dutch called out.

"Are you sure you even left it here?" Susan asked for the tenth time.

"Yes I'm sure, damn it. I'm just not sure where. Crane, did you check the chart desk?" Crane looked up from the pile of clothes he was scavenging."

"Yes, of course I did. Nothing there. You sure you didn't throw it away?" Crane asked for the twentieth time.

"No, I didn't throw it away," Dutch screamed. Susan shook her head in dismay and headed up to the galley as Dutch and Crane continued to scour the staterooms.

"Got it," Susan called out from above. Dutch and Crane immediately scrambled up the stairs.

"Where was it?" Dutch asked.

Susan triumphantly held up the crumpled bill of lading. "Stuck between the cushions of the dining table bench. It must have fallen out of your pocket."

Dutch took the shipping document from Susan and studied it. "I had a feeling this would come in handy when I visited the British High Commission.

"You mean broke in," Susan added.

"Whatever," Dutch replied. "Okay, so now we've got an address for Lord Hainesborough," Dutch said holding up the invoice.

"So what do we do now?" Crane asked as they all sat down at the table.

"Well, since no one is coming to us, I think we had better go to them," Susan suggested.

"You've got that right. But first, I want to verify that the number on the spyware on my phone is Hainesborough's." Dutch checked his watch. "Crane, could you call Ted and Keith from the pay phone at the ship's store? They should have an answer on that cell phone number."

"You going to talk to her?" Crane said with a note of determination as he left, giving Susan a long look. Dutch nodded, Susan looking on dumbfounded.

"What's all that about?" Susan asked.

"Well, you know Crane. He feels responsible for Vicky being taken. And we all know how quick you are to shoot people."

"What do you mean? It's not like I go around shooting people every day. Jeez, you make it sound like I'm some crazy gun toting maniac or something."

"No, it's not that. It's just, well, Crane made me promise that he and I would go check these places out."

"You mean without me?" Susan replied, a hurt look on her face.

"Yeah, I guess."

"Well that's not going to happen old man. No way. No how."

"I'm not old."

"Really?"

"Okay, fine. But will you at least agree to let Crane shoot someone?"

"You mean the person who took Vicky?"

"Sure, okay. That'll do."

Crane appeared at the door to the upper salon with a look of satisfaction on his face. "I found our friend stalking us again." Crane pulled Menton Moore into the salon.

"Menton Moore," Susan and Dutch said simultaneously. Menton hung his head as smiles spread over everyone else.

"Get in here you nut," Susan said with warmth.

"You don't have to track us anymore Menton. You're officially on the team. Right?" Dutch said to Susan and Crane.

"Yes, of course," Susan said as she put a welcoming arm around Menton's shoulder.

Menton took out a hanky and dotted a tear from his eye as he sat down. "I don't know what to say. I've never been part of a gang before. Just formal audits and such, but never a gang."

"Well you're part of this gang," Susan said as she gave him a hug. "Did you get the info Crane?"

"The phone number is registered to a corporation. But the address belongs to Lord Hainesborough," Crane replied.

"He must have loaded the spyware onto my cell phone when we met him at the Hilton reception," Dutch surmised.

"Well, if we've learned anything it's that our Lord Hainesborough would do anything to keep his family name from being tarnished."

"What's your point Ice?" Dutch asked.

"This is where we use us knowing what we know," Susan said with a smile that was more devil than diva. "How's your acting voice Dutch?"

CHAPTER 27

Menton Moore walked into the lobby of the British High Commission dressed in proper British attire of white Bermuda shorts, a short sleeved dress shirt and straw panama hat. He approached the receptionist who gave him a quizzical once over.

"I would like to see Mr. Wilfred Engleton please."

"What does it concern sir," said the receptionist.

"Passport issues. Personal you see. Very personal," Menton replied in a hushed tone of self importance. The receptionist flipped through an appointment schedule, running her finger down each page. She returned to Menton with a sanctimonious smile.

"I'm afraid Mr. Engleton is rather booked today Sir."

"No worry dear. I'll just wait." Menton took a seat under the glare of the receptionist, oblivious to her consternation. He patiently sat until the receptionist finally lost interest, turning her attention back to the trivial typing of correspondence that was her daily burden. Menton checked his watch and then approached the receptionist.

"Excuse me. Would there be a convenient lavatory?" The receptionist pointed to the far corner without looking up from her work. Menton retreated, going directly to the men's room as he checked his watch again. Once inside, he took out a handkerchief and carefully unwrapped a small pocket recorder along with Dutch's cell phone. He set both on the sink counter and wiped the sweat from his brow with the kerchief. His watch hand shook as he checked the time once more while he unfolded a piece of paper from his breast pocket. Menton silently mouthed the numbers on the paper and then picked up the cell phone and carefully dialed the numbers on the paper. Menton listened for an answer and then fumbled with the buttons of the recorder until the device finally emitted Dutch's voice. Menton held the recorder to the cell phone as it recited Dutch's salutation to Susan who listened on the other end. Menton stopped the recorder and bent his ear to the cell phone to listen to Susan's reply. He hit the start button on the device. The recording, in Dutch's voice, stated that he was at the British High Commission waiting an interminable amount of time in order to speak with Wilfred Engleton regarding what he had discovered during his trip to London. The recording went on to assure Susan that it would be a revelation that would put a whole new light on Lord Hainesborough. Menton paused the recorder and bent down to listen to Susan's reply, the recorder slipping out of his hand and sliding across the tile floor of the bathroom and under a toilet stall. Menton scurried after it, only to find the stall door locked. He bent down and frantically swung his arm about as he blindly grasped for the recorder. His hand landed on an object. Menton tugged on it, unsure of what he had. The door to the stall opened and a stately elder Englishman looked down on Menton from his perch on the toilet, the recorder in his hand.

"Sir, I sincerely hope this is the object you are groping for," the man said.

"Yes, most certainly. I assure you that is the only object of my desire," Menton said in as manly a tone as he could muster. Menton took the recorder and hurried back to Dutch's cell phone. He held the recorder to the phone and pushed the play button, letting Dutch's voice sign off. Menton collapsed over the counter from nervous overexposure as the Englishman approached. Menton moved to the side as the man began washing his hands. The man glanced at Menton, who was sweating out his anxiety.

"I am not sure what you are doing sir, but perhaps I can be of some help?"

Menton reached into his pocket for the relief of his handkerchief, a small revolver coming out with the handkerchief. Menton fumbled for the gun as it dropped to the floor at the feet of the gentleman.

"Perhaps not," the man said. The gentleman briskly walked out of the bathroom, his head on a swivel.

Dutch and Susan crouched low in the branches of a large Kapok tree across the road from The Royal Westmoreland Resort in St. James on the West Coast, just up the way from Mullins Beach, ten minutes from Hole Town. Susan pocketed her cell phone as Dutch used binoculars to scan the grounds beyond the high masonry wall that surrounded the upper class development of million dollar homes and villas.

Dutch pointed to one of the villas. "That's the one. Number sixteen. That's where our lord should be leaving from, if you're right."

Susan took the binoculars from Dutch and studied the building as Crane nervously paced around the trunk of the tree below. "Let's hope I am. I see one large guard in uniform by the side of the house. And an even larger guard by the second floor window. He's sitting in a chair." Susan grabbed Dutch's arm as she continued to survey the area. "There it is. A large Range Rover. It looks like there's three, no four men in it."

"Do you see Hainesborough?"

"No, not yet. Wait a minute, there he is. He's coming out of the garage and getting into the front seat."

"I'm impressed Ice. One of your ideas actually worked," Dutch said as the vehicle drove away from the house toward the front gates. Susan attempted to slug Dutch in the arm, causing her to almost lose her balance and fall out of the tree.

"Anyone else?" Dutch asked.

"No, that's all I can see. Not much movement. But there's a lot of house there." Susan lowered the binoculars and took out her Glock. "I say we storm the place."

Dutch gently pushed her gun hand down with a smile. "Love the enthusiasm, but I'm thinking a subtler approach may work better. Stay here and use those binocs to report anything." Dutch hoisted himself out of the tree and joined Crane on the ground. He spoke in hushed tones to Crane as Susan looked on from above.

"What are you saying Dutch? What are you two planning?" Susan called out as Crane darted across the road.

"Just keep an eye on the house Ice. Let me know what's happening."

Susan raised the binoculars and focused on the house just as Crane scaled the outer wall in one bound like a cat. Like a ninja set on invisibility, Crane disappeared from view for a moment, and then like a ghost, he reappeared behind the guard on the side of the house. Susan winced as she observed Crane land a direct punch to the back of the guard's neck. The guard dropped as if his heart had been ripped out. "The outside guard is down," she reported to Dutch, not sure if that was the diminutive Crane she had come to know or some killing machine. Susan continued to watch as Crane moved to the back of the house. He withdrew his pick tools and worked on the lock for a moment before opening the door. "He's in the house now." Susan focused on the second floor window through which she could see the other guard quietly sitting in the chair. The guard stood up as the sound of the house alarm went off. "Crane's tripped the alarm damn it. We better get in there!"

"Wait for it," Dutch calmly replied.

The alarm went silent as did the rest of the house. Susan refocused her attention on the house, Crane appearing at the back door and waving them in. "Son of a bitch," Susan muttered as she shimmied down the tree.

"Amazing little guy, huh?" Dutch mused.

"Maybe I can trade you in for him?" she wondered out loud.

Within minutes Susan and Dutch had scaled the outside wall with the help of a step ladder they brought along. They crossed the yard with as much stealth as they could. Once inside the house, they quickly took stock of the first floor of the vacation home, ornately furnished in the style of impersonal vacation decor. Dutch tried a pair of locked French doors. He kicked open the doors as Susan withdrew her gun. Inside the study were several shipping boxes including the long rectangular box Dutch had taken the shipping docs from at the High Commission. Dutch and Susan called out for Crane and then made their way up the stairs to the second floor, finally hearing Crane's reply from one of the bedrooms. Dutch motioned Susan to the bedroom door and they burst into the room, their weapons in the ready. Crane sat on the bed cradling Vicky in his arms, her body as limp as a rag doll. Tears streamed from his face as he rocked her back and forth. Dutch and Susan rushed to their sides, Susan immediately checking Vicky's pulse.

"Is she?" Dutch asked.

"No, she's alive. But barely." Susan checked Vicky's eyes and listened to her chest. "She's drugged. Not sure with what. We've got to get her to a hospital and fast."

Dutch hoisted Vicky into his arms and carried her down the stairs.

"Should we call for an ambulance?" Susan wondered.

"Screw that. I'll get her there twice as fast." Dutch turned to Crane. "You know what to do."

Crane bounded out the back door of the house as Dutch carried Vicky out of the front, while Susan covered them from behind. Dutch walked boldly down the main road toward the gated front entrance occupied by two guards.

"What are you doing Dutch? Shouldn't we get her over the wall? What about the guards?"

"Screw that," Dutch said with a look of stoic determination. "Hey, assholes," Dutch hollered out to the two guards at the front entrance gate as he gently placed Vicky onto the grass in the roadway medium. The two guards came out of the guard shack and approached Dutch and Susan, their guns drawn just as the short metal gate exploded off its hinges. The guards turned around as the car driven by Crane approached at full speed, the gate flying off the hood. Dutch immediately punched both guards in the backs of their heads with full force, the two crumpling to the ground as Susan looked on in stunned silence. The car braked at full speed and did a full one eighty, its tires squealing. Dutch turned to Susan as he collected Vicky. "We've done this before," he said with a shrug. Susan opened the back door and Dutch placed Vicky onto the seat of the waiting car. "Let's go."

With Dutch behind the wheel, they arrived at Queen Elizabeth Hospital in Bridgetown in twenty minutes. Susan's forceful aplomb to the hospital's admission staff had Vicky in a room with a doctor within minutes. Crane and Dutch stood guard outside the room as the doctor and two nurses examined Vicky, the whole time, Susan refusing to let go of Vicky's hand.

Dutch put a reassuring hand on Crane's shoulder. "Don't worry old friend. She'll be fine. This doctor will do his best, otherwise Susan will shoot him. I'm sure of that." Crane managed an unconvincing smile as Dutch paced back and forth. "What's taking them so long?" After twenty minutes Susan joined them in the hallway, her expression hard as nails.

"What is it? What did they say?" Crane demanded.

Susan wrung her hands as she stared down at the floor. "It seems she was drugged all right. Flunitrazepam."

"Flunit what?" Dutch said.

"Rohypnol. Rufilin. Ruffies. That's what they gave her. It's a powerful hypnotic used to treat severe insomniacs. They're treating her now with a drug called Flumazenil which blocks its effects."

"Will she be okay?" Crane asked.

"Yes, she will. The drug also causes short term amnesia when it's used. Which in Vicky's case is probably a good thing."

"What do you mean by that?" Crane asked.

Susan looked into both of their eyes. "She was raped Dutch. Violently raped. Several times."

Dutch and Crane stood motionless as if the air had been taken out of the world. Susan placed a hand on their shoulders. "The important thing is that she is going to be okay. That we got to her in time."

Crane pounded his fist against the wall. "It's my fault this happened. I should have been more careful. It's all my fault." Crane turned and ran down the hallway as Susan and Dutch looked on. Susan turned to go after him, but Dutch held her back.

"Let him be for now. He needs some time alone. I know how he is. He'll be okay."

"What do we do now?" Susan asked.

"We get even."

CHAPTER 28

Dutch left Crane to watch over Vicky while he drove Susan straight to the Caribbean Court Hotel in Hastings. The whole way Dutch didn't say a word. Susan began to speak several times, thinking better of it as she studied the steely look on his face. She had seen that look just once before, when Dutch had arrived in Miami to avenge her father's death. It was a look that struck an uneasy feeling even in his close friends and relations.

Dutch parked the car and walked straight into the office, motioning for Susan to stay put with a wave of his hand. He returned moments later with what was obviously a long range rifle draped in a blanket. He placed it in the trunk and started up the car, wheeling it around in the direction of the airport.

"Look Dutch, I can only imagine how you're feeling," Susan finally raised the nerve to say. "But killing Hainesborough is the wrong thing to do. I know you're angry, but I can't let you do that."

"Relax," Dutch said without looking over, "I'm not going to kill that son of a bitch. At least not yet. No, I'm not going to do that."

"Then what's with the rifle?"

"Just to provide cover. Nothing more."

"Is that what you spoke to Keith and Ted about?"

"That, and a way for us to finally get our hands on Lady Melody and finish this thing."

"What's the plan?"

"They're going to get their contact at the phone company to monitor the Carringtons' cell phones."

"What good is that going to do? They're not going to use their cell phones. Especially after you dropped in on them with the helicopter."

"No, but they'll take a call. Especially if it's from someone they trust."

"And who would that be?"

"I don't know. A neighbor, a close friend. Some family relation on the island."

"I don't follow. How are we going to find out who that is?"

"We're not. We're just going to get them to call. And when they do, we'll get their location on St. Vincent."

"So where are we going now?"

"To the airport. We've got to make sure we have plane tickets waiting and ready for when we get their location."

"Once more, how are we going to get someone to call the Carringtons?"

"We're going to burn their house down."

By the time Dutch had calmed Susan down and reviewed the plan three times with her, they had gotten the standby tickets at the airport and dropped by the ship's store in Bridgetown to gather the supplies they needed. As they sat on the deck of Dutch's catamaran checking their weapons, Crane carefully mixed three parts potassium nitrate with two parts sugar into several pans in the galley. Using a long spoon, he slowly heated and stirred the concoction with the care of a master chef. Once the mixture was liquefied, Crane poured the pans' contents onto several pieces of tin foil sheets, carefully positioning string fuses into the globs with an artist's eye.

"We're going to need some fountains Crane," Dutch called out from the deck.

"Can't you see I'm busy here," Crane shouted back. Dutch cracked the first smile of the day.

"Fine. I'll make them." Dutch hoisted himself down into the galley and gathered up the rolls of paper towels that they had bought. He removed the towels and covered the bottoms and sides of the cardboard tubes with aluminum foil as Crane made a new batch of material, this time mixing even parts of potassium nitrate and sugar. Crane carefully poured the mixture into the tubes, stopping an inch short of the top. Dutch pushed short fuses into the mixture as Crane proudly looked over his work. He nodded with satisfaction and began taking the legs off of the small charcoal grills that Dutch bought. Susan entered and looked over the armory, her arms cradling several guns and the long range rifle.

"You sure this is going to work?" she said for the tenth time.

"No problem Ms. Susan," Crane replied. "Dutch and I have done this many times. No problem. Not one house has burned down yet."

"Except that one in Eleuthera," Dutch said.

Crane wriggled his nose. "Yes, that was a bad one. Whole place went up in minutes."

"More like seconds. Remember?"

"Yes, seconds."

Susan slapped her forehead with the palm of her hand. "God, please tell me this isn't going to turn into Dutch's wrecking crew?"

"Just kidding Ice," Dutch said as he checked his watch. "It's time."

"Hey guys, what's happening?" Menton asked as he appeared at the doorway of the galley causing Susan to drop the guns.

"Menton, you startled the crap out of me. You've got to stop doing that," Susan fumed.

"Sorry," Menton said with a sheepish look. "It's just that when Crane told me over the phone what happened, I just wanted to see if I could help."

"This isn't something you should be involved with," Dutch replied.

"Come on Dutch. If this has something to do with getting Melody back and keeping her safe from that lunatic, then I want to help. There's got to be something I can do?"

Dutch studied Menton for a moment and then shot a short glance at Crane. "You know what, there is something you could do Menton. How about you go to the airport and wait for our call?"

"Okay, then what?"

"We'll need for you to book the tickets I've got on hold for the next flight out. We won't have any time to spare."

Menton enthusiastically jumped about with glee. "Yes, I can do that. You'll see. You call and I'll make sure to get the tickets on the next flight out."

Menton and Crane gathered up the smoke bombs as Susan collected the weapons from off the floor. With Menton trailing behind, picking up errant bombs and pistols that fell behind as they made their way to the parking lot. Menton left for the airport and within twenty minutes Dutch had driven to the Carringtons' house, the first signs of night crowding out the evening sky. Dutch parked the car by a vacant lot just around the corner from the house.

"What do you want me to do?" Susan asked as Dutch and Crane gathered up the smoke bombs.

"Just keep an eye on your cell phone. The minute Keith gets the location of the Carringtons he'll call you."

"You mean, if they get the location," she replied.

"Don't worry, by the time we're through the Carringtons will be able to see the smoke themselves from St. Vincent."

"You just watch Ms. Susan. This will be fantastic flames," Crane said, looking more like a mad scientist than a humble Asian.

Susan's stomach grumbled as she thought about her insurance premiums and what the punishment would be for arson in Barbados. "God be careful," she said as the two headed down the road, their arms chock full of potential disaster. Susan tried hard to mentally distract herself for several minutes until one of her father's favorite sayings passed through her mind. "Hang around with fools and the fools will get you hung."

Susan felt her neck as she imagined swinging from the large Baobab tree in Queens Park. "Crap," she said out loud in self recrimination and then took off down the road after Dutch and Crane. As she approached the Carringtons' house, a large pillar of flames suddenly shot up from behind the house. Susan stopped dead in her tracks as the flames were joined by two more along with smoke that began to billow from out of the front windows and door. Susan stood frozen, not sure if she should run toward the house or away from it, momentarily mesmerized by the spectacle. She decided that getting a good distance from the house would be the better part of valor.

Susan turned and feigned walking casually back up the road toward the car when the unmistakable sound of crackling firewood caught her ear. Susan turned just as the front door burst into flames. The fire soon ran over the front of the house, covering it in a golden cast. She stood there, her mouth agape, as the flames leapt to the roof. Susan took a few steps toward the house and then turned and ran as fast as she could back to the car. Dutch and Crane were already in the car, calmly sitting in their seats. "What the fuck!" Susan shouted through the open car windows.

"Beautiful, huh?" Dutch smugly replied.

"We do good work, right Ms. Susan?" Crane added from the backseat. "We cut across the backyards to get to the car so no one would see us."

"You idiots. The whole frickin house is on fire. It's burning down. Burning. All burning!" she shouted.

Dutch and Crane looked at each other and then scrambled out of the car and ran down the road as Susan steadied herself on the car door. A single ash lazily floated down in front of her eyes gingerly landing on her nose as the smell of burning wood filled the air. Susan slumped down into the front seat of the car burying her face into her hands. She looked up at the sounds of Dutch's and Crane's voices as they slowly shuffled back to the car.

"I told you, not so close to the walls," Crane said.

"And I told you that unless they're close to the walls, the smoke won't seep through the windows," Dutch countered.

"I still think they could have been a little farther away," Crane replied. Susan glared at them as they got into the car and Dutch started up the engine.

"What?" Dutch finally said to Susan.

"What?" Susan incredulously replied. "That's all you have to say? Don't worry Susan. It won't burn down Susan. We know what we're doing Susan. You two idiots! You burned down the man's frickin house." The sound of Susan's cell phone cut off her tirade, Dutch holding up his finger for silence as he answered the phone. Dutch momentarily listened, a smile coming over his face.

"It worked. We've got the address." Dutch turned the car around and headed for the airport. Susan looked back at the house fire that lit up the skyline.

"It worked. Really?" she said in disgust.

Within fifteen minutes Dutch had reached the airport, having called Menton on the way. He parked the car in the nearby lot and rushed everyone into the terminal, Susan lugging the bag of firearms with her.

"Dutch. Susan," Menton called out as they approached the ticket counter. Menton stood by the security line. He held up three tickets in his hand which he wildly waved.

"Menton, good job," Dutch said as they approached him. "When does the flight leave?"

"I was able to get us on the next flight. It leaves in ten minutes. I got a ticket for myself as well."

"Ten minutes? What are we going to do with this?" Susan asked as she held up the bag of weapons. "We don't have time to check it now."

"Someone will have to stay behind." Dutch gave a knowing nod to Crane who took the bag from Susan.

"You three go. I'll stay behind and wait for your call," Crane said.

"But what will we do for guns?" Susan asked like a drug addict headed for rehab.

"We don't have a choice Ice. We've got to go now or we chance the Carringtons changing location and never finding Lady Melody." Dutch took the tickets from Menton and abruptly headed for the security line. Susan and Menton shrugged and followed him, as Crane took the bag and left the terminal.

Within thirty minutes the plane touched down in St. Vincent at the Joshua International Airport. Moving quickly through the small terminal, the group was soon headed in their rental car toward the Carringtons' location using the GPS in Susan's cell phone to guide them down the dark roads. As they drove into the mountains on the Vigie Highway, Dutch glanced at Menton who nervously squirmed about in the backseat.

"You okay Menton?"

"I'm not sure. It's just been so long since I've seen Lady Melody. I'm afraid I'm a bit nervous. I'm just not sure what to expect. And these ruffians who've captured her. How do you propose to handle them? I mean, we don't have any firearms."

"Don't worry Menton. I've got a feeling that Ice and I can handle them." Dutch stared through the darkness and pointed to a narrow gravel road that led up a short embankment by the Villa Lodge Hotel.

"Can this be right?" Susan asked as she drove up the narrow road overgrown by brush.

Dutch squinted at the map on Susan's cell phone. "According to this, we're right about on it. Maybe we should park and walk up?" A whirring sound caused Susan to look up as they exited the vehicle, a helicopter passing by high overhead.

"Hope that doesn't spook them, considering last time," Susan said as Menton looked on from the backseat.

"I'm sure it won't. Those choppers are always ferrying tourists from the airport to the other islands. Mostly for sailing charters or remote hotels," Dutch replied.

"Menton, you coming?" Susan asked.

Menton hesitated and then slowly left the backseat. "You don't think they'll have guns, do you?" he wondered out loud as Susan and Dutch led the way up the narrowing roadway, the vegetation on each side of the road closing in on them.

"They did last time," Dutch casually replied as a small brick building laying at the bottom of a hollow came into view. A single light shone through the threadbare curtains that lazily flapped in several open windows.

Susan raised her hand. "That's got to be it." She looked through her binoculars for some sign of life. "I don't see any movement," she said as they all crouched low on the side of the roadway.

"I say screw it. Let's all go in and get this over with," Dutch said with blind bravado.

"I don't know Dutch," Susan said.

"Yes, what she said," Menton added as he nervously looked about for routes of escape.

Dutch massaged his jaw as he considered the situation. "I think it will be okay. I say we just walk up to the house and let them know who we are." Dutch started toward the building with Susan and Menton following a cautionary distance behind. He approached the front door and with a stature of aplomb, vigorously rapped on the large wooden door. "Carrington, it's me. The guy in the helicopter. We need to talk." Dutch, Susan and Menton waited as his knock was met with silence.

"See, nothing to worry about. No one's home," Dutch said just before the door exploded in a hail of bullets. "Holy crap," Dutch shouted as he jumped out of the way. Susan hit the dirt as Menton turned and ran back up the roadway toward the car as fast as a short, overweight man could.

"Carrington, it's me, Dutch. Stop your shooting. We're here to help." The gunfire stopped, but Dutch and Susan remained plastered against the block wall of the house. They studied the rays of light that streamed through the numerous bullet holes in the front door, both thankful that it wasn't them.

"Reggie, Mr. Carrington, it's Susan Berg. We don't have any weapons. We're here to help you. Just give us a second of your time." Susan and Dutch waited for a reply. Susan motioned for

Dutch to go to the door, Dutch vehemently waving her off. "Mr. Carrington, you have my word. All we want to do is talk. Nothing more. Look, if we could find you, it's just a matter of time before the police do the same thing. We'll come in with our hands up, I promise."

Dutch motioned for Susan to go to the front door, Susan vehemently waving him off. The front door slowly opened, Dutch and Susan starting a staring contest. Dutch finally gave Susan the finger and raised his arms as he walked through the door. Susan followed behind. A bright light momentarily blinded them as they struggled to see their surroundings.

"You wanted to talk, so talk," Mr. Carrington said, his voice coming from a dark corner of the small room.

"Can we lower our arms?" Dutch asked as his vision adjusted to the light. In one corner stood Carrington with a .45 Magnum trained on him. In the other corner stood Reggie, a furtive look of concern on his face.

"Okay, but if you're here to take my son in, you're already dead."

"That's the last thing on our mind," Susan said.

"How did you find us?" Carrington asked.

"We heard you had a house fire, so we traced the call to your cell phone," Dutch replied.

"Damn sister. I told her not to call me for any reason except for an emergency."

"Well that probably qualifies, don't you think?" Dutch wondered out loud with a knowing smirk, Susan rolling her eyes.

"You have homeowner's insurance, right?" Susan asked.

"Yes, thankfully. I can only think it was that scumbag who burned my house down."

"Which scumbag would that be?" Susan replied.

"Lord Hainesborough, my father," Lady Melody said as she appeared from the bedroom. Reggie took a protective position by her side. Dutch and Susan gazed at her as if she were the golden child.

"Yeah, I'm sure it was him," Susan finally said.

"Melody, we should leave," Reggie said as he took her hand. "It's not safe for you here."

"No Reggie. I'm tired of running and I don't want to cause any more trouble for you or your father." Lady Melody approached Dutch and Susan. "You see, this is all my fault. I met Reggie at Club Xtreme in Worthing. We just fell in love with each other, you understand. I know we shouldn't have run, but he would never have allowed us to be together."

"You mean your father, Lord Hainesborough?" Susan asked.

"Yes, he's just frightful. I'm afraid all the time. The only reason I was allowed on this trip is because he was on the island, showing our family heirlooms."

Susan approached Melody and took her hand. She looked into her sad eyes and for the first time saw what Dutch had seen. "It's true, isn't it?"

Lady Melody sadly nodded. "Yes, it started when I was ten. Not anymore, now that I'm older. But I hate him for it. I despise him." Lady Melody broke down in tears as Susan hugged her.

"Do you see why my son had to act?" Mr. Carrington said, his words angry and defiant. "That son of bitch should be fried. What he did to his daughter is an abomination. And no one does a damn thing because of Hainesborough's position. It's bullshit."

"I don't blame your son or you one bit," Dutch said as he looked upon the girl. "You did the right thing Reggie."

"So what do we do now?" Reggie said.

"What you do now is hand over my daughter," Lord Hainesborough said as he came through the door. He was flanked by two of his house guards, both bearing automatic micro Uzi's. Hainesborough proudly held at his side a gold sword as he swaggered into the room. Hainesborough pointed the jewel encrusted sword at Mr. Carrington, who had his pistol squarely trained on Hainesborough. "I'd suggest you put your weapon down, unless you would like to lose your life, as well as that of your son." Carrington slowly lowered the pistol in defeat as Hainesborough looked on with smug satisfaction.

"How? How did you find us?" Susan wondered out loud.

"You Americans. So common. Always thinking so basic. No sense of history or tactics. I made sure to guard my interests Ms. Berg, knowing Americans' penchant for backwoods' justice as well as your lack of propriety."

"What the hell does that mean?" Susan asked.

"Come on in Menton," Dutch shouted out.

"Very good Mr. Holland. Did you just figure that out?" Hainesborough said as Menton Moore entered through the front door.

"You bastard," Lady Melody shouted at Menton, as Susan tried to restrain her.

"Menton? You? But why? She's your niece." Susan blurted out. "What about your sister?"

"Ms. Berg, we are dealing with royalty here. A lineage, that goes back for centuries. My sister and I are nothing more than commoners, like yourself. You Americans just don't understand. I was the one who arranged for my sister to have Lord Hainesborough's child. It was her fault she turned to drugs. She was a weak fool. Thinking she could be anything more than a vessel for his child. She couldn't handle not being able to be Lady Melody's mother. Can you imagine? Her, the mother to Lady Melody! A commoner? So she turned to drugs."

"What she couldn't handle was that asshole molesting his own daughter!" Mr. Carrington shouted.

"But you helped us rescue Vicky," Susan said.

"An easy tradeoff to secure your trust in Menton. We planned it all along," Hainesborough said with a stately air.

"Did you plan to rape her too?" Dutch asked.

"I'm afraid that was the act of a blatant failure to observe orders. I can assure you that the responsible party has been reprimanded."

"And who would that be?" Dutch asked, Hainesborough's quick glance at Menton telling Dutch all he needed to know. "So, I imagine it was little ole Menton there who saved me from the Captain, huh?"

Menton beamed with a smile of satisfaction. "As well as taking care of him and his other associates," Menton added. "Yes, I started the fire on the dock that saved your ass. I'm afraid my interrogation of the Captain may have gone a bit overboard."

"Just a bit," Dutch said.

"So I guess that you were responsible for London as well?" Susan asked. Again Menton smugly smiled.

"That's enough of that," Hainesborough said with a dismissive wave of his hand. "Well, it seems Ms. Berg that you and your associates have done your jobs. You can now leave the clean up to my men. My secretary will deliver your fee tomorrow."

"Clean up what?" Dutch asked.

"These two kidnappers, of course. Surely I can't allow them to go about spreading these lies about me and my daughter? Besides, I'm not so naïve to think they won't try again, do you? Melody has a very convincing way you know."

Dutch scratched his head as if in thought as Susan incredulously looked on. "Well, I'm gonna have to give that some thought," Dutch finally said. "You mind if I smoke? It helps me to think."

"Fine, but be quick with it. My men have very itchy fingers," Hainesborough said as his guards pointed their weapons at Dutch and Mr. Carrington.

"I've got just one more question. Why did you come to us Menton with the story about finding that stupid sword?" Dutch asked as he withdrew a lone cigarette from his shirt pocket along with a disposable lighter.

"I'm afraid I was being too clever. I never dreamed you would find the historical records," Menton replied. "I just used it to stay close to you two. But it worked out rather well in the end, don't you think?"

Susan, her mouth agape, looked on as Dutch lit the cigarette and clumsily puffed away. "So if you shoot the Carringtons, what do we tell the police?" Dutch asked between puffs.

"You don't tell them anything," Menton said. "We'll take care of them. Some of the mountains here have never seen a human foot print." Mr. Carrington moved to his son's side as if to shield him from the evil that had befallen them.

Lady Melody stepped forward. "No father, you can't. I won't let you," Lady Melody pleaded. "They were just trying to help. It was all my fault."

"She does have a point," Dutch said with a smirk.

"Yes, my dear, it is all your fault. Spreading those rumors about me. And their blood is squarely on your hands," Hainesborough said. "Perhaps this will teach you to not rely on the lesser class. Your place is with me. With the privileged. When will you see that Melody?"

"Well Ice, I think we have no choice but to do what they want," Dutch said to Susan as he subtly glanced toward the open window behind her and the Carringtons. The reason for Dutch smoking a cigarette for the first time in Susan's memory suddenly dawned on her. "Ok, so how much are you willing to pay for our silence?" Dutch continued.

"Ah yes, like all Americans. We are down to the money now. Well, I would think double your fee would be appropriate."

"Double!" Susan shouted. "No way. We want at least triple or nothing."

"Triple?" Harrington said through a smirk of bemusement.

"Let's just shoot them all," Menton suggested as Dutch dropped the lit cigarette from his hand. The second it hit the floor, a hail of rifle fire split the curtains of the open windows, the first shots taking out the lights in the room. Dutch crouched down in the pitch black and in one swoop gathered Susan and Lady Melody into his arms, literally hurling them through the open window. As the rifle fire continued overhead, Dutch reached out for Carrington and Reggie, his foot kicking something metallic. Dutch instinctively picked it up as he grabbed the Carringtons' arms, leading them out through the other open window.

The sound of Uzi fire erupted in the room behind them just as they hit the dirt, the rifle fire continuing to fill the house from the top of the hill. Dutch and the Carringtons scrambled around the house and then ran up the side of the road. Dutch approached Susan and Lady Melody who were already in the car, as Susan fired up the engine. He opened the back door motioning the Carringtons in as he held up the golden sword for Susan to see.

"Looks like we got the girl and our pay," Dutch said triumphantly as a hail of gunfire splattered the ground in front of him from the direction of the house. Susan spun the car around. Dutch jumped into the passenger's side as she roared down the road, the brush slapping the car as it went.

"Are you crazy?" Susan shouted at Dutch as the car skidded onto the Vigie Highway, her foot to the floor. "You could have gotten us all killed."

"I wasn't worried. We had a backup plan."

"We? *We* had a backup plan? And when were you going to tell *we*?"

"I didn't want to say anything unless I was wrong. That's why I had Mardrid bring Crane over in the helicopter. He did some great shooting from the top of the Villa Lodge Hotel, huh?"

"Yeah, just great. And how did you know that Menton might be a plant?"

"When I spoke to his sister, right before she died," Dutch said in hushed tones on Melody's behalf. "Her last words were fuck, my brother."

"Fuck, my brother?" Susan whispered back.

"Yes. But I wasn't sure if she meant fuck, I'm shot, my brother. Or just fuck my brother. See what I mean? I didn't want to say anything until I was sure. I mean, what if it was the other way around? I didn't want you to think ill of Menton if it wasn't true. It wouldn't have been fair to him, now would it?"

"Oh right. Menton. The guy who set us up, sold his sister to that creep, and tried to kill us. Poor old Menton, let's not hurt his feelings," Susan fumed.

"Okay, okay. I made a mistake. You can take it out of my pay."

"Pay? Really? It's a good thing you grabbed that sword. That's all I can say."

"Just get us to the airport. The helicopter will be waiting there to get us back to Barbados."

"Don't want to hurt Menton's feelings," Susan repeated under her breath as she stamped her foot on the accelerator.

CHAPTER 29

Although it only took forty minutes to chopper back to Barbados, it was none too soon with Mardrid complaining the whole way about Dutch wrecking his other helicopter. By the time they had landed, Susan had capitulated to his demands for her to cover his deductable on the repairs, as well as have Dutch attest to the aviation authorities that he had forced Mardrid to continue flying in an effort to save Lady Melody.

As Dutch drove back in the middle of the night to the marina from the Barbados Airport, everyone slept in the crowded car, except for Susan who was plastered between Crane and Dutch in the front seat.

"What the hell do we do now?" Susan said in a hushed voice.

"We need to get off the island. Think things out," Dutch replied. "We need to head out to safe waters where we can't be tracked."

"I'm not going out on open water in that tin can of yours," she replied.

"We've got no choice Ice. We're not even sure if Hainesborough or his guards are alive. What if Crane killed one or all of them? I mean he's a great sniper. I should know, since I trained him. But who knows? And what if Hainesborough is alive and he calls the police? Where do you think they'll look first to find Lady Melody or the Carringtons?"

"Maybe I'll just catch a flight back to Miami. I could just phone it in," Susan suggested.

"Okay, if you want to leave it in my hands, including getting any money out of all of this, then that's up to you."

Susan thought hard on the alternatives. Although Susan had grown up on the water in Miami, she was one of the "non-waters" that inhabit Florida. "Christ Ice, you might as well live in

Montana," Dutch always said when she refused to go sailing. Susan knew this was definitely not one of those times. The gun play and their perilous position regarding Lady Melody made the ocean their only safe harbor.

"Okay, but no screwing around. No fast sailing or wave riding," Susan demanded.

"I promise," Dutch replied making the sign of the cross.

By the time they had made it out to sea, Lady Melody and the Carringtons were sound asleep in the staterooms below. Dutch and Ice sat at the dining table as Crane brewed some warm grog in the galley.

"So maybe we should take a heading for Miami and get Lady Melody and the Carringtons safely to land," Crane said.

"We can't do that Crane, you know that," Dutch said.

"Well are there any better ideas?"

Crane sat the two grogs on the table, Susan taking a small sip as she thought about their options. "First of all, the Carringtons can't just leave their home, or at least what's left of it. What would they do for money? How would they live?" Susan wondered.

"Yes, there is that. Hey, they could stay with you for awhile," Dutch suggested, Susan's scowl sucking the breath out of that idea.

"And then there's Lady Melody's age," Susan said.

"Her age?" Crane asked.

"She's only seventeen. In Barbados, she's still considered to be a child. As her father, Lord Hainesborough could make our lives impossible. And let me point out that England and Barbados have extradition with the United States. Even if we get Lady Melody and Reggie to some safe place, with all his money, Hainesborough would dog us forever."

"How about we take it to court? Have him charged with child abuse? The courts would have to let her be," Crane suggested.

Dutch shook his head. "She'll never testify. You saw the way she looked when Hainesborough showed up. She was scared stiff. No, Melody won't do that. And even if she did agree, with his power and money, Hainesborough could keep it tied up in court for years."

"So what can we do?" Crane asked in exasperation.

"There's only one thing we can do. We make a trade," Susan said.

"A trade?" Dutch asked.

"Lady Melody in exchange for Hainesborough dropping all charges against the Carringtons."

Dutch rubbed the back of his neck, his lips pursed in consternation. "I don't know if I can stomach that. Putting that girl back with that sadist bastard."

"We've got no choice Dutch," Susan replied. "That's the best deal we can get. Besides, she'll only have to be at home for a year. Your friend in London, what's his name?"

"Mickey?"

"Yes, Mickey. We have him keep an eye out for her. Let Hainesborough know that he's being watched. The last thing someone like that wants is scandal. If he knows he's being watched, he'll behave."

"So what's our next move?" Crane wondered.

"We arrange for an exchange," Susan answered.

"But on our own terms," Dutch firmly stated.

Every weekend, the small village of Oistin's, just past St. Lawrence Gap on the South Coast, has a street side fish fry and barbeque during the evening. Susan spotted the weekly funfest the first week she arrived. It was a perfect place to arrange for a delicate meeting, where a chance of double cross and gun play was possible. Along with dancing and low prices, it's the best bet for getting a feel for the real Barbados. Dutch brought the boat to dock right outside of St. Lawrence Gap, the group taking a taxi to the street fair. Everyone sat at one of the open air tables, Crane dodging the crowds as he shuttled plates of barbeque chicken and fresh flying fish to the group. Lady Melody and Reggie dolefully sat together, holding hands. Mr. Carrington sipped at a beer as he vacantly stared off into space.

"Look, as long as we all stick to the plan, it will all work out," Dutch finally said with forced optimism.

"They'll be here any minute," Susan said.

"And your minute is up, Ms. Berg," Lord Hainesborough announced as he stepped out of the crowd along with his two guards. Everyone at the table stood up except for Lady Melody and Reggie, who held onto each other like a seawall against the storm. "I hope we can complete this transaction as quickly as possible," Hainesborough said as he looked about the street fair with disdain.

"Do you have the document?" Dutch asked.

"And the check," Susan added.

Lord Hainesborough reached into his jacket and withdrew an envelope. "Just as we agreed. A letter signed by me stating that it was all a misunderstanding with the Carringtons. And a certified check made out in the amount we agreed upon."

Susan withdrew her phone. "One thing before we take the envelope." She dialed a number and then hung up.

"Come Ms. Berg, what type of game are we playing now?" Hainesborough said. From out of the crowd, Wilfred Engleton of the British High Commission appeared along with the sergeant of the Barbados Police. After a discreet call to him from Susan, with veiled mention of their unfortunate meeting in his office, Wilfred "Willie" Engleton had agreed to listen to the Carringtons' story. After speaking with Mr. Carrington regarding the gory details, Engleton was securely on board and offered to provide an official presence at the meeting.

"Willie, so glad you could come," Dutch announced. Engleton gave Dutch a dirty look as he summarily took the envelope from Lord Hainesborough and opened it. He withdrew the signed paper and read it over. He then handed it to the sergeant.

"This all looks in order," Engleton said. "Lord Hainesborough, Mr. Carrington took the liberty of recounting *all* that he has learned about this unfortunate circumstance," Engleton continued as he held up a hand to silence Hainesborough. "I will be certain to make a confidential report to the home office. I have no doubt that you will maintain a proper and civil position from this point forward. I am confident that the last thing anyone would want is for these details to become public."

Lord Hainesborough begrudgingly nodded acceptance, Engleton bearing a resolute expression. "Yes, of course. I never had any intention otherwise," Hainesborough said.

"Good. Then we will consider this matter and any other associated matters resolved," Engleton said. Engleton gave Susan a furtive glance as he handed her a certified check from the envelope.

"One last matter," Hainesborough said. "It seems that one of my family's greatest heirlooms, a sword of gold, seems to have gone missing. I might wonder if someone here may be able to return it?"

Dutch and Susan looked on with mock expressions of dismay. "I have no idea of what you're talking about," Dutch said. "Do you, Ms. Berg?" Dutch asked turning to Susan.

"No, no I don't Mr. Holland," Susan replied. "But if you'd like, you could hire us to try and find it," Susan said to Hainesborough as she looked over the certified check. "We'll be docked at the marina for a day or two. You can contact us there Lord Hainesborough."

Lady Melody slowly rose and flanked by the two guards, left with Lord Hainesborough and Engleton, her eyes remaining on Reggie until she disappeared into the crowd.

"Where to now?" Susan wearily asked.

"Back to where we came from. The Bridgetown Marina. I still have a score to settle."

CHAPTER 30

Dutch took no pleasure in the sail back to the Bridgetown Marina. Not a word was said as everyone tried their best to stomach the reality of the day. Even the dolphins seemed forlorn as they swam alongside the helm of the catamaran. Mr. Carrington decided to go stay with his sister while his home was being renovated. Susan offered to cover the deductable, much to the surprise of Mr. Carrington. He warmly thanked them before they left, Dutch doing his best to assure Reggie that his love would not be in vain.

Upon Dutch's suggestion, Susan and Crane retired to their staterooms early, Susan taking a calculator with her to determine how much money, if any, she had made on what she now referred to as "this frickin island". The ultimate outcome had drained the smiles from everyone, as life and love often do. The only respite was sleep, which the last few days had stolen from them all.

In the middle of the night, a shadowy figure stealthily walked down the marina docks, shrouded in the dense fog that often settles in off the ocean. Dressed in black, with face paint to match, he was almost invisible. He carried a small doctor's bag in one hand as he made his way to the slip where the boat "Sailher" was birthed. At three in the morning, not even the waves were awake, the utter silence adding to the stealthy intruder's confidence. With skill, the figure opened his bag and with the tools he withdrew, he picked the lock on the main salon door of the catamaran.

The man withdrew a gun with a silencer attached, leaving the satchel on the deck. Keeping low, the interloper crept through the main deck's galley, certain where his objective was located. He descended the stairs to the owner's stateroom, making sure each step was silent. With the moonlight sneaking in through the porthole curtains, he could make out the faint figure of a person sleeping in the queen sized bed at the end of the stateroom. Taking steady aim, the man fired three silent shots into the figure, the only sound being the faint noise of the silencer as the bullets met air. It was then that he knew he was set up, his past experience alerting him to that fact, the absence of the distinct thud that occurs when a bullet hits a human body. The man spun around just as Dutch burst out of the closet, Dutch's arm knocking the weapon from the man's hand. The man instinctually raised his knee, landing a blow to Dutch's groin knocking Dutch back into the closet. The man scrambled to retrieve the gun that had fallen to the floor, Dutch falling onto him. Dutch crashed his elbow onto the man's back. The man dropped to the floor on his side with a groan. Dutch bent down to punch the intruder, but was met with a side kick that made Dutch stumble back. The assailant crawled for his weapon which had settled at the foot of the stateroom stairs. He grabbed the gun and spinning on his back, stopped Dutch just as he was ready to pounce.

"Not so fast old man," Menton Moore said with a satanical smile. Dutch stood frozen in his tracks as Menton fixed the gun on Dutch. "Actually, I'm glad you created this little ruse. It will give me the pleasure of watching you die. Or would you rather give me the golden sword that you stole from Lord Hainesborough?"

"You mean that golden sword?" Dutch said with a smirk just as Crane leapt from the top of the stateroom stairs, sword in hand. Crane brought the sword downward as he landed, the blow striking Menton's gun hand at the wrist. Menton screamed out in pain, the sword cutting straight through his wrist before Menton could react. Blood streamed from his handless arm, covering everyone and everything as Dutch and Crane stood frozen. Menton pushed past Crane and ran up the stairs as Dutch and Crane gazed at the lifeless hand on the floor, its fingers still wrapped around the gun.

"Pick it up Crane," Dutch finally said.

"You pick it up," Crane replied.

"No, you."

"No, you."

"Crap, you're such a baby," Dutch said as he bent down and gingerly picked up the gun, hand attached.

"You want me to go finish him?" Crane asked, a note of relish in his voice.

"Then we'd have a body to get rid of. It's bad enough having to get rid of this." A devilish smile came over Dutch as he tossed the hand at Crane, Crane batting it away with the sword.

"You're such a child," Crane said as he dragged himself up the stairs, sword in hand.

"Hey, whose gonna clean up all this blood? Crane?"

Susan appeared at the top of the stairs, sleepily rousing her bird's nest of bed head. She looked at Dutch who held the gun, still with hand attached. She shook her head, and then without a word went back to bed.

The next day, the sun arose as always. The sea air filled the catamaran with the expectations of another day. Susan had left early for the airport to collect her secretary, Patrick. He had flown down with the checkbook and ledger from the Miami office to help Susan settle accounts. She had also instructed him to bring a first class ticket back to Miami with her name on it. Pronto. As she put it to him in no uncertain terms, "I've got to get off of this frickin island today!"

After depositing Hainesborough's cashier's check in the local branch of her bank, Susan and Patrick made their rounds delivering checks to Mardrid, Keith and Ted, and the Carringtons. Susan had discovered long before that the only salve that helped to heal the wounds that Dutch inflicted was money. She then met Vicky's parents at the hospital, where she gave them a sizable sum for Vicky's care and recovery. Dutch had already assured Vicky and her parents that he would visit her once a month, or more often if and when Vicky wanted. Susan had one last stop to make.

Walking up to the Sailher's berth, it was apparent that Dutch and Crane were preparing to set sail. Crane was busily storing provisions from boxes on the deck as Dutch was checking the riggings on the foredeck.

"Hi sailor," Susan said.

"Ah, I see you brought your muscle with you," Dutch said, motioning to Patrick. Patrick unabashedly admired Dutch's bare chest. Dutch immediately put on his shirt.

"Mr. Holland, we are here to pay you," Patrick said.

"Then I'm glad you came," Dutch replied as he approached them.

Susan stood on the dock's edge and held out a check as Crane carried boxes of provisions down below. "You got lucky Dutch. Even after all of your mayhem, there was still enough left to pay you."

"Lucky is as lucky does," he mocked as he took the check. Dutch smiled as he read the amount to himself. "Nice, very nice. Of course, I do still have some expenses to send you."

"Don't even think about it," Susan bluntly said.

"We've got to go if we're catching the afternoon wind," Crane shouted out from below. Dutch smiled at Susan. He reached out and gently touched the side of her face before retreating to the helmsman's seat and checking the control lines. Crane quickly released the mooring lines and in the blink of an eye pushed off from the dock as Dutch started up the dual Yanmar diesel engines.

"You take care Ice. You know how to get me if need be, right?"

Susan nodded. "You never did tell me what you plan to do about Hainesborough," she said.

"Me?" Dutch said with mock innocence. Dutch looked off into the horizon. "People like him always seem to get what's coming to them. Somehow. Someway."

"Where are you headed? I mean, just in case I need to follow up with something?" Susan asked.

"We've got a need for breeze and the taste for Jamaican rum on our tongues," Dutch said with a smile as the Sailher motored away from the dock. The mainsail rose along with the spinnaker and in moments the catamaran was gliding across the open bay on its way out to sea.

Susan and Patrick watched the idyllic scene without saying a word. A sudden look of realization chased the smile from her face. "Damn it! He never gave me those frickin deeds from Costa Rica!"

EPILOGUE

One Year Later
London, England
Perse School for Girls

It was only midday, but the student at the prestigious Perse School for Girls situated in London's Cambridge area had plans. It was her birthday, and not just any birthday, but her eighteenth birthday. She had meticulously planned for this day for nearly a year, following the instructions she had secretly received, anonymously placed in her backpack while at recess in the school yard.

The night before her birthday, the girl had stuffed all the essentials she could manage into her school backpack. Doing everything she could to act nonchalant, the student said goodbye to her father and sat quietly in the backseat of the limo that delivered her to the Perse School that morning. It took all the effort she could manage to remain calm, even though her heart had been racing for days before. She worried if her casual response to have dinner out with her father on her birthday seemed authentic. At lunch, she walked to the gym, knowing that the gym would be deserted during that time. She quietly slipped out through the emergency exit, the siren having been disabled by someone the day before. There on the street a black nondescript sedan waited. The back door opened and she got in.

"How goes it love?" Mickey Farer said from the driver's seat, dressed in a chauffer's outfit. Lady Melody forced a nervous smile from the back seat. "Don't you worry about a thing. 'Ole Mick and Dutch have everything ready like clockwork." Mickey held up a flask filled with whiskey. "You want a pull?" he asked. "Seeing how it's your eighteenth birthday and all."

Melody nodded and took a short sip, coughing as she did. Mickey smiled as he pulled away from the curb and headed straight for the Port of Tilbury. Twenty minutes later, Mickey pulled up to a small cargo ship where cranes were busily loading pallets of goods into its hold.

Mickey got out of the car and opened the back door, Melody exiting like a cat touching water for the first time. Mickey pointed to the gangplank of the ship, at the top of which stood a young sailor. Lady Melody instantly recognized the young man and without hesitation she ran to him. The two met at the bottom of the ramp, Reggie Carrington taking Melody into his arms. The two kissed in a warm embrace as Mickey looked on with a smile as wide as the English Channel.

Mickey wiped a tear of joy from his eye and then approached them, carrying a sealed package. "This is from Dutch," he said as he handed Melody the package.

"What is it?" she asked.

"Let's just say golden swords fetch a whole lot more nowadays," Mickey said with a smile. Melody and Reggie gave Mickey a hug and then walked up the ramp and onto the boat, the destination of their new lives only known to Mickey and Dutch.

When Lord Hainesborough returned home that evening, he was met by the maid. The maid's concerns about Lady Melody's absence were answered by the sealed note from Melody which Hainesborough found on her bedroom nightstand.

Many say you can still hear Lord Hainesborough's screams of despair in the mansion before he hung himself from his bedroom chandelier later that night, an apparent suicide. What wasn't apparent on that day was the early arrival and late night departure of Mr. Richard "Dutch" Holland from London's Gatwick Airport.

Made in the USA
Middletown, DE
21 December 2019

81624907R00139